Whistling for the Elephants

To Anna

Whistling for the Elephants

SANDI TOKSVIG

love

Sandi T

BANTAM PRESS

LONDON • NEW YORK • TORONTO • SYDNEY • AUCKLAND

TRANSWORLD PUBLISHERS LTD
61–63 Uxbridge Road, London W5 5SA

TRANSWORLD PUBLISHERS
c/o Random House Australia Pty Ltd
20 Alfred Street, Milsons Point, NSW 2061, Australia

TRANSWORLD PUBLISHERS
c/o Random House New Zealand
Poland Road, Glenfield, Auckland, New Zealand

TRANSWORLD PUBLISHERS
c/o Random House Pty Ltd
Endulini, 5a Jubilee Road, Parktown 2193, South Africa

Published 1999 by Bantam Press
a division of Transworld Publishers Ltd

A catalogue record for this book is available from the British Library.
ISBN 0593 044800

Typeset in 12/14 Ehrhardt by Falcon Oast Graphic Art

Printed in Great Britain by
Clays Ltd, St Ives plc.

To Julie

I would like to thank the following people for their invaluable assistance in writing this book: my editor, Ursula MacKenzie, and all the staff at Transworld; my agent, Pat Kavanagh; The Born Free Foundation for all the work they do and for introducing me to Cynthia Moss, elephant expert; the staff at the British Library Reading Rooms, Bloomsbury; the Gladys Society; and for love and support, my family and friends, my children and Alice.

Whistling for the Elephants

Chapter One

There are two basic types of creature in Nature's kingdom. The first, like frogs and turtles, produce many offspring and simply hope that some will survive. The second, like elephants and people, produce one, or two at long intervals, and make great efforts to rear them. My mother belonged in a class of her own. She produced two at short intervals and made no effort to rear them whatsoever. Some people agonize over these things but I thank God. A hint more attention from my own family and things might never have turned out the way they did.

We need to go back a bit. 1968. I was ten. Almost certainly I was wearing a short tartan kilt (Clan McLadybird), a white shirt, a very neatly tied tie, a blue blazer and a peaked sailor's cap which hid my long curly ginger hair. No-one made me dress like that. It was a kind of school uniform I had invented for myself. In the photos the combination tie and skirt make me look a strange boy/girl hybrid. My face, born with a frown, was obscured by the peak of my hat. I had spent most of my early child-hood shielded from a full view of anything. The cap and I were inseparable. I was, even in my tender years, trying to develop a rakish look. I spent many hours trying to persuade people to call me Cap'n instead of Dorothy. It didn't work. Not a popular child. Not even with my parents.

Mother and I were, as ever, travelling. It was what we did. Always first-class and always a long way. This is not a story about coming up the hard way. At least not financially. It should have been idyllic. It was, I suppose, an education of a sort. I could read a wine list and order any meal combination in perfect French by the time I was seven. My first sentence was reputed to have been 'What the hell's happened to room service?', but that may be family myth. I know that my brother Charles and I thought laundry came out cleaned and ironed if you left it in a bag overnight. Our life only came home to me as strange when Father rented a car the summer I was nine, in Berlin. The car-hire woman wanted our permanent home address and none of us could think of one.

My grandmother thought we were growing up 'as gypsies', which is why Charles finally went to boarding school. The crunch had come during an annual visit to Granny.

'What's for dinner?' said Charles, then probably six to my four.

'Roast beef,' said Granny.

'What else is on the menu?' asked my brother, sealing his fate.

We didn't know about everyday life. We didn't know it was possible to have just roast beef. Charles was dis-patched to Father's old school on the Sussex coast. He went off to learn a smattering of Hardy, an ability to distinguish places of interest on an Ordnance Survey map of the Rhine Valley and to decline absolutely anything in Latin – except occasional buggery by the Latin master on exeat weekends when Granny wouldn't have him. Charles received the dubious honour of a public-school education because he had been clever enough to be born with a penis. I, rather more stupidly, had come without and so carried on travelling with Mother.

Both my father and brother were called Charles. Always Charles. Never Charlie. It gives you some idea about our family that we didn't indulge in pet names. It wasn't deliberate. I just don't think anyone thought of it. Nor did we find it in the least bit confusing to have two males of the same name. This was probably due to the fact that on the whole we were not given to addressing each other directly. Anyway, my brother went off to learn 'to interact with the world'. I don't think he wanted to go. He cried for days before he went but he had no choice. In fact I think his crying rather confirmed the need for him to go. Learning to interact, not crying, was what men did. It was what Father did. I knew that because, wherever we were, he went off on the train every day to do it.

Mother didn't interact with anyone. It was not required. She was, even with the distance of time, a curious creature. Rosamund Amelia Dorland Kane. Everything about her was perfect. Her nails, her hair, her voice, all strictly first-class. I remember her as having golden hair but I can't find a single photograph to make that true. Perhaps it is because I can only see her as a kind of aura. Not so much the woman but the fine mist of   *13* perfumes and powders which always hung about her. A woman whose entire appearance was constructed to suggest that she had never had a secretion in her life. There was absolutely nothing moist about Mother.

I can see her on that trip in '68. Sitting up in bed wearing a lace-trimmed morning jacket surrounded by her most devoted companion, Louis Vuitton. It is hard to imagine quite how much travel has changed in just these three decades or so. It makes me sound like an old fogey but it was so different then. There were no ziplock bags, absolutely everything was crushable and we always carried wooden hangers with our name embossed in gold on them. Mother and I were bound from Southampton to New York aboard the SS *Hallensfjord*. A five-day odyssey of cocktail wear and endless food. Mother, always indescribably elegant, and I, almost certainly, an indescribable disappointment.

We were an odd combination, Mother and I. Early on in life she had discovered the pointlessness of enterprise. Being a married woman of some means, she had escaped the burden of usefulness. You have to understand – women's lib was still on the cusp then. No one talked about it or thought inactivity strange. Mother followed Father and his work round the world utterly disengaged from it and him. I don't know if she was bright. It never came up. She might have filled her time with religion, with some wider sense of responsibility, but being English she had escaped that too. Not for her the drive of the Protestant work ethic or the guilt of the Catholic. The Church of England was a comfortable backstay which 14 functioned only on a social level, and then on predictable but limited days of the calendar. Mother travelled on. Going everywhere and seeing nothing. A shimmering varnish on life's great table. It didn't matter. There was plenty of surface life for her to lead.

I was, for as long as I could remember, seeking something else, but I didn't know what. I couldn't see a fresh ocean of anything but I wanted to dive headlong into it. Even at ten I longed for desperate romance, nerve-jangling drama, or even just a minor vision from God. I thought I was precisely the right sort of person to appreciate the significance of a burning bush or two and could never understand why I was not 'chosen'. Together Mother and I formed an ill-fitting jigsaw puzzle. It was not a picture which screamed 'Mother and Daughter'.

On the boat, apart from supper, we didn't spend a lot of time together. In general I was expected to entertain myself. But we had two moments of scheduled daily closeness, one in the morning and one in the evening. After breakfast on my own, where I quite often ordered steak just because I could, I would go to my cabin for a while and look at my 'present'. The 'present' was the only unsolicited thing I had ever received. (I'm sure I'd had gifts from my parents at Christmas and birthdays and so on. They weren't unkind, just rather given to good form.) We had spent a short time in Singapore, I can't remember why, and I had a nice lady who looked after me called Anna. When we left she cried and she gave me my present wrapped in a silk scarf. I didn't open it for ages because I liked the idea of it so much. When I finally did it was a framed piece of illuminated manuscript. A strange thing covered in drawings and animals. Father explained that it was a tenth-century classification of the animal world according to the Chinese. It wasn't an easy order to come to terms with, not when I was young and not really even now:

1. Those Belonging to the Emperor
2. Embalmed
3. Tame
4. Suckling Pigs
5. Sirens
6. Fabulous
7. Stray Dogs
8. Included in the Present Classification
9. Frenzied
10. Innumerable
11. Drawn with a Very Fine Camelhair Brush
12. Et Cetera
13. Having Just Broken the Water Pitcher, *and*
14. That From a Long Way off Look Like Flies.

I studied the list every morning, partly to see if I could work out where I came and partly at the wonder of my unasked-for gift.

Then – 'Not too early!' – about eleven o'clock, I would knock on the connecting door between our cabins. When Mother was ready, I would sit beside her bed on a chair reading from the *Hallensfjord News*, which was slipped, freshly printed, under the door just after midnight each evening.

'There's clay-pigeon shooting on the top deck at twelve.'

'Oh no, dear, I couldn't stand the noise, the what do you call it, guns et cetera.' Mother lay back against the pillows, exhausted by the very thought of finishing a sentence. She often started quite well and then drifted away as if everyone knew what she was going to say anyway. She eyed me carefully. I knew even then that I wasn't right. Would never be right. I was like some very expensive appliance which she had bought in error. On paper I had all the functions of the required daughter, but she couldn't seem to make me connect to her system. I caught sight of myself in a mirror. A slightly plump girl in a tie. Too much nearly a boy. A miniature monsieur-dame that no frock could ever feminize, with impossible red hair for which there was no genetic explanation. Mother never directly criticized me. That would have been too close to an actual conversation. She looked at me closely.

'Darling, aren't you . . . hot . . . in that tie and jacket, you know . . .?' She waved a hand at my ensemble.

'No.'

Mother patted my cheek and sent me off while she powdered and dressed, which left me free till supper.

After my maternal moment, I spent my day exploring the boat. It was all old wood and reeked of polish and a tidy absence of children. I spent most of my time pretending I was a spy, but I don't think I was a very good one. In four days all I had worked out was that the lady in the Royal Suite was very kind to servants. One of the waiters visited her constantly and each time he came out he looked very happy. I took my time each morning making 'observations' as I worked my way from the Saloon deck down to Commodore. Through the library, past the ballroom and down near the shop, there was a *17* closed, frosted-glass door. A green line on the carpet underlined the imprinted words *Second Class*. I longed to go through it. I knew that beyond there was a world of mystery, where people ate chips with their dinner, fathers drank beer and children slept in the same room as their parents. This side of the door, ours, was an unreal world.

We had breakfasts of freshly peeled tropical fruit, bouillon on the Sports deck at eleven, grilled lunches on the afterdeck, tea in the casino, supper in the Polar Room and late snacks in the cabin. Not that Mother ate. She just ordered brilliantly. I don't remember there being any menus. I know the waiters might occasionally suggest things but mostly people ordered as the fancy took them. Gold-trimmed plates would emerge in triumph from the kitchen bearing a constant stream of seared steaks wrenched from the whole side of a cow, wild birds festooned with wilder berries, lobsters dancing with lemon sole, crabs clutching other crustaceans and flaming batches of Baked Alaska. Caviare nestled in the curved back of an ice swan as Mother's laugh tinkled over melting martinis.

Our other moment of closeness came every night after supper. We played bridge in the library with some cheerful octogenarians in evening wear. It was the only time I think Mother found me useful. She could never be bothered to remember what cards had been played. I usually bid rather wildly so that Mother was assured of being dummy. She liked the shuffling and the dealing of the cards because she thought it showed off her long fingers. After that she much preferred to lay her hand down and just pretend to watch while she sipped Brandy Alexanders.

'Oh, Dorothy has such a good brain, clever, numbers, et cetera. I'll leave it to . . . her,' she would announce, smiling as if genuinely pleased.

Nothing stopped the elegant routine of those lazy days. At least it shouldn't have. I don't know what caused more stress to Mother that trip – the talent contest, my hair or the hurricane.

I signed up for the talent contest in secret. Before the New York posting we had been about five months in Paris. Usually Father's postings involved some nod towards my continuing education, but I don't remember even an attempt at school there. The only concession had been a Mme Henri who had provided pianoforte lessons on a Thursday afternoon while Mother rested. (Thursday lunchtime was the weekly gathering of the Parisian International Ladies Lifeboat Association and she was always exhausted.) Mme Henri and I had worked rather hard at what I now realize was a simplified and possibly repetitive version of Beethoven's *The Bells*. I thought it sounded wonderful. My new notion was that I was actually a child prodigy whose talents had inexplicably been overlooked. I was ready to sweep everyone away with my bit of Beethoven and the boat talent contest was, I knew, the place to do it. Mother had never heard my musical expertise and I thought to surprise her. I suppose in a way I did. We had gone to the lounge to watch the show and Mother had joined the captain and a group of socialites for coffee. She gave the tiniest murmur when my name was called and for a brief moment I swelled with pride at her unaccustomed full attention as I marched to the piano. I sat down and prepared myself. *19*

My hands went to the keyboard and I began. My left hand carefully pounded up and down on the same two notes for the one-minute duration of the piece while the right plodded out something close to the tune. When I had finished there was complete silence. So, rather carried away, I played it all again. There was an even deeper silence when I had finished but I feigned exhaustion and left my instrument. Mother never opened her eyes once as I walked back across the dance floor to some belated but kind applause.

Had I been older I would have realized that I never had a chance. The prize was easily swept away by a man who did impersonations of World War Two bombers using only his tongue, a paper cup and a great deal of microphone technique. As the only entrant under forty, I got a consolation voucher to spend on board in the establishment of my choice. Mother never said a word but I knew I had let her down. Perhaps she too had expected that I was about to reveal a light under my rather ample bushel. I don't know which of us was the more disappointed. I should have been brilliant and I wasn't. I was just a kid. A regular kid. Mother went straight to bed. The next morning she didn't even want the newspaper read out. I wandered down to the Commodore deck a failure.

The Commodore deck was home to, amongst other amenities, the barber's shop. It had the most lovely smell outside it. I suppose it must have been bay rum or something. Men came and went in the big red leather chairs. It looked so comforting. Great hot towels gently wrapping their faces. A bit of jovial chat with the man in the white coat, who snipped away with hardly any hair falling on the floor at all. I had been to the ladies' hairdresser with Mother and that was quite different. All rather shrill. Lots of bright pink bottles of things, hundreds of little stabby hairpins and everything happening at too high an octave. The barber's looked and smelled more like Christmas. I stood there for about an hour looking in the window and watching customers come and go. After a while the place emptied as everyone went to change for something. There was always something to change for. The barber came out into the corridor in his white coat and shook a small towel in the air. He was about to go back in when I surprised myself.

'I've got a voucher,' I said. He looked at me as I produced the talent-contest voucher from my blazer pocket. 'Can I have a haircut?'

'What's your name?' he asked.

'Dorothy.'

'Well, Dorothy, I don't really do little girls. You need to go with your mother to see Mrs Harton down the hall at the ladies' salon.'

'But I want you to do it.'

'What sort of haircut?'

I wanted to say 'like a spy' but I knew that involved having a moustache as well so I said, 'A boy's one.'

He shrugged. 'Okay, it's your money.' And he did it. It seems odd now. Maybe he was sick of rich people and didn't care any more. A short haircut. A really short haircut. I didn't have the hot towel on account of not having a moustache, but otherwise it was wonderful. When he had finished I looked in the mirror and for the first time in my life I saw myself. An absurdly small, slightly freckled child with short red hair, now swept into a neat side parting. A young snake released from a confining skin.

The hurricane occurred that night and I remember feeling that somehow it was my fault. Had I known about Shakespearean portents in the weather then I would have been sure that my Samson-like shearing had angered the elements. I don't know why we didn't avoid the storm but we didn't. We steamed straight into the worst of it. The weather meant Mother didn't emerge for supper so I hadn't seen her between the haircut and going to bed. I awoke in my cabin to find a heavy blue-leather-and-mahogany chair walking slowly by itself across the room towards my bunk. Outside the porthole the sky had disappeared and been replaced entirely by sea. I wasn't a child given to panic but this didn't seem right. I crawled off my bed and had to clamber uphill to Mother's room. In my hurry I quite forgot my cap. All the pillows from her bed had slipped and she was now lying quite comfortably on what had previously been the wall. She was doing her nails and didn't look up as I came in.

'All right, darling? I didn't want to wake you, et cetera,' she said against the rasp of her file.

'I think we're on our side,' I said, looking at yet more water beyond Mother's window. Mother looked at the window.

'That can't be right, darling. Aaagh!' Mother fell back into almost a dead faint on the pillows.

'It's all right, Mother. I don't think we'll drown. We've been on our side for some time.'

'Dear God, what will your father say?' I couldn't think

what Father would say if we drowned. Something appropriate.

'I expect he'd have a word with the shipping company,' I replied.

'Oh darling, how could you? Your beautiful hair.' Mother began to weep. In the face of a potentially watery grave only my appearance was causing my mother grief. I looked out of the porthole. Under the strain of the storm, the ancient stabilizers of the *Hallensfjord* had simply given way and we were, to put it mildly, listing. The Atlantic wind continued to whistle outside. Mother, unable to face anyone with me by her side, went back to sleep and I went to have a look. There was no danger of sinking and no one seemed in the least bit distressed. At least no one in first class. They had paid far too much money to do anything as undignified as drowning. A rope had been strung up in the ballroom to assist passengers with cabins on the raised side of the vessel to get to them. I spent some time with a Polish waiter hauling myself to the top of the shiny wooden floor and then sliding swiftly down to the other end. The only person I remember being at all put out was the chef. He sat drinking gin in the Polar Room and weeping and weeping.

'My kitchen is ruined. I can do nothing for you. Steaks and lobsters. I am reduced to steaks and lobsters.'

'Nonsense,' said one of my octogenarians. 'We don't mind one bit. Come on. Chin up, man.'

Everyone was most sympathetic but there was an underlying sense that the chef was behaving rather badly. It was far too much emotion, even for a person allowed to be 'creative'. I think some attempt was made at a lifeboat drill in the Columbus Bar but Mother refused to go. She said her nails weren't dry yet and anyway what shoes could she possibly wear at this angle?, but I knew she didn't want to be seen with me. Mother liked the idea of lifeboats. She had raised money for them even when we lived in landlocked countries.

Everything was like a strange *Alice in Wonderland* dream. The library tables stood all askew. People picked a spot to walk to and then sort of fell towards it. That evening, in full dinner dress under large orange life-jackets, my octogenarians and I played gin rummy on the floor. As I was going to bed I met my Polish waiter in a corridor on the Boat deck. He was trying to push open the door to the wooden deck outside. I don't know why. There was no job to do out there. No one had had a drink on deck all day. He pushed at the door but the wind was too fierce. At last he managed it and the heavy door almost ripped from his hands as he flung himself outside. It was utterly foolish but I followed. The storm was blowing itself out but the wind didn't want to let go of the boat. The waiter turned his face to the blast and then slowly put his hands up as if arrested. He smiled as he leaned his whole body forward at an angle and began doing press-ups against the wind. It was so strong it held him easily. I struggled to his side and put my hands up in a great act of faith. We did press-ups on the wind and I wanted that. I wanted that feeling all my life.

Father was waiting for us at Pier 96 when we docked. We saw him from quite a long way off, like a patient fly waiting on a great wooden arm. I don't know what to say about Father. I didn't know him that well. I suppose a lot of people have never seen their father naked; I had never seen mine without a tie. We could see him from the embarkation deck. An immaculate, entirely white-haired head. His back ramrod straight and his collar so tight that he constantly twitched his head sideways to relieve the pressure. He saw us but he didn't shout. He never shouted. A cricket ball with an unlucky bounce had once hit him in the throat at school and I never heard him speak above a whisper. He didn't need to be any louder. You always knew where you were with Father. He was a man of few but clear notions in life. They were mostly to do with men:

Manners maketh man
Coloured shirts on a man are a sure sign of homosexuality *and*
Never trust a man in a ready-made bow tie.

Ex-Army, he had a surprising amount of chin for an Englishman and rather more hair than must have been thought sensible in the mess. He had not been 'fast track' enough for the services and they had tipped him out as major, fit for nothing except to be in charge. After a comfortable and extended bacherlorhood, at the age of forty-five he had made up his mind to marry and picked the first attractive woman who came along. Twenty years younger than him, Mother had rather shocked him by producing two children. I don't know what he thought about fatherhood except that it was an awkward announcement to make at his club.

After the Army, Father travelled with the Foreign Office. I'm not entirely sure what he did. I desperately wanted him to be a spy but in my heart I knew he wasn't. His shoes were too squeaky and he was clean-shaven. I think he was something to do with protocol. It was both his business and his passion to know exactly how one ought to behave in any given situation.

'Hello, my dear.' He patted me on the back and kissed Mother politely on a proffered cheek. 'No trouble, I hope?'

We were three days late. Mother dismissed it with her hand and frowned at the customs officer examining her lingerie.

'Hey, lady, whatja got here?' the Bronx officer shouted, holding up an intimate item. The family shuddered. We were not ready for New York.

I didn't know why but Father had done a very strange thing. We had had many postings and had lived in one city-centre flat after another. This time, he had rented us a house. Not just any house but one outside the city. The sort of place that families actually lived in. With a garden. I suppose it should have been the first hint that things weren't quite right. Now that I think about it, certainly it was a place where no one Father knew would ever bump into Mother by chance. It was a hideaway but I didn't take it as that. I was too excited. I had also fallen in love with Father's car. A station wagon. I had never heard of such a thing. Powder blue and unbelievably long. Longer than necessary for any conceivable car purpose. A huge, pointy, chrome-covered, road-eating monster. It was too big to be

just for business. It was a family car. Our first family car.

'It's a Pontiac,' whispered Father.

I kept saying the word over and over to myself like a kind of mantra. 'Pontiac, Pontiac, Pontiac.' We headed off on the expressway. 'Pontiac, Pontiac, Pontiac,' all the way upstate, about fifty miles to Sassaspaneck. I didn't know I was going home. Pontiac. Pontiac.

'Indian name.' I leaned forward to hear as Father whispered to me on the back seat. Mother slept bolt upright in the front, seeing nothing. 'Sassaspaneck. They say it's Algonquin for "Where the fresh fish meets the salt". Been reading up on the history. Fascinating bit of colonial stuff.' If Father had a passion for anything it was for history. He liked anything which had already happened. Where you knew the end of the story. He was not given to fiction. 'Place used to be packed with Algonquin. Tricky fellows. Europeans had a terrible time. No crops, smallpox, and no one could calm the Indians down. Then the British sent in General Amherst. Jeffrey Amherst. Tremendous chap.'

We crossed over the Amherst River which ran down into Sassaspaneck Sound. Congregational and Methodist churches, so white that they had to have been touched by God himself, dominated the street corners. Past Tony's Pizzeria and the Dairy Queen, and then we turned down into the residential area. I couldn't imagine the Indians living here at all. Clapboard houses with porches needing paintwork and swing seats that had lost their swing stood shielded behind acres of ripped flyscreening. Everything looked big and expansive to our English eyes but I guess even then the town must have begun to feel a little down-at-heel. It was ex-grandeur rather than grandeur.

'Know what he did? Amherst? Gave all the natives blankets from the smallpox hospital. I think it must be the earliest example of modern germ warfare. Tremendous. They all died of smallpox and the settlers used the Indian stores to survive the winter.'

It was what the town was famous for. The spreading of smallpox. The killing of Indians.

'Here we are.'

The house was right on the waterfront. 5 Cherry Blossom Gardens was in what the Americans call a dead end. The French call it a 'cul de sac', which sounds slightly exclusive. The English call it a 'close', which breathes their horror of proximity, but it was a dead end. A dead end of five houses. Four of them were rather large, with one lawn running casually into the next. Ours was the smallest and the only one with a holly hedge at the front. I think that's why Father chose it. I'm sure he could never have hired a house without boundaries. The house itself was a large bungalow covered in light green clapboard which on closer inspection turned out to be made of aluminium. (It would take me a while to learn it was a ranch-style house, not a bungalow, and it was made of aluminum, not aluminium.) The clang of halyards against masts rang out across the water. A real house. I couldn't believe it. It was wonderful. Mother got out of the car and stood in the driveway looking at the new place. Father didn't look at her. He busied himself with the luggage. Mother never travelled light. He would be busy for some time. I took my own bag and headed for the front door.

'What the hell is this?' Mother didn't yell. She didn't

even raise her voice but it was enough to stop us porters in our tracks. We looked at her. Standing in the driveway at Cherry Blossom Gardens, her expensive coat flung casually across her cashmere shoulders, Mother was patently entirely out of place. The Empress of Russia come to rest in some peasant quarter.

'You need somewhere quiet,' whispered Father. 'You've not been . . . yourself lately . . . have you? I thought by the water . . .'

'Charles, I am not living here. People with smallpox wouldn't live here.' She had been listening.

Father looked at me, his neck surging around his collar looking for air.

'We need to tighten our belts a little. It will be fun, won't it, Dorothy?'

I think I was supposed to help him but I wasn't sure how. I nodded, trying to imagine us having fun.

'I am not living here,' said Mother, raising her chin but not her voice.

Father addressed a large hatbox firmly. 'I spent the money on your tickets. This is what there is.'

It had been quite close to a row and everyone felt most uncomfortable. I didn't know about money then. We had always had it and I had never thought about it. If not having money meant living in a real house then I thought it was great. Father opened the door and began staggering in with luggage. I dumped my bag and wandered around. The lounge was at the heart of the house. A vast room with plate-glass windows on to a flyscreened porch overlooking Sassaspaneck Harbour. Dense flyscreening protected all the large windows and made the view of the bright harbour endlessly grey. Off the sitting room were the dining room and the kitchen. The kitchen was absurd: thirty feet of fitted shininess which Mother would never set foot in. It had the most enormous fridge I had ever seen. Taller than me with a great silver lever of a handle, it bulged as if it had already overeaten. The other side of the lounge was a large bedroom for Father and Mother, again facing the harbour, a small bedroom for me and a third room for Father's study. The furniture was all 'early American' – a heavy, semi-quilted look straight from a catalogue. There was nothing about the house which suggested that it was ours but I loved it. I wandered from room to room, trying to soak it all in and ignore the strong smell of mothballs. When he had finished with the bags, Father went and stood by the front door. He held the screen open until Mother had no choice but to come in. She stood in the lounge looking down at everything. Father got her a drink of water.

'Have one of your pills,' he said quietly, getting them from her bag. Mother took it and handed him back the glass without looking. Each word she spoke came out like a telegram.

'We are not staying here. I won't. I can't. You know how I get all . . . et cetera.'

'I'll see what I can do,' he soothed. He always soothed her in the end. Mother went to lie down. Which was probably just as well. Father had just helped her into the bedroom and was looking out to the boats with me. We were trying to think of something to say. I thought maybe I should ask what had happened and why we were here but I couldn't think where to begin. Anyway, I liked it. I didn't want to not stay. That was when the front screen door banged open and a woman with skyscraper hair appeared.

She was the most carefully constructed woman I had ever seen in my life. Everything about her was carefully polished and planned but it didn't quite work like Mother. It was a much cheaper imitation. A market-stall run-up of a Gucci bag. A whole beauty shop of smells enveloped me as I stood, gawky and unsure in the face of such blatant womanhood. Mother often complained about women who 'hadn't made the most of themselves'. This woman had made the most of herself some time ago and then just carried on, not knowing when to stop. Nothing, not a hair was out of place. She wore very tight trousers. Black pedal pushers in spray-on form. I had never seen my mother in trousers. Indeed I don't think at that time I even had a pair myself. Her fluffy white sweater finished rather too early around her midriff and her high heels stopped rather too late. She wasn't young. I guess she must have been as much as forty but she carried her youth preserved in pancake and powder.

In her arms she carried a very elderly white poodle, a hatbox of a cake and a large black bag. The poodle too had been manicured to within an inch of its diamanté collar. It looked down its nose at me as water ran from its slightly yellow, rheumy eyes.

'Hey, honey. Judith Schlick. You have gotta be Dorothy. Ain't you cute? What do they call you?'

'Dorothy,' I said.

Mrs Schlick raised a pencil-line eyebrow. 'Well, I never. Is your father home?' She swept in, moving towards Father in a spectacular series of curves as if avoiding unseen sharp objects. 'Charlie, so they came. Finally. How fabulous. A little cake. What else could I do? Think of it as a kind of Welcome Wagon.'

'Mrs Schlick . . .' The dog wrestled its way to the floor and Father had no choice but to take the violent cake. I had never seen an American layer cake before. It was incredible. I couldn't take my eyes off it. For a start it was green. And not just any green. Mesmerizing green. A sort of poor-man's-St-Patrick's-Day celebration green. A green you couldn't imagine anybody coming up with for anything, let alone a cake. The bright green icing was raised up all over in sharp little spikes which spat from its sides. At least a foot and a half in diameter, the cake gave rather more the impression of having landed than having been baked. It was an alien thing.

'Charlie, Charlie! Mrs Schlick! Really, you English and your manners. Judith, remember? He is *sooo* polite, your father, such a gentleman.' Mrs Schlick settled carefully on the settee like a rather rare butterfly come to rest, and crossed her legs. 'Charlie and I have had such nice talks, haven't we, Charlie?'

This was impossible to imagine. Her right foot swung rhythmically in the air. Perfect pink polished toenails peeked out from her mesmerizingly tall sandal. I took a sharp breath. She had an ankle chain! I gawped. I know I did. Mother had talked about women like this. Women who were genuine floozies. Women who didn't use door-bells. Women who wore ankle chains.

'Rocco, you dirty devil. Stop that.' She began to giggle. The elderly poodle was standing on its hind paws and had firmly attached itself to Father's leg. It had a slightly strange grin as it humped hell out of his highly polished brogues. Sex had entered our house. Father's neck twitched uncontrollably against his collar but he did not move.

'And your wife?' Mrs Schlick scanned the room with rapid radar.

'Sleeping, the trip, you know, et cetera,' he whispered.

'Of course, of course.' Every word sprang straight from her nose.

When Mrs Schlick and Rocco finally left, Father was still standing in the middle of the sitting room, with a stain on his trousers, holding the green cake.

'She lives across the road,' he whispered, his neck going double speed. I felt I ought to say something.

'Father?'

'Yes?' he mouthed.

'What flavour is green?'

'I don't know.'

We stood and looked at each other for a moment. He never mentioned my hair. I went outside.

A group of children were playing in the street. I didn't know what they were playing. It involved a rugger ball and a lot of shouting. They stopped when they saw me. No one said anything. There were about six of them and they circled warily towards me. One of them, a girl, older and bigger than me, picked up a bottle of squash or pop or something from the edge of the road. She thrust it towards me.

'Hey you, you wanna soda?' I wasn't sure that I did, any more than I wanted green cake, but they were all watching so I carefully put the drink to my lips and sipped. The place erupted, the children screaming and jumping about.

'Cooties! Cooties!' They pointed and jabbed at me. 'Urgh, you got cooties!'

There was no two ways about it. I had got cooties and I didn't know what they were. I did know one thing. I did not have the language for this place. Not yet, anyway.

Chapter Two

America. Land of therapy. Where something or someone is always to blame. They say the Americans have such a restless frontier ethos that when they got to California and couldn't go any further they carried on exploring inside themselves. It hadn't reached a national obsession yet in '68. The country was only just beginning to put itself on the couch. No one knew that pets could have 'abandonment issues', that cheese was a dangerous food-stuff or that America could lose the Vietnam War. The US had not yet adopted for itself the onerous role of the world's policeman, but the foundations of the place were beginning to shake a little. Martin Luther King was dead a month and it pricked the conscience of people who had thought he was nothing to do with them.

Although there were only a few weeks to the endless American summer holidays, Father registered me in the sixth grade of Amherst Elementary School. The school was big with hundreds of students and there was a lot to learn. Not so much in the lessons as in the structure of the place. Even Adam and Eve knew that, if you want a little control, first you have to learn to name everything. Lesson one – everyone had a 'homeroom'. This was where you belonged. Your sorority as it were. You might spend part of each day elsewhere but your homeroom and, more specifically, your homeroom teacher, was base. Outside the homeroom you had a long, thin, metal locker with a combination lock. In this you kept everything of value and your lunch. My locker was number 69. I was the last to join class 6A and locker 69 had been empty all year. I didn't know but it had belonged to a girl who, at the age of eleven, had been kicked out of school for 'going down' on the assistant football coach. There was a general sense that her unnatural precocity was catching and no one had wanted her locker with its sniggering number. I didn't know any of this. I didn't know sixty-nine was a funny number. I thought going down was something you did in a lift. I didn't know why everyone whispered when I approached my locker down the long, dark corridor. I was blinkered. I just liked having a locker with a lock. I thought it was a secret place for secret things.

My homeroom teacher was Mrs Shepherd. She was a nice woman with black glasses which swept up into great wings at the side of her head. She counted us in and counted us out again each day and, in her own way, also covered history. I suspect she even liked history. She was certainly enthusiastic but her broad Brooklyn accent made all life, past and present, impenetrable to me.

'So, class, let us awl look again at Waallwor One. It was

a tearable wor. Lots of people doyed all over Yarrup. It was really tearable.'

Yarrup? I spent the first week trying to work out what Yarrup was. It was only when Mrs Shepherd showed us a map and combined pointing at it with the word that I understood. Europe. It was where I came from. Although Mrs Shepherd's picture of a Britain where everyone still blessed Yanks for gifts of silk stockings and Hershey bars was somewhat remote from my own experience. I didn't tell Mother or Father about coming from Yarrup.

I got to grips with school basics quite quickly. 'Colour', 'neighbour' and all other words ending 'our' lost their U with no grief on my part. I went to baseball games and learned to shout, 'We want a pitcher, not a glass of water,' although I hadn't the faintest idea what it meant. I concentrated hard to pick up everything else. The whole school was too big for everyone to get together each morning. Instead of having an assembly we sat listening to tannoy announcements in homeroom.

'This is Coach Harding. All football tryouts will take place on the field this afternoon. Remember – no show today, you don't get to play.'

'The Recorder Group will not be meeting in first lunch period due to the unexpected demise of Mrs Baxter. Our condolences to the Baxter family and if anyone's mother teaches recorder could she please call Principal Markowitz.'

I learned the pledge of allegiance by the second day and would leap to attention, hand over my heart, once the announcements were over. 'I pledge allegiance to the flag of the United States of America and to the republic for which it stands, one nation indivisible before God with liberty and justice for all.' It was like the Our Father in English assemblies only a bit shorter.

I knew my locker combination, I knew the way to the sports field and where to sit at lunch. It was the big stuff I wasn't sure about. Suddenly I was supposed to have an opinion on a bewildering range of things. No one had really asked my opinion before. America was in a new state of doubt and even as kids we seemed to have to hold an awful lot of truths to be self-evident. Television was beginning to have an impact and every night Huntley and Brinkley intoned the dead of Vietnam. Forty thousand US soldiers dead. Two hundred fifty thousand wounded. On my second day the whole school had a sit-in. I don't think Amherst Elementary was particularly current-affairs-conscious. It was happening across the country. That year there were more than 1,800 student demonstrations in every type of educational establishment. Our age didn't mean we didn't have to be involved.

Everyone in the class wrote off for silver bracelets bearing the name of an American PoW. You ordered them from the back of some magazine which involved children wanting a Better World and Mothers Calling for Peace. Lots of kids had a bracelet. Each one had a different prisoner's name inscribed on it whom we supported. The idea was that we weren't supposed to take the bracelets off until the men got home. Mine was Lt James Hutton.

Nixon was campaigning for the fall elections on a pledge to get the US out of South-East Asia. Although I wasn't exactly sure where Vietnam was, I learned to chant, 'LBJ, LBJ, how many kids did you kill today?', wore a badge that said *Give a Damn* and one that said *We Try Harder*. The first was for black equality and the other was from a car-rental company, but in my mind the message was much the same. I learned the routine. I was for the Black Panthers, against the war, for free milk in schools, against the SST airplane, for free love but against overpopulation. Maybe it was my age, maybe we had traveled once too often, but for the first time anywhere I wanted to belong. I really tried.

I persuaded Father to let me go to school on the yellow school bus. I thought I would meet people. That's how I met Gabriel. Gabriel Aloisi worked for Jacobson's Garage up on the corner of Palmer and Lindhurst, but in the mornings he drove the school bus. He was handsome. Italian handsome. Singing-gondolier handsome. Gabriel wanted to be a racing driver. He drove the big yellow bus fast, swinging into Cherry Blossom Gardens at a quarter of eight like he was Mario Andretti. He was nice to me. He always stopped the bus in front of our house and I was always first on. I'd be standing there as he reached forward for the handle to unfold the door. I guess he must have been around eighteen because I remember the morning he got his letter from the Draft Board.

'What's it say?' Gabriel thrust the letter at me. He wasn't exactly a high-school graduate. Gabriel knew cars, not words. I read the letter over.

'It's from the Draft Board.'

'It's from the Draft Board, right?' Gabriel was a little slow.

'You've been called for your "pre-induction physical exam",' I continued.

'Pre-induction physical exam. Geez.'

'Tuesday the fourteenth.'

'God damn. God damn. I am a good American, you know that?' I nodded. I knew this. Being American came with a presumption of goodness. 'I am a goddamn good American but I am not going to fight no goddamn foreign war. You know what you need to know to be a good American?' I shook my head. The other kids were piling on the bus and I leaned forward, desperate not to miss what he was saying. This was information that I needed. 'All you need to know is that the Chevy is a primo car and Bud Harrelson is the greatest shortstop of all time.' Gabriel slammed the door shut and took off.

Since 1964 draft dodgers had been gathering force in the US. They had a fairly straightforward slogan which even Gabriel could come to terms with: 'We won't go.' Gabriel was not the type to run to Canada. It was too far and too foreign. So he just decided not to sleep any more. It was not an uncommon dodge. He figured if he didn't sleep for ten days or so he would fail his physical and go back to the garage. Gabriel was about four days into his plan when it started affecting his driving. At first we helped him out. The kids took turns standing beside him and steadying the wheel as he drove. Unfortunately our house was the first one on his route (pronounced 'rowt'). There was no one else on board to correct Gabriel as he made a wide turn into the Gardens, ploughed right through our holly hedge and came to a stop next to our front porch. It so happened Father was sitting there that morning, reading the *New York Times*. To give him credit he never flinched.

'What, may I ask, is going on?' he demanded.

'It's just Gabriel,' said Donna Marie, who had been waiting on the corner. Donna Marie lived next door but one. She was the one who thought I had cooties so I never sat with her on the bus. She attempted to unjam our mailbox from the bus door and get in.

'He probably fell asleep at the wheel again. Asshole,' Donna Marie's cousin, Dirk, volunteered. Dirk lived over on Hampshire. He was a senior and he didn't exactly approve of Gabriel. Dirk had very short hair and wanted to be a Marine. I tried to explain to Father.

'No one else's house would have been a problem. You see, we're the only ones with a hedge around our lawn. No one else has anything on their lawn that Gabriel could have hit and it's only that he hasn't been sleeping so the Army will say he can stay home. After all, the escalation of the Vietnam War was done without the will of the American people. It's up to the goddamn Commies to sort themselves out, not the US Marines.' I took a deep breath. Normally the word 'goddamn' would have caused a stir but Father wasn't listening. He was only fixed on one thing.

'He doesn't want to do his military service?' Father's quiet disgust cut through the noise of the bus horn which Gabriel had chosen to rest his head on.

'He doesn't want to kill people he doesn't know,' I explained. 'It's . . . uhm . . .'

'Un-American,' said Donna Marie. We nodded to each other in political agreement. It was thrilling. Father folded his paper and came quite close to slapping it down on the porch railing.

'But he appears perfectly happy to kill people he does know.'

Father drove the bus that day and forbade me to wear my Vietnam PoW silver bracelet any more. I felt disloyal to Lt Hutton, but it was probably just as well. The inscribed bangle had already made my wrist go a slightly green colour. It was odd seeing Father drive a bus. I don't believe he'd ever been on a bus in his life. He sat rigid, driving on the right with disapproval, and never said a word.

I never heard what happened to Lt Hutton. Gabriel made 4F (Physically Unfit for Service) and wasn't made to join up. Dirk reported for duty a week later on his eighteenth birthday and was thrown into uniform. He ended up as a stores clerk at a supply base in Santa Monica. Ten days in, he was killed when an unstable consignment of baking powder collapsed on him in the warehouse. After that we used to watch the news with a slightly different atmosphere in the house. Every night Huntley and Brinkley would start by telling us how many Americans had now been killed in action. I would feel sad for Dirk, while Father sat upright with his gin and tonic. I couldn't help feeling he saw them all as a bad lot and did not mourn.

Father was coming to grips with America in his own way. Each night after dinner he would spread a US map out on the dining-room table. He had blocked out the names of all the states and he and I would sit trying to remember their names. It was a British Empire attitude.

That which can be mapped can be ours. Within a week I could have made my way across the Midwest blindfold, but it wasn't enough. Once we had done the States we moved on to county Ordnance Survey. Through the evenings Mother slept and my fingers passed over new frontiers.

I carried on making my adjustments. I gave up ham sandwiches for lunch and moved on to peanut butter with Welch's grape jelly, marshmallow fluff and baloney stuffed in a brown-paper bag. That part was easy. Mother never looked at what we were buying anyway. I never drank some-one else's soda without wiping the top off first, I put a peace symbol on a rainbow up on the inside of my locker and I learned all the words to 'Leaving on a Jet Plane' by Peter, Paul and Mary. I still didn't have any friends. I tried hang-ing around my locker between classes to see if anyone would bump into me. There was one girl who looked hope-ful. Connie Emerson. She was in my homeroom and I often caught her looking at me. One day I was just turning my combination when she leaned on the locker next to mine.

'Hey,' she said.

'Hi,' I responded, trying not to look too pleased. Cool, I needed to be cool.

'Can I ask you something?'

'Sure.' God, it was going so well.

'The others want to know if you're a boy or a girl.' I looked across the hall. A small group of giggling girls were watching. I flushed.

I pulled my peaked cap low over my short hair. 'Dorothy. My name is Dorothy.'

'Yeah, but the tie and everything. We thought you must really be a boy.' Connie collapsed into laughter and ran off with the others. I watched them run. Their arms flailed out sideways and their legs looked all bendy. It was a hopeless girly gait and somehow I knew I would never be able to run like that. I did make one or two other friendship efforts after that but it was no use. I thought about giving up the tie but before I had had time to make all the necessary changes the summer vacation came and I didn't know anyone. It was only June. The unoccupied months stretched interminably ahead of me.

Like a colour-blind chameleon, I fumbled at adapting. Mother, however, refused to play the game. As I let my accent grow as wide as the American continent itself, hers shrank to a small town in Kent. She began making pinched little noises as if she were simultaneously speaking and unwrapping toffees with her bottom. I think everything was too big for her and so she withdrew further and further from life. I suppose if she liked anything about America it was the ephemera. She was particularly taken with the concept of the Dixie cup. A childhood in the war had taught her never to throw anything away. She had spent a lifetime hoarding and counting. Until the Dixie cup. It was a very American concept. The Dixie cup was a brand-name paper cup. It was quite small and came in many colors with a matching dispenser. The Dixie company encouraged the notion of a different-colored dispenser in each room in the house. We had yellow in the kitchen, blue in the bedrooms and, rather shockingly, the all-new avocado in the bathroom. If you wanted a glass of water or a glass of anything in any room you simply reached for a Dixie cup, used it and threw it away.

Quite often Mother had drinks for no reason at all, so if we shopped, when we shopped, we always stacked the trolley high with multi-colored cups. About twice a week Mother would make the effort to be up and out before the banks closed and we would go to town. It was a small circuit that we did. First to Johnny on the Spot, the dry cleaner, to collect Father's shirts, where I got a free Bazooka bubblegum. Then on to the A&P supermarket, which Mother patronized because you got free pink and white dinner plates with any purchase over $10. She would let me buy Oreo cookies and Kool Aid in different flavors just to make sure we got the plate. It wasn't long before we had enough plates for twenty people to be able to drop in unexpectedly for dinner but they never did. I liked the A&P because of the fruit and vegetable man, Alfonso.

Alfonso wore a red apron, a white short-sleeved shirt and the obligatory small black bow tie. He was very thin with a crewcut, which made him look like a pencil with a rubber on the end. Alfonso was quite old by then. He had lines all over his face like one of his prunes but he smiled all the time. A sort of grandfather but without the beard or the rocking chair. He was a man happy in his work, for Alfonso loved fruit.

'It's a wonderful world of fruit, Dorothy,' he would say, letting me polish some of the apples with a special cloth. 'Look at this banana. See this label? That came from a banana tree in the Caribbean. Can you imagine that? That little yellow fruit has traveled further to be with us in Sassaspaneck than I have in my whole life. The Caribbean. Why, they have pirates and palm trees there and everything.'

Alfonso stroked the Caribbean product as if it had been entrusted to him by Pirate Pete himself. He laid the yellow offering back on his regimented display and carefully picked up an apple. He smiled at me. It was a big-toothed smile. Probably from so much healthy eating. He stood polishing the apple on his apron with pride while I did another one with a cloth.

'Did you go to the zoo yet?' He leaned confidentially toward me. 'I do the fruit for the zoo, you know. Miss Strange used to come in for it but now I go out there.' He stood to attention as the manager strode past. Alfonso smiled another flash of teeth and straightened a pineapple before going on. 'Used to be the main attraction in town. People came from miles around to see the Glorious Burroughs Animal Collection. Even after the shoe plant closed down it kept us on the map for a while. Now pretty much no one is interested. TV, that's what did it. I think sometimes families go to the zoo on Labor Day or something, but that's about it. That don't mean the animals don't have to eat. Every Tuesday, out I go with the fruit. Course, it's not as exciting as it used to be. Nothing really escapes any more. You know, when I was a young man I was going home from work one evening and a polar bear come right up Amherst Avenue. You see, Mr Burroughs, John Junior, he was back from one of his trips. He was always traveling. Seen more fruit growing round the world than I have here on my stand. So he'd got this polar bear and he thought he would take it fishing down at the river. It seems people used to do it all the time.' Alfonso moved a grapefruit for emphasis. 'You know, Miss Strange told me, Henry the Third of England, he kept a polar bear in his menagerie way back in the thirteenth century. He often took it down to that Thames River in London to catch fish, and he was a king. So it seems John took the bear down to the Amherst River and took off its muzzle. This was probably a mistake but it was brave. They can be mean, polar bears. John was like that. Always trying new stuff. He didn't care. Well, the waters move fast down by the old house. They were streaming by and so, pretty soon, was the bear. It wasn't thinking about fishing, it just jumped right in the water and swam off. So you know what John Junior did?'

'No.'

Alfonso chuckled. 'Why he thought it was long gone so he just ordered another one. I called him to say I'd found his bear outside the store. Gave me a start, I'll tell you. Not what you expect in Sassaspaneck. You should go out there. To the zoo, before they close it. Take a banana for the gorilla.'

After the A&P we would go and fill up the car at Jacobson's Garage on the corner of Palmer and Lindhurst. It was really a Mobil station and it had a huge stopwatch in the window. When Mother drove the Pontiac over the rubber tube in the driveway the clock would start ticking and Gabriel had thirty seconds to get out, wipe the wind-screen and start filling her up or we got a prize. Gabriel worked full-time at Jacobson's since he got out of the draft. Sometimes he was in the office when we came but mostly he was under some car. Other times he would be welding and the sparks would shower round him like he was covered in fireworks. Mother would get out and lean against the car while he twirled the petrol cap off.   *47*

'Fill you up, Mrs Kane?'

Then she would need the bathroom and Gabriel would show her where it was round back. He would wait for her for ages round there while I stayed in the car. After that Mother would be tired. One time she was so tired she let me drive her home. The car was automatic. Sitting on an old fruit box, I found it no problem to drive.

That summer, Charles was allowed to go sailing in Greece with a friend's family, so Father let me buy a bike. He was busy commuting and Mother was, I don't know, in bed, et cetera. Anyway I know I went to Milo's Toy Store on my own. I spent ages deciding but in the end I chose a blue chopper bike with a long white banana seat. It was trendy but not too girly. Milo came out on the sidewalk with me to watch me take the first ride. As I came out a red pick-up truck was going by. The sun was shining on the windscreen and I couldn't see the driver real well. Old white writing stood out on the passenger door: *Burroughs Zoo*. The back of the truck was empty but wisps of hay and straw blew about against the sides. A woman was driving with one hand on the wheel and one out the window holding the edge of the roof. I could see one side of her face but when she turned the corner there must have been a trick of the light. It was as if the rest of her head melted away. As if one side of her face didn't exist at all. Milo shook his head.

'Goddamn freak.' I didn't think he was talking to me. 'You have fun now,' he said and went back into his labyrinth of Slinkys, footballs and bikes. I loved that bike. I felt so grown-up as I rode it away from the store. I felt confident that it would impress potential new friends. It didn't. What it did was make me the Marco Polo of our neighborhood.

Cherry Blossom Gardens was off Amherst Avenue. The old railway track ran along Amherst between the avenue and the river. Where the road left the last houses and curved away toward the Expressway the railway track took off over the river into the woods. Once there must have been a bridge there but now the tracks hung silent, unprotected and naked across the river. They hadn't been used in years. Not since the mills had moved south to the cheap labor in Georgia. I rode my bike down to the crossing most days. Sometimes I would ride along the side of the track, pretending I was following the line south to freedom. Sometimes my bike was a horse called Rusty and we lived on the trail eating baked beans and wearing bandannas. Different games, different people. Never me on my own. Always exploring.

One late afternoon I had been playing a particularly complex game in which I was an ambulance, the ambulance driver, the doctor and the patient when I came to a halt by the tracks. It had been hot all day and the river looked inviting. I was too scared to swim but I put my bike down under a tree and stepped out on to the shiny track. It hung over the water but the metal was still hot. Even through my sandals. I took my time. I found if I was careful and balanced with my arms I could make my way slowly across the river. The water was calm below me and before I knew it I was into the woods over the other side. That was when I saw the Burroughs House.

I guess it was beginning to fall down in those days. The world hadn't yet gone history-crazy, running around preserving everything more than ten years old in aspic. The theme-parkization of the world hadn't started yet. No one knew about the past as a money spinner. The waterfront was so overgrown that I hadn't seen the building from the other side. It was breathtaking. I was ten. I didn't know about architecture but I knew that I had found a palace. What I didn't know was that it was an exotic Venetian palazzo, an Italian Renaissance villa. To me, what stood before me was a Sleeping Beauty draped in ivy and long grass. A princess's place. They've made it into a museum now and not surprising. It was incredible. Two hundred feet of terrace in green and white variegated marble ran along the whole of the back of the building. Thirteen steps, the width of the terrace, ran up to the enclosure of terracotta balustrades. Between the terrace and the main house lay what was left of a formal Italianate garden. The careful squares of grass had long since spread, tentacles of green capturing the attention of the tiled walkways. A group of rather Bacchanalian men with horns held up a long-rusted fountain. A statue of a fat man stood above them in the middle of a half-shell, his weight sitting heavily on his left buttock as he looked over his shoulder in a slightly camp manner.

In the evening sun the building seemed to be made entirely of gold. A cream edifice with every inch of every corner picked out in gleaming terracotta brick. It was an architectural fantasy. At once beautiful and barmy. It was part-Italian, part-French Renaissance, part-baroque, part-art deco, part-madness. An American whirlwind tour of Europe in one building. A kind of 'If this is the east wing I must be in Paris' building.

Above my head an outside staircase rose to a sixty-foot-high square tower encased in colored glass and topped by brilliant red barrel tiles. Four Muses swathed in flowing robes kept guard on each corner, watched over by a selection of cat and parrot gargoyles. The colored glass was repeated in all the Moorish windows of the second floor and all along the western façade. The center section of the house, overlooking the gardens, had seven pairs of french doors glazed in a rainbow of rich colour. Handmade bricks in shiny yellow, blue, green and ivory finishes flung diamond patterns across the walls. Everything which could have been filigreed or ornamented was. There was absolutely nothing plain about any of it. I followed the building round to the front and found the door ajar. With the idiocy of youth and made bold by loneliness, I entered.

The door opened straight on to an immense two-and-a-half-story roofed courtyard. I was inside the tower. The central room rose to a coffered, cypress-wood ceiling which framed the inner skylight of colored glass. I could just see ornamental paintings of mythological figures and signs of the zodiac which covered each octagonal section of the ceiling. From the center, a huge chandelier hung down on a great iron chain, its loops of crystal suspended like a Folies Bergères headdress. Spectrums of light rained down on the black-and-white-tiled floor. A room of rainbows. On one wall hung the most enormous oil painting in a golden frame.

It was a busy picture, painted in what seemed like the gardens of the house, but the house itself looked quite different. It was square and plain. Not the fancy edifice I had just come into. In the middle of the painting stood a large man holding aloft a golden birdcage containing a single golden bird. He was immensely tall, with the chest of a sea elephant, the chin of a prize fighter and an Atlantic Ocean of wavy black hair. No clothing could adequately encompass him. His what used to be called 'rude health' burst from every button of his dark suit and his brilliantly colored waistcoat. Nature's only flaw in him, her little aside, seemed to be terrible eyesight. He squinted at the world from behind small round spectacles. Perhaps because he couldn't quite see everything that was happening, he stood laughing as a giraffe, twelve lions, three tigers, two leopards, a polar bear, assorted antelope and a sealion ran riot around him, chased by exhausted assistants of various ethnic origins. A hyena was stalking a peacock on the lawn while a polar bear with a collar, muzzle and chain was standing on its hind legs trying to reach a quivering black man up a tree in what looked like a red dress.

In the corner of the picture sat a young woman in a wheelchair. Her body was withered by some illness. She was very small and her tiny frame lay twisted in the large mahogany-and-cane chair. She had no lines on her face so I guessed she was young, but her hair was thin like an old lady's. Only her eyes still suggested youth. She looked like she was having fun. She was dressed for the jazz age – a beaded flapper frock in pearl gray and a small matching gray feather in her hair – but didn't look like she was ever going to be part of it. She was never going to get up and boogie, that was for sure. The wheelchair woman was smiling at the man with the birdcage. A man in command of his world and all that was in it. A small brass plaque was fixed to the bottom of the painting. I read it out loud: 'Phoebe and John Burroughs Junior. 1925.' Phoebe. His wife? The woman in the wheelchair. Feeble Phoebe . . .

'We shall have a Chinese Garden of Intelligence.' I jumped as a voice spoke behind me. I thought for a second it came from the picture. 'A Great Menagerie. Like King George at Windsor or the Duke of Bedford. Tropical princes shall come and bring us barbaric offerings of tigers, leopards and creatures no man has ever seen before. We shall have such a collection that the Emperor of Abyssinia will hear of it and wish to come.'

I turned but couldn't see anyone. Then, amongst the great drapes which covered the walls, something moved. A giant insect woman. All in brown. Its wings closed about itself. It spoke to me.

'No one, not even in Egypt, China, India or Rome, will be able to boast of such exotica.'

The huge bug shimmered toward me. She was maybe in her late thirties but when you're a kid everyone just looks old. She was probably as old as Mother, just less set in aspic. She wore brown corduroy pants, a brown turtleneck and a vast brown cardigan. Her face was plain and thin and looked severe with her matching brown hair pulled back from her face into a brown rubber band, but she smiled at me and I smiled back. There was nothing about her which suggested 'friend', but I didn't think to run. She stood and looked at the painting for a moment.

'Were they here? The animals?' I asked.

'Yes,' she said.

'How?'

'The SS *Uritania* from Europe and then Amherst's finest railway. They had to walk from the station. Couldn't get the giraffe in a cab.' It sounded like a joke but she said it seriously so I didn't laugh. The brown woman reached her hand out to the picture for a second. 'Poor Phoebe.'

Then she sort of fluttered off. I followed her into the next room. The room beyond, with the french windows overlooking the terrace, was entirely white. Well, ex-white. Ghost white. The carpets, the curtains, the walls and all the furniture had once been polar. Now they had a gray sheen of cobwebs. Despite the dust, I could see the river flowing purple through the rose-colored glass of the windows. A real moth fluttered from the gray curtains and made me jump. The insect woman nodded at it. What did I know, maybe they were family.

'They say the first primitive moths fluttered over giant dinosaurs a hundred and forty million years ago. Imagine that. The butterflies came much later. Forty million years. Really they are the new kids on the block. The moth is beautiful. Here, look.' From inside her folds of brown clothing she removed a large black-rimmed magnifying glass, which she held up to the moth near my head. 'Look. See how it has a tiny kind of hook-and-bristle thing linking its fore and hind wings? It can fly better than an airplane. Land more accurately than a helicopter. Of course some female moths can't fly at all.' She put down the magnifying glass and looked at me.

'Did you know that there are more species of beetle than any other type of insect?'

'No.'

'Butterflies and moths are unique. Almost every part of their body from their wings to their feet is covered by thousands of delicate scales. That's what gives them color and pattern, but we don't see them. Do you like insects?'

'I don't know. I don't like spiders.'

'A spider could catch this moth. Some spiders can make a smell like a female moth and attract the male.' She nodded at me confidentially. 'Attraction is all about chemicals.'

'Whose house is this?' I asked.

'It is mine.' She gently touched a cobweb which glistened against the tinted glass. 'My father built it for my mother. John, big John. It was the house of love. He wanted to marry her before they even met.' The house of love stood silent as the woman sighed.

After a moment she pointed to the spider's work. 'See this web? See how it is shaped like the sun and its rays? Spiders always spin them in the morning to remind people of their divine ancestor. It was Grandmother Spider who brought the sun.' Behind her the tinted glass made ripples of palest crimson, aubergine, blue, yellow and green on the river. 'Do you think spiders feel?' she asked. I had never thought about it. I was sure my family had never thought about it. We were English.

'I don't know.'

'Do you know why people hate spiders? Because they aren't cute. I like trapdoor spiders. They live in the ground and make silk-lined tubes. Sometimes they have silk trapdoors and they can shoot out from them to capture passing insects. I put one in alcohol once.'

'What?'

'A trapdoor spider. They twitch awhile if you put them in alcohol but after that you can keep them for ever. She had babies on her back. I took them off with tweezers and put her in alcohol. After a while I thought she was dead so I dropped the babies in. The babies floated down in the jar and as they passed their mother, the spider reached out her legs, folded her babies beneath her and clasped them to her till she died. I think it was a reflex. I figure she would have seized anything floating near. Of course it wouldn't have happened if I had used chloroform instead of alcohol. That kills them stone dead.' The insect woman clutched herself smaller. 'Then I thought about it. The spider's web is very complicated. If they can do that, why can't they love their kids as well? You don't know what's in the mind of a spider, do you?'

The light was fading but we sat there on the floor, trying to imagine the silent spinning spider with the potentially rich inner life harboring a riot of emotions. Had I known what it meant I think I would have felt almost philosophical. Until a single word cut through the silence.

'Cunt.'

Even in the richness of the English language there are not many words which can have so immediate an effect. I had never heard it before and it had much the same impact on me then that it might still have in the middle of a BBC wildlife documentary. Cunt. It is a splendidly satisfying, sharp sound. The least onomatopoeic word in the world. I looked through the doors to the tower room.

High up on a balcony I could just see someone standing. The last rays of the sun were behind them, spilling down from the tower windows. I couldn't see if it was a man or a woman. Certainly it was a person. A tall person with what appeared to be a parrot on their right shoulder. My storyteller folded up like a moth and scuttled away.

I ran. Out of the house, back through the gardens, across the tracks over the river and on to my bike. I was frightened but all the way home I couldn't stop thinking about spiders. Even steeped in alcohol I couldn't imagine my mother reaching out to haul me in.

Chapter Three

Donna Marie Dapolito lived next door but one at Cherry Blossom Gardens. Although she was twelve, and two years older than me, I wanted her to be my friend. I thought if we became pals she could tell me if I still had cooties from sipping her cream soda. After my visit to the Burroughs House I held off exploring for a while. Most afternoons I would just drift up and down on my bike past Donna Marie's house. Mother and Father might be beautiful people with perfect manners but the Dapolitos – that was a family. They had the untidiest house in the street but it also looked like the most fun. There was the best part of a '59 Oldsmobile, several abandoned bikes and most of an old bathroom on the front lawn. Round back they had a trampoline. It was the noisiest house on the block. Boy, could the Dapolitos yell. Aunt Bonnie yelled and her kids, Donna Marie and Eddie Jr, yelled. The noise was as much part of the neighborhood rhythm as the banging of

the halyards across the water. I couldn't believe it. I

wasn't used to noise. Not just because Father's voice never rose above a soft breath and Mother rarely got up, but because it wasn't welcome in our house. Everything, every footstep, was taken quietly, carefully and with much planning, preferably by map.

Three of the houses in our dead end had their own floating docks with gangways from the backyard down to the harbor edge. There was ours, the Dapolitos', and Sweetheart's, who lived between us. The Dapolitos' dock ran way out into the harbor. Uncle Eddie was in salvage. He wasn't a yeller. He left that to the family while he worked the waters of the harbor all day on his flat-bottomed boat with a large crane. When he wasn't pulling things up from the bottom of the river and the sea he was helping rich people move their yachts. Uncle Eddie knew every inch of the seabed. He'd either dragged it or fished it. Other than recycling from the deep, fishing was Uncle Eddie's life. He was a big man. Everything about him was big; he was maybe six foot four and as wide as an ox. Every year he won the 'Biggest Hands in the County' competition at the Harbor Island Carnival. Eddie Jr said his dad could catch a shark by just scooping it out of the water with his bare hands.

Aunt Bonnie was the thinnest woman still actually breathing in the United States. She was thin because she never ate anything. She just sat on the back stoop drinking Budweiser straight from the can and watching over her kids. The Dapolitos didn't have much money but whatever her kids wanted they got. She was always there for them. Never asleep when they got home. I guessed it was because she spent so much time on her family that Aunt Bonnie didn't really 'make the most of herself'. She always wore trousers (pants) and I think she even cut her own jet-black hair. Maybe she had been pretty once. Now she just looked kind of used up. If she were a Dixie cup you would take a new one. Of course they weren't my real aunt and uncle but that was what they said I should call them.

I tried making friends with the Dapolito kids a few times before I finally got invited over, but it wasn't a big success. I kept getting little things wrong. Like the time I was waiting with the Good Humor man on the corner, trying to decide what kind of ice cream I wanted from his truck. He stood there patiently in his short-sleeved white shirt, skinny black bow tie, black pants and matching peaked cap. Donna Marie and Eddie Jr came tornadoing over from their house.

'Hey you, English, you wanna go to the zoo later?'

I did. I desperately did but I didn't want to look keen. 'Sure. I mean in a minute. I was just getting a lolly.'

Eddie Jr, who was only seven, looked at me and started laughing. 'A lolly? What the hell is a lolly?' And they began to chant the word. 'Lolly, lolly!' It was a cooties kind of chant and then Father arrived from the station and I could see him eyeing the Good Humor man's ready-made bow tie with disgust so I went inside and never got the ice cream or went to the zoo.

The second time I was trying to see if I could 'pop a wheelie' on my bike. Mother was asleep and Father was at work so I concentrated on my chopper. Trying to make the whole thing rear up on the back wheel like a high-spirited horse. I had just fallen heavily onto the hot tarmac when Aunt Bonnie drove past in her car piled high with kids. I had a leg full of grit and I could feel a small rivulet of blood making its way down the inside of my knee-socks but I got up and smiled.

'Hey, kid, you oughta come. Get in,' she yelled. It seemed like an order, so I leaned my frisky bike against the stop sign and got in. I felt really pleased with myself. I had sussed car-getting-in technique. The very back of the Dapolito station wagon had a large window which was always wound down. You could open the back like a door if you wanted, but that was not cool. The trick was, if the window was down, never to open the door. You climbed in through the window. I climbed in and landed on a pile of kids. I don't remember seatbelts in those days. I don't even know if cars had them. If they did no one used them. Certainly in Aunt Bonnie's car you were mostly held in by the sheer number of other kids. There were a lot of big boys in the back of the car. I listened as they talked, making myself as small as possible.

'The minister is so weird.' It was an argument not a statement. 'He says he talks direct to God.'

'Yeah, right. That's only since he found his wife giving head to that Cuban refugee in the belltower during the Christmas service. You'd need to talk to God after that.'

The big boys laughed. The world was becoming more and more incomprehensible to me. It wasn't till we got to the Methodist church that I found out what we were doing. Boat safety classes. Presumably under God's supervision. Being right on the water, Sassaspaneck was a big sailing community. All the kids in the neighborhood took 'Boat Safety' down at the Methodist church. About a dozen of us, most from Aunt Bonnie's car, fell into the church, where we stood giggling. The minister, Reverend Harlon, was wandering up and down the aisles babbling loudly. A man in desperate conversation with his Lord. He had once been famous for talking in tongues. Apparently it had been very impressive. Then his wife left him and he had a kind of breakdown. After that he *only* talked in tongues and no one liked to be the first person to be less than impressed so they just let him get on with it. Harry Schlick, Judith's husband, boomed into view.

'Come on, you bunch of little jerks. Let's go. Hup two.'

We filed into the hall at the side. No one argued with Harry. Harry had been in the Army in Europe or, as Mrs Shepherd would have it, Yarrup. He had fought for Yarrup. Indeed if you met him you might think Yarrup owed its freedom to Harry. Apart from his role as Freedom Fighter for the old country, Harry had two claims to fame. He was Mayor of Sassaspaneck and he had been quarterback in his senior high-school year when the Sassaspaneck Senators had scored a perfect season. Amherst's gift to women, he owned Schlick's Corset Place (*Est. 1946*) next to the drugstore. He also ran Boat Safety. He was older than Judith. I guess he must have been around fifty that summer. A little younger than Father anyway. Still good-looking though. A large man with a chiseled face chipped straight off of Mount Rushmore. It was a hundred percent USA. He had a huge jaw and a fantastic number of straight teeth set under a neat pencil-line mustache. Far too many teeth to be of practical value except possibly to look good in team photos.

'Okay, shape up, here we go. Grab a life preserver, your port and starboard reminder cards and take a look at this.' Like a magician with an oversize rabbit at his disposal, Harry produced a large life-size rubber doll.

'This,' he announced proudly, 'is Resussa-Annie, and she is going to teach you mouth-to-mouth.' The boys snickered. Resussa-Annie was clearly what they went to Boat Safety for. Not only was she shaped like a full-grown woman, she was naked and actually pretty good-looking for rubber. She had long blond hair which spread down over quite realistic breasts.

'What do you know about Annie here?' bellowed Harry in a voice which had carried him to victory on the football field.

'She's naked,' chortled Nathan Crystal, who lived over on Edgemont. Nathan went to remedial summer school and was into leather at a surprisingly early age.

'Don't be a wise ass, Crystal,' warned Harry. 'Your father can't pass a ball worth a nickel. Yeah, so she's naked. She is naked for a reason, okay?' Harry held the doll up by the neck so that she sagged from his grip. 'This woman is going to drown and you are going to save her. She does not have a top on . . .' There was a great wave of snickering. 'Thank you . . . she does not have a top on as we are supposed to be able to see her chest moving when one of you wisenheimers has successfully expelled air into her lungs. Who wants to be first?' The answer was no one, but Harry had dealt with reluctant recruits before. 'Come on, Donna Marie, let's go, hup two.'

Donna had no choice but to shuffle up to the front. She looked at naked Annie. Harry clipped on.

'Okay, let's get the head in the right position. Here, give me your hands.' He took Donna Marie's hands and moved them toward Annie's head. Suddenly he stopped.

'What the hell is this?' he demanded, holding up her wrist. Donna Marie looked at her wrist as if for the first time. I think it took her a minute to know what he was talking about.

'It's my PoW bracelet.' There was a terrible silence. The fate of Lt Hutton aside, I knew I was glad I wasn't wearing mine. Harry looked at Donna Marie.

'How old are you?' he demanded.

'Twelve.'

'Twelve, huh. You go out with boys?'

The boys snickered but one look from Harry and they stopped instantly.

'No,' said Donna, blushing.

Harry looked at her in disgust. 'Not a goddamn idea in your head.' He grabbed her wrist and pulled at the offending chain. 'Do you know where this kind of thing can lead, huh? Do you have any idea? Give me the bracelet.' Donna Marie took it off and handed it to him. 'Sit down, I'll talk to your father.' Harry cleared his throat. 'Anybody else want to be a smartass?'

I don't know why I put my hand up. It wasn't like me to push myself forward. I certainly didn't want to be a smartass. It was pathetic but I had a terrible longing to breathe life into the sleeping creature, Resussa–Annie. Harry looked at me strangely. I don't think he knew what to make of me. I was a girl but I looked like a boy. My hands stuck firmly in my pockets, the hair under my cap, neither one thing nor the other. A gender-non-specific. I could see that he had no idea whether I needed the hail-fellow-well-met slap on the back of a lad or the pinched cheek of a princess. Harry did neither but waved in the general direction of Annie and let me approach.

He had laid her out on two chairs covered by an altar-cloth. There was something religious and yet pagan about it all. Annie had a very big but quite realistic mouth which was permanently open to allow easy passage down into her big bags of lung. I wasn't sure what to do. I never touched anybody. I wanted to stroke her hair. I mean, if she had been drowning I thought that would be nice but I knew all the boys and Donna Marie and Eddie Jr were watching. Maybe stroking was not cool. Harry became businesslike.

'So the person needs your help. She can't breathe. Whatcha gonna do? First tip her head back and make sure her airways are free of obstruction.' He tipped Annie's head back and her glazed eyes stared up into mine. 'You put your hand on her chest like so, then take a deep breath and blow, one, two, three.' Harry blew into Annie and her chest rose like a swelling wave. 'Head to the side, blow out, one, two, three. Okay, kid, you're on.'

I shuffled to Annie's side and looked down at her. She was dying. I had to save her. In fact, only I could save her. Gently I tipped her head back and looked down her mouth. Her pink rubber passageway was very free of obstruction. So free that on a clear day and with her legs at the right angle to the window, you could have seen our house.

'Come on, kid, she's dying for Christ's sake.'

I took a deep breath, leaned down and blew so   *65*

forcefully that her lungs popped up and shot my hand off her chest. I'd save her, I would. I got into the rhythm of it. Breathing in, one, two, three, blowing out, one, two, three. Annie's chest rising and falling. It was the most incredible feeling, breathing life into something. I had an overwhelming sensation of usefulness, of purpose. It was as close to a religious feeling as I had ever had. At which point I fainted.

When I came round I was lying on Annie's chairs and she was looking decidedly deflated in a corner. All the kids had gone. Harry was looking down at me with disgust.

'Listen, kid, you're new, right?' I nodded vigorously. 'Don't rush the plate. Girls oughtta take their time. That's what girls do. Let the boys rush the plate.' Harry nodded, pleased with his own statement on life. He really was trying to be helpful. I thought I ought to comment on this unexpected piece of advice but I didn't quite know what it meant. He drove me home in silence. As we pulled up to our yard he spoke out of the corner of his mouth. Not looking at me but talking quite intently to the steering wheel.

'Be smart, kid. Don't wear the tie. Don't be so . . . different, right? Kids'll tease you. You know, give you a hard time in school and like that. Don't be so . . . different.'

I knew he was trying to tell me something important but I didn't really get it. I still hadn't gotten used to the idea of conversation with adults whose first names you knew. I nodded again.

'Thank you.' I got out of the car and carefully shut the door. 'Sorry I was such trouble,' I mumbled into his exhaust.

I didn't go to Boat Safety again. Partly because Father didn't let me and partly because of what happened with the zoo and everything. Most of the other kids got their certificates but I don't think Harry had his mind on the course that summer. He didn't really pay attention 'cause for a while the boys were happy just breathing on Resussa-Annie. Then Harry got caught up in the election and stopped taking the classes. The minister took over but he never noticed what was going on. Unsupervised, Nathan discovered he could jerk off in Annie's wide mouth. I learned so many things that summer. Pretty soon all the boys wanted a go. After a couple of months she was full up with semen and went a strange color. A kind of black pallor developed all over her, as if it were the plague she needed rescuing from, not drowning. Not surprisingly, none of the girls wanted to save her and there was an almost entirely male pass rate for Boat Safety in town. Not that it mattered at the certificate ceremony. Reverend Harlon was supposed to call out the successful students, but no one could understand a word he said so in the end a lot more kids got a certificate than should have.

That was my first outing with the Dapolitos. Then there was the time I went to dinner.

'Hey, kid,' Aunt Bonnie yelled as I cycled past for the twentieth time one afternoon. 'You want a meatball wedge?'

I had no idea whether I did or not but I nodded. I just wanted to come inside their house.

'The kids are watching TV . . . in the den.' Aunt Bonnie nodded into the dark interior.

I knew it. What a great place. They didn't have a

lounge. They had a den. A dark, snuggly place for baby lions. That was the first time I ever saw a color TV. It was a huge wooden box with a panel of three lights at the front – green, blue and red. We sat on their endless sofa (dark wood with quilt-pattern cushions from the Pioneer collection – Sears, Roebuck Catalog 1961) and watched *Gilligan's Island* followed by *I Dream of Jeannie*. Aunt Bonnie was unpacking things from a large brown cardboard box.

'Donna Marie,' she would call and toss cellophane packages at her daughter. 'Eddie J.' More packages rained down on the sofa. Clothes, endless clothes. Donna Marie opened her packets. Shorts. Shorts in bright colors, and really soft. Not tailored at all. Shorts with pockets. And T-shirts, striped T-shirts to match the shorts. Maybe six or more sets in different colors. It was the most fantastic box of clothes I had ever seen.

'Excuse me, Mrs Dapolito,' I said quietly.

'Mrs Dapolito! For Christ's sake, Aunt Bonnie.' Aunt Bonnie dragged on her Salem cigarette. 'Everyone calls me Aunt Bonnie.'

'Where do you get such a box?'

'Sears, Roebuck. Goddamn finest store in the country. Here.' She tossed a catalog the size of a small child at my feet. Then my new-found aunt went into the kitchen. She returned with great submarines of bread overflowing with Italian spiced meatballs. Wonderful food that you just couldn't eat neatly. Food that you ate with your hands! In the lounge. The den! On the settee. Not at a table. I ate, I looked at pictures of smiling girls in shorts in my catalog and on the TV Barbara Eden came out of a genie's bottle with a bright green face. I had died and gone to heaven.

Uncle Eddie sat silently in a huge reclining chair with a great footrest. He didn't really watch but occasionally he would click his fingers to show he wanted the channel changed. He was definitely in charge of the TV. Looking back, maybe it was a testosterone thing.

Father rang the doorbell and Aunt Bonnie went to answer.

'Good evening, Mrs Dapolito,' he whispered. 'I was wondering if you might have seen my daughter, Dorothy?'

'You got a problem with your voice?' asked Aunt Bonnie straight out.

'Yes.'

She shrugged. 'Too bad. She's in here.' Aunt Bonnie nodded toward the den. Father was unmoved.

'Perhaps you might call her?' he suggested, it never occurring to him to enter someone else's home without prior arrangement.

'Hey, kid, your dad's here,' Aunt Bonnie yelled with a paint-stripping voice.

'You have been most kind.'

Father was cross. I knew he was. I had eaten between meals. I had red sauce down my tie.

'They have color TV,' I said as we walked home.

'It is vulgar,' whispered Father, even less audible than usual.

I didn't think so but I didn't say anything. I thought I'd never seen anything more exciting in my life, but I knew Father wanted me to stay away. He never banned me, or   69 anything as straightforward as that. I just knew I wasn't to go to the Dapolito family. At home Father sat reading at the dining-room table. Mother's door was closed and the air was thick with silence. My tie was ruined. In my room I took it off and put it in the bin.

Chapter Four

The dead end that we lived in had five houses. Ours was next to the stop sign on to Amherst. Next to us, on the same right-hand side of the street, lived Sweetheart, Harry Schlick's mother. Next to her and at the head of the close were the Dapolitos. Next to them was the drive to the Yacht Club. Then on the left side were Harry and Judith and next to them Joey Amorato, the dog catcher, who lived alone.

The Schlicks invited us for a barbecue as part of the Welcome Wagon's welcome to the neighborhood. I guess it was the barbecue which started everything rolling but I didn't pay that much attention to the invitation. I was still obsessed with the idea that, like the spider, Father and Mother might be harboring a rich, internal emotional life about which I knew nothing. I hadn't been up to the Burroughs House again after that first time. I spent most of my time hanging around our road, improving on the number of things my bike could be. Whatever the bike was, a horse, a pioneer wagon, I was mostly alone. Cherry Blossom Drive was not a great address for activity. Rich people mainly used it to get to the back entrance to the Yacht Club.

At weekends Father was home but he spent most of his time sitting at the dining-room table working on his project. Our family, the Kanes, came originally from a small village in England called Ickenham. Father had been researching the town's history for some time. This was difficult as Ickenham was pretty much the sort of English town which history had entirely passed by. It was not mentioned in the Domesday Book and no one of any consequence had ever thought it was a good place for a battle. It suggested somewhere not worth fighting over. However, Father had a trump card. While examining the guest register of the Ickenham Arms he had discovered the signature 'ER 1598'. He was convinced that Elizabeth I had once slept there *en route* to whatever it was she was *en route* to. Consequently he was in endless correspondence with specialists in the field. Father always meant to be nice. If I came in he would look up from his work and I always felt I had to stop by the table. Neither one of us could ever think of a suitable subject for conversation.

'How's school?' he would whisper.

'It's the holidays.'

'Absolutely.' He paused. 'When it was school, how was it?'

'Fine. We did World War One.' I searched around in my mind for a fact. 'It was a terrible war.'

'Second one was better. I fought in the Guards, you know.'

'Yes.'

Father nodded. We had done enough bonding and I would go to my room. There I pulled out my secret weapon from Aunt Bonnie. I spent even more hours with it than my Chinese present, until at last I felt ready. The night of the barbecue, I wandered down the corridor with it to Mother's room. I thought she might be up as she would need to get ready for the outing. I knocked and heard her light, 'Come in.'

Mother was sitting in a white slip and stockings at her vanity table. She stared blankly in the mirror. Small bottles from the drugstore littered the glass top among an array of powders and puffs. Mother took a lot of pills. They all came from the doctor so I guessed she needed them.

'Mother, can I speak to you about something?' She nodded but never swayed her attention from the mirror. 'I want to get some new clothes.' For one brief second we had a mother-and-daughter moment. Mother smiled in the mirror. I smiled back. In her mind I think she had leaped with me to the finest stores in New York. In mine, my Sears, Roebuck catalog purchases had already been delivered. Then we looked each other in the eye and the moment was gone. She was so beautiful and I was so strange-looking. I put the catalog which I had borrowed from Aunt Bonnie on the vanity table.

'They're in here.'

'What are, darling?'

'The clothes I want. Some shorts and some shirts. Maybe . . .'

I don't think a stray dog relieving itself in the

bedroom could have had a worse effect.

The barbecue hadn't really started by the time we got there. Father always got us too early everywhere. He had a dark suit on and held Mother's arm as we crossed the empty road to the Schlicks' house. Mother was wearing her cream Jaeger suit. I didn't think either one of them was really in barbecue mode. We walked slowly and carefully. No one ever said there was anything wrong with Mother. I just knew we were always careful. The Schlicks' house was clapboard like ours, but it was two stories high and made of real wood painted a dark gray. A large brass eagle flew over the front door with a Stars and Stripes clenched in its beak. On the front lawn, a small cannon stood sentry. We knew the barbecue would be in the backyard and we could easily have just gone round but Father insisted on ringing the front doorbell. We stood waiting on the step. Mother looking lovely but smiling vacantly, Father's neck twisting like the clappers against his collar, and me. Funny old me. Mrs Schlick took some time to open the door. We could see the handle being wrestled long before it opened.

'Come on, Rocco. You have to move, sweetheart.'

It was with something of a wrench that she finally fell out of the screen door, which banged against the wall and caused the flag to flutter above in the eagle's beak.

'Charlie, I am so sorry. It's Rocco. He's old and I cannot get him away from the front door.' Mrs Schlick leaned rather longer on Father than was necessary. She had very high-heeled shoes on. Maybe she needed the support. Her outfit was a little startling. It was a brocade 74 jacket, very close-fitting, which finished somewhere on her upper thigh. After that there was nothing till you got to the shoes. It was a long way to the shoes. She smiled at Mother while pushing her mountain of hair a little more heavenward. I swear it creaked as she did it. I don't know who was more dumbfounded, Mother or Father. I knew Mother wouldn't think these were our sort of people. I just hoped she'd remember not to say so till we got home. Father was very tense. We'd had some bad times with Mother at cocktail parties in Paris before we left. I don't think he had ever thought that Cherry Blossom Gardens would be a place where he had to deal with socializing. Slowly the front door closed behind our hostess.

'So, you must be Rosamund. Such a beautiful name. We hadn't seen you. I was beginning to think Charlie had given you a cement overcoat in the Amherst.' Mrs Schlick's body jiggled all over at the joke and then stopped as she spoke confidentially to my mother. 'It has happened, you know.' Mrs Schlick tutted for a moment, brushed an invisible piece of lint from her remarkably exposed cleavage and turned to me. 'Why, hello, Dorothy.'

'Hello, Mrs Schlick.'

'Dear God, listen to you. I told you, honey, Judith, everyone calls me Judith. Funny kid.' No one disagreed. 'Come on in, come on in.'

Judith turned to push the door open again. It would not budge.

'Rocco, darling, you have to move, honey,' she called, but nothing shifted. Mrs Schlick shoved again and her Empire State heels began to slip on the front step. Father had no choice but to leave Mother to stand on her own for a moment and help push. The door became less and less helpful until Father and Judith were shoulder to shoulder against the wretched thing. With a small yelp from the ancient Rocco, it finally gave and they rather collapsed into the house. I helped Mother in. The dog had suffered something of a decline since I had first met it. Now bits of moisture dripped from every possible opening, not just the eyes. Fading fast from this world, Rocco had taken to lying across the mat by the front door. Bewildered by the onslaught of people, he swayed slowly to his feet and released a loud, dissatisfied explosion of gas as we stepped into the hall. It mingled with Judith's overwhelming perfume.

Judith sighed. 'Oh God, ain't it terrible. I cannot get him on his feet any more. Not even for a walk. A WALK.' She screamed the word at the dog but it was unmoved. It had, I suspect, determined to dedicate the remainder of its life to flatulence. 'He won't move from the door. I said to Harry we oughta just cut a piece off the bottom of the door and open it over his head. Don't stroke him,' she said to Mother, who could never have been further from such a thought in her life. 'You look so lovely but he doesn't expect it and it'll make your hand smell. I don't know what it is. I've had him cleaned. It stays with you for days. Judith sighed and then instantly brightened into a good hostess. So come in, come in. Welcome to Our Home.'

It sounded like a welcome but in fact Judith was pointing out a large needlepoint which said *Welcome to Our Home* in bright orange with a border of small pumpkins. 'I made it for Halloween, but everyone said it was so lovely I just kept it right there.'

The house was perfect. I mean in that nothing was out of place. It was also tapestried knick-knack heaven. Everything which could have been made out of canvas and thread had been. Everything which deserved an embroidered motto got one. The keyring holder by the hall window said

> *You Don't Got to Look Far*
> *For the Keys to the Car*

with hooks shaped round pieces of an Oldsmobile in quilted fabric. The hat rack poked out from a major piece of sewing of cats wearing fedoras with the words

> *Hang Your Hat on a Cat!*
> *You're Purrfectly Welcome.*

Small wooden ducks rested on embroidered ponds, the banister of the main stairs had an embroidered cover of ivy leaves, every door had a cheery sign indicating its function in words with follow-up pictures in case you got confused. If I stood still long enough I was fairly sure I too would be committed to wool in surprising shades. Any remaining wallspace was filled in by God blessing the house in every possible manner, and at least ten different designs assured me that Jesus was my friend. I liked that. I had been thinking about having Jesus as my friend since I had seen the advice on a bumper sticker. I thought Jesus being your friend would be a good deal because you wouldn't have to worry about getting cooties from drinking soda wrong. While I was having these revelations Father was staring at me. My hat. He wanted me to take my hat off. I removed it reluctantly and hung it on a cross-stitched Siamese.

Through an arch in the hall we could see into the sitting room. Judith swept us in on a brief tour. It was obviously not where the party was happening. The furniture was not designed for sitting on. It all looked very nice but was entirely shrouded in clear plastic fitted covers. If you sat down you would either stick to it or slide off in a second. In one corner there was a huge tropical-fish tank, but the focus of the room was a fake fireplace surround above which hung a painting of a girl. The picture was lit so that you couldn't really look at anything else. In another country you might have guessed that it was some mystical shrine. Judith tottered toward it and leaned on the mantelpiece.

'That's our Pearl. The pearl of our heart. Her papa's pride and joy. Taken on her sixteenth birthday. The photograph, that is. This is a real painting. Milo, at the Toy Store? He does them from the photograph. He's doing one of Rocco too.' Judith sighed in wonder at the painting. 'So much talent in a storekeeper. She's twenty now. Be twenty-one before you know it.'

'She looks lovely,' murmured Father. Mother didn't say anything. She was just looking at the plastic on the sofa. 'Uh . . . I'm looking forward to meeting her.' Father marched the conversation on, his hands clenched behind his ramrod-stiff back.

Judith pulled a lace handkerchief from her sleeve and ran it along the bottom of the picture frame.

'Oh, Charlie, she's not here. I miss her.' She choked suddenly, emotion welling under her mascara. I don't think we knew if this meant the daughter was dead or what, and no one dreamed of asking.

'Perhaps a drink?' suggested Father.

'Of course,' Judith replied, and the bright hostess returned.

She sparkled her way through the house to the backyard. As we left the hall I could just see Rocco in the corner under the hat rack. He was still swaying at the unexpected sensation of being on his feet. He took the scene in for a moment and then simply fell sideways. The tremor shook my captain's hat free from the rack and deposited it on his head. We moved on.

'We are so glad you moved to the neighborhood. Harry and I have been here for ever but every time we think of moving something interesting happens and we just have to stay.' Judith giggled the sort of laugh I had spent a young life avoiding. I knew if such a girly sound ever came out of my mouth I would have to kill myself.

Father whispered something which Judith must have taken as a compliment. 'Oh, Charlie,' she giggled and whispered back, 'Don't mention Pearl to Harry, okay? He gets kind of funny. Fathers, huh? He's a good man, really.' Judith pushed open the back door.

In the garden, Harry was wearing a large chef's hat with a blue and white striped apron bearing the words *I'm in Charge*. Smoke poured from a barbecue which an ox might have found a little roomy. He was cooking steaks so big they had to have been stitched together from several cows. A great dustbin of ice was filled with cans of beer and soda.

'Great, great, the Kanes, start the party.' It seemed unlikely. 'Charlie, grab a beer.' Harry twinkled at my mother. 'You have gotta be Rosamund. What do they call you? Rosie?' He lowered his voice confidentially and leaned too close to Mother. 'I tell you, Rose, we were beginning to think Charlie had given you a cement overcoat in the Amherst.' Harry roared at the joke and Judith did some more jiggling. The evening was going to be impossible. Father could never drink from a can. Mother could never cope with that much meat. I moved to put the picnic table and chairs between me and Harry. I didn't really want to talk to him. I was feeling very exposed without my tie and didn't want him to say anything. I did the top button of my shirt up and stood watching the grown-ups.

'It's a good job you arrived, Rosie,' confided Judith. 'Your Charlie is much too handsome to be left alone. We had such talks, didn't we, Charlie? And you know what we have been talking about?' I couldn't imagine. 'History. Ain't that nice? Who woulda thought we had somethin' in common? We just adore history. Course, mine ain't as refined as Charlie's.' She sat down on a deck chair and gently patted the one next to her. I couldn't tell if it was for Mother to sit down or because the cover was slightly wrinkled. Anyway, I knew it wasn't for me so I didn't move. Judith waltzed on.

'Dorothy, you're a girl.' She looked round at me as if to check. 'You'll appreciate this.' Her tone turned confidential. 'I am writing the total history of fashion in cheerleading through the whole century. People didn't always wear saddleshoes, you know.' I nodded. I don't know why. I had no idea what a saddleshoe might be. 'And look at this. I just finished this. Isn't this keen?'

She picked up a large black bag from beside her chair. On the side in multicolored diamanté was a portrait of Rocco in what I could only imagine was a full cheerleading ensemble. The dog looked slightly demented wearing a short, pleated skirt and holding its paws aloft with two giant pompoms. Above the pompoms were the words *Notre Dame 1952*.

'It's Rocco. Ain't it the spit?' Mrs Schlick let out a shrieking yell. Everyone nodded.

Harry torpedoed in. 'Want to see my tanks? Come see my tanks.' I think Father thought it was some war thing but Harry opened the door to a large wooden building at the back of the yard and led us in. Inside was a crescent-shaped aquarium divided into several different compartments. The walls had a few shelves with fish food paraphernalia on them, but everywhere else there were photos. Black and white pictures of Harry with a baby Pearl on his lap. Harry and Pearl laughing in a rowing boat, Harry and Pearl playing baseball, Pearl blowing out birthday candles. Apart from the fish, she was everywhere. Harry stood proudly in front of his mini-ocean and put his arms out to take in the joy of it.

'Twelve thousand gallons. That's the cubic capacity of the underground reservoirs and that's just the salt water on this side. There's six thousand gallons of fresh water in those tanks over there. Of course the amount of water you see is only about a fifth of what's in circulation.' Harry tapped on the glass. 'The water is constantly on the move. The water flows out of the tanks through a series of very elaborate sand filters and then returns to underground reservoirs to feed the tanks again. Everything from salamanders to shrimp. Took me and Eddie a helluva time.' Harry beamed with pride at his own creation. Above his head an old poster announced

A College of Trained Animals and Cephalodian Monsters of the Deep.

'It's all here, you know: drama, sport, domestic idylls, monstrosities and horrors.' Harry leaned toward Mother. 'Did you know that prawns play football?'

She smiled uncertainly. 'Really? How absurd. I mean they're so small and . . .'

'Sure they do. If you drop tiny pieces of fish in the tank and they're not hungry then they dribble the food along with their forelegs to each other.'

Father chuckled. 'Perhaps you could have a Touring Prawn Football League.' Harry laughed and dropped some food into one of the tanks.

'Watch this.' He reached into another tank, pulled out a starfish and without a word tore a leg from it.

'I say!' said Father ineffectually.

'Don't worry.' He threw the starfish and its leg back in the water. 'You tear a leg off and it makes a new one. The old leg makes a new starfish.'

Mother looked faint at the whole operation and gave a slight moan. Harry reached for her arm and soothed her.

'It's all right, Rosie. It's natural.' He smiled at Mother and turned to me. 'So, you feeling better, Dorothy?' Harry asked. Father looked at me. 'Fainted right away at Boat Safety.' They didn't even know about Boat Safety. It was terrible. Father would think I was turning out like Mother.

'Hello,' an elderly voice interrupted. It was my savior. Everyone turned. Sweetheart was in her late sixties by then but she was what people in those days used to call spry. She had such a lovely soft face under her white hair. A face that had aged with nothing but laugh lines. I wanted her to adopt me straight away. I thought about adoption a lot in those days. I stood stock still, holding on to myself so I didn't run at her for a hug. She had on a pink and white striped dress and white nurse's shoes. Harry smiled.

'Hey, Mom. Everyone, this is my mom, Sweetheart.'

Sweetheart smiled and nodded. 'Have you done the drinks, Harry?'

'Just coming, just coming.'

Harry ushered us outside again where Judith was looking in a small compact to apply yet another layer of lipstick.

'So, Sweetheart, these are the Kanes,' she said, pursing her lips to herself and then snapping the pocket mirror shut. 'I can't believe you haven't met yet. Sweetheart lives right next door to you. Isn't that nice?' It clearly wasn't that nice. Her tone to Sweetheart was less jovial as she spoke to her out of the corner of her mouth. 'Sweetheart, didn't you want to change? You still have your uniform on and there's Rosie looking so . . .' Judith took in Mother's pristine suit, '. . . nice.'

'I'm fine. Thank you.'

'Hey, Mom, look at the size of these steaks,' Harry called.

She smiled at her son. 'That's nothing, Harry.'

'I know,' he laughed. 'When you've eaten eland, steaks are nothing.'

Sweetheart worked as a volunteer at the local hospital so I guess she knew instinctively that Mother shouldn't stand long. She took Mother's arm and settled down with her on a bench. Aunt Bonnie, Uncle Eddie and the kids arrived in a great display of noise. Eddie Jr and Donna Marie bombed into the house as if they owned it and within a minute Aunt Bonnie was chucking a beer down her throat on the grass and Uncle Eddie was gutting fish over in a corner. It would be fair to say that Aunt Bonnie had made no effort for the party at all. She was at the other end of the sartorial spectrum to Mother. She wore jeans and a T-shirt before even folk singers thought it was a good idea. Father stood uncertainly in the middle of the patio. Now he didn't have Mother to hold up he wasn't sure where to go. Judith minced over to the barbecue and put her arms around Harry's waist. He patted her hand and prodded at his task with a huge fork as flames spat up from the grill.

'Honey,' wheedled Judith, kissing his back after each word. 'Do you think maybe you put the steaks on a little too soon? I mean the fire looks a little hot.'

It had all been going so sedately that Harry's speed surprised everyone. He turned Judith under his arm with one hand and grabbed her by the neck. She kept smiling but sagged slightly as he held her like his own personal Resussa-Annie.

'Darling!' he hissed, smiling. 'What does it say on here?' He held her face close to the words on his apron. Judith laughed as she tried to release herself.

'Oh I know it . . .'

Harry squeezed his hand closed on the back of her neck. He spat the words through his big teeth.

'In charge. It says I am in charge.'

No one said anything. We all saw, we all watched, and

no one said anything. I like to think Father would have but I know he wouldn't. I should have but I didn't. I was too busy thinking about girls not rushing the plate.

'Harry.' Sweetheart spoke quietly to her son. He looked at her and I thought something was going to explode. Instead he stroked Judith's neck and pulled her to him for a hug like he was just kidding. Judith laughed and moved away to smooth her hair. Harry carried on as if nothing had happened. Happy couple banter.

'Hey, Dorothy, you're not wearing one of those anti-war bracelets, are you? Eddie, you know your Donna Marie has one?'

Eddie shrugged and pulled the liver from a trout. 'Kids.'

'It's not just kids. That goddamn Martin Luther King riling up the black people against our boys.'

'He's dead,' said Aunt Bonnie, opening another beer.

'That's not the point. It's un-American. Why, I never even questioned serving my country. When I signed up . . .'

Sweetheart interrupted quietly. 'Don't upset yourself, son.'

'I am not upset, but if those goddamn Commie people had never . . .'

We didn't hear what the goddamn Commies should never, because the fire alarm went off on the other side of the harbor. As the siren started, Harry threw off his apron.

'I'll get the car,' yelled Uncle Eddie, divesting himself of fish scales on the run. The hooter carried on giving the signal as Aunt Bonnie counted.

'Three-two-four. Over on Palmer, Eddie,' she yelled after her husband. Harry nodded.

'Come on, Charlie. Sounds like a big one.' He gave Father no choice but grabbed his arm and in a second the men were gone.

Almost every guy in Sassaspaneck was a member of the Volunteer Fire Brigade. It was partly to do with economic necessity in the town and partly to do with some kind of sperm-count display in the men. It was about as macho an organization as it was possible to find. Sassaspaneck was not a rich town. There had been a boom in the twenties when the Burroughs Boot Factories were going full-throttle, but nothing had been the same after the Depression. Fifty miles upstate from the city, it was a little too far to be commuter belt and no industry had ever settled along its shores again. Now the town didn't have the money for a full-time fire brigade. The big horn over at the boatyard would suddenly start blasting and men from all over the town would close down stores, drop fishing rods and race to be first on the engine. They all wanted to drive the fire truck, or at least race through town clinging on in a yellow hat and big boots.

Each street had a different series of blasts and the council printed a list of them so everyone in the neighborhood could tell exactly where the fire was. The signals didn't tell you where in the street, as it was generally reckoned if you couldn't see the fire by the time you got there the owners had no business calling out the brigade in the first place. Mr Angelletta from the pizza parlor (*Tony's Pizzeria – 25¢ a slice – Your Mother Should Make it so Good*) was nearly always first on the engine as the firehouse stood between the pizza parlor and Torchinsky's (*It's Your Funeral*) Funeral Parlor. Mr Torchinsky always stayed behind.

'Please God there are no fatalities,' he would mutter outside his door as the engine pulled away. Then he would turn and polish the brass plate on his door. 'Still, if it should happen . . .'

The women sat quietly on the patio. Within a few minutes we could hear the sirens of the first engine pulling out toward Palmer. Judith went to get some sewing to do and Aunt Bonnie grabbed a fresh six-pack out of the garbage can. Sweetheart sat looking at Judith.

'He means well. He's not been himself since . . .' Judith interrupted with a stab of her needle.

Sweetheart shook her head and changed the subject. 'So, Rosie, isn't this nice? We have time to visit now the boys have gone off to play. What do you do with yourself all day?' she asked. My mother smiled uncertainly. I was curious to hear the answer.

'Oh, you know, the house, Dorothy . . . et cetera.' The others nodded. It was a full life. Sweetheart smiled. Judith settled down to her Christmas tapestry in the warm summer air.

'Sweetheart works as a candy-striper. You know, a volunteer at the hospital. Kind of fancy cleaner, isn't it, Sweetheart?'

'I work with the patients,' replied Sweetheart quietly. It was obviously an old exchange. Judith hardly took a breath.

'I mean, I think it is wonderful to give your hours

but being *married* I just don't have the time.'

There was some problem here but I couldn't work out what it was. Judith was getting at Sweetheart but I didn't know how. Aunt Bonnie flipped open another beer. Judith stabbed at a festive reindeer and ploughed on.

'I don't know how you stand that hospital. The place is full of people who don't pay their bills. Harry was talking to Doc Martin today. Doc had a woman up there who had been admitted with terrible back pain. Turns out she only works as a furniture remover! She said to the doc, "What can I do?" He said, "You can start by behaving like a lady and stay home." '

Aunt Bonnie nodded. 'Doc Martin, he's a funny guy.'

Sweetheart fanned herself. 'Going to be a hot summer.' She shifted to get more comfortable and sighed.

Judith looked up. 'You still haven't been down to the store, have you, Sweetheart? I keep telling you. Do you have an eighteen-hour girdle yet, Rosie? They are fabulous. Harry can't get enough of them. They just sell the minute they come off the truck into the store. I keep telling Sweetheart. Your own son and you won't go.'

'I like my old girdle just fine,' said Sweetheart, fanning herself.

'A woman shouldn't have to suffer.' Judith pulled herself upright. 'You should try one, Bonnie, might give you a better shape.'

'Who gives a hang?' barked Bonnie into her beer.

Judith eyed Bonnie, who was slumped on the grass. 'Might give you a shape at all. I'm sure Eddie would like it.'

'If Eddie don't like my shape he knows what he can do.'

I looked at the four women, Bonnie, Judith, Sweetheart and my mother, and I knew I didn't want to be any one of them. I wanted to be driving the fire truck.

Chapter Five

Inside Harry and Judith's house Donna Marie and Eddie were watching TV in the den. I was shunted away from the women's talk 'to make friends'. I stood in the doorway of the small room where the black and white TV blared. Eddie Jr looked at me.

'Hey, English, where's the tie?'

'I took it off,' I answered, trying to make my vowels sound right. He turned back to the TV.

'Made you look like a freak.'

'They got freaks out at the zoo.' Donna Marie never looked up as she spoke. 'Maybe you oughta go out there.'

The friendship wasn't going that well. I was still too different. I went and looked in the sitting room. On a nest of tables a small, strange-looking goldfish was making its way erratically across the waters of a crystal bowl. It was strange-looking because it couldn't swim straight. It tumbled pathetically through the water.

'It's the way they're bred.' Sweetheart came quietly up

behind me. 'It's called a tumbrel. They are bred and rebred to encourage the spine to curve unnaturally. It's a fish freak. Here, look.' Sweetheart took a small pocket mirror from her bag and held it down into the bowl. The tumbrel stopped its bumbling course and seemed to stare at the mirror for a moment. Then the ridiculous fish turned painfully and swam awkwardly back where it had come from.

'Donna Marie called me a freak,' I said.

'Curvature of the spine. That's what's wrong with it. They say goldfish only remember things for a few seconds.' Sweetheart laughed. It was the light sound of a small bird.

'I used to know a man called John Junior who knew all about animals. He used to say goldfish would be a nightmare for a fish doctor. You'd have to keep on telling the tumbrel it was sick, because it wouldn't remember. Of course if the doctor was a goldfish as well the whole thing would take for ever.' Sweetheart pretended to play both parts but her light voice made the two indistinguishable. 'I'm afraid, Mr Tumbrel, we have bad news. Oh no! Yes. I'm afraid, Mr Tumbrel, we have bad news. Have I already told you this? We have bad news. Oh no! Yes.'

Sweetheart looked at me and put her hands on my shoulders. 'I once knew a man called Fred from Chicago. He had a very strange throat. Kind of wide. It didn't look right. I guess he was a kind of freak. He changed his name to Monsieur Cliquot from Paris and took up sword-swallowing. Eventually he could swallow an electric light bulb connected to an eight-volt battery while juggling and made a lot of money. I knew a bearded lady too but she was never very happy. Really she wanted to be a bare-back rider but she could not get the hang of it. The lovely Madame Josephine Clofullia from Switzerland.'

'Did she really have a beard?'

'Of course.' Sweetheart winked at me so I wasn't sure. 'She finally did get to work with horses but it didn't go well. John Junior, he had shows all over the country. He put her in the Western Wonder Show of the World with Stupendous New Equine Features, but she sued him.'

'Why?'

'It only had one horse in it. That always made Phoebe laugh. She said Madame Josephine had no imagination. The taking of Troy was a one-horse show and that was pretty spectacular.'

I remembered. 'Phoebe. In the wheelchair. And John Junior – the big man?'

'Yes.' Sweetheart looked at me. 'How do you know that?'

I blushed. I was sure I shouldn't have been there. 'The big house . . . there's a picture . . . I saw it.'

Sweetheart sat down on a plastic-covered chair and smiled at me. I plumped down on the floor in front of my new friend.

'I forgot about the picture. That day! The day the painter came, the noise was unbearable. I think he was quite a distinguished artist as well. If you can imagine the collective noise of a giraffe, a bunch of lions, several tigers, a leopard, a polar bear, assorted hyenas and a sealion making their way home from the train station after a long day's journey then you might have it about right. The poor painter. He did his best but the giraffe ran off and got entangled in the garden pagoda. It stuck its head through the top and proceeded to drag the entire thing toward the house. It caused havoc with the rhododendrons. Phoebe was crying with laughter. All the time John was shouting to her, "Look what I brought you! You told me to get you a souvenir from Africa. Look!" Not that there weren't enough animals already. He just kept bringing more.'

'Did you know him – John?'

Sweetheart stared into the fish bowl. 'I sure did. It was a long time ago. John Barton Burroughs Junior. He was a good man. Rich and bored, but he was a good man. He built that house for his wife.'

'Phoebe?'

'No, Phoebe was his sister. Billie. Billie Blake. Of course, that's not the house in the picture. That was the old Burroughs House. It was nice too, just not grand like the new one. It was square, red-brick, nothing fancy. Billie pronounced it "a thoroughly reliable, respectable and dull building", so John built her a new one.'

'The house of love,' I said. Sweetheart looked surprised, but I wasn't a trainee spy for nothing.

'Yes, the house of love. Whatever Billie wanted. They had the money then . . . 'twenty-six or 'twenty-seven . . . must have been nineteen twenty-seven, before the Crash anyhow.'

'What was wrong with Phoebe?'

'Polio, and then I guess she was always weak. You see . . .'

Judith tottered into the room, patting her hair. 'There

you are. What are you two doing in here? I've been looking everywhere.'

'I was telling Dorothy about the old Burroughs' house.'

Judith looked at Sweetheart for a moment and didn't say anything. She glanced at Pearl's picture and gave a slight shake of her head.

'Yes, well, I never go there any more.'

'You should,' said Sweetheart.

Judith gave a little jiggle of her head. The weight of hair made the move work its way right down to her feet.

'Look, Sweetheart, you know it makes Harry uncomfortable, and . . . yes, well, Dorothy, you kids could eat now. We'll wait for the men, of course, but you kids could start.'

It was two hours before the men returned from the fire. Donna Marie, Eddie Jr and I had burgers but the women waited for the men. Judith fussed over everything while we munched.

'The men will be hungry. We had better save as much food as possible, don't you think? Eddie Junior, another cheeseburger? Men eat a lot anyway, don't they, but after tonight . . . well, they will have been doing men's work.' Judith sprayed the side of the ketchup bottle with disinfectant and polished it with a cloth. Men's work? I couldn't imagine what Father would be doing.

Sweetheart got everyone another drink but no one else moved. Aunt Bonnie was still on the lawn with a can of beer. She had made a little necklace out of the beer-can tabs. Sweetheart went and sat on the porch swing with

Mother.

The women's abstinence from food turned out to be pointless. In fact, the men returned fully sated. The fire had been at the General Amherst Restaurant. Once they had realized it was out of control, the brigade of boys had fanned the flames round the kitchen to roast all the meat in there and enjoyed the biggest cook-up the town had ever seen. They came back full, filthy and pumping with their own virility. Even Father had a smudge and had loosened his tie. Harry steamed into the yard and plunged his hand in the iced garbage can. He threw a beer at Father who, always alert to unexpected bouncers, grabbed it deftly. To my surprise he opened it and began to drink without asking for a glass.

'Hey, great catch, Charlie.'

Joey Amorato arrived with Eddie. He was the last of our immediate neighbors. Joey was really small for a man. Small and wide. I knew if I grew up to be a man, which I knew I wouldn't, but if I did, then I would look like Joey. Not that I would want to, but life isn't fair. He wore light brown pants and a matching work shirt but it had been some time since either one had seen a washing machine. Apparently it was because he lived alone and his mother had died. No one said why he couldn't do it himself. The shirt was tucked into Joey's pants but it protested at every button. His belly hung like a precipice over his work boots, which had also seen years of service. There was a popular men's hairspray ad on TV at the time announcing, 'The wet head is dead. Long live the dry look.' Joey hadn't heard about it. He was going bald with some speed. What was left of his hair was greased back into a DA you could fry an egg on. I'm trying to think of good things to say about Joey. He smiled a lot, which was good because he had no chin to speak of. His face kind of fell off at the smile, but at least the smile was a good finish. I don't know how old he was. Everyone was just a grown-up. I think he went to school with Judith, which would have made him her age, but he was so short that he looked like a man who wasn't done with growing yet. Anyway he was whatever you are when you're more than thirty and not dead yet.

Donna and Eddie Jr went back inside when Joey arrived.

'Hey, it's the dog catcher,' yelled Eddie Jr as he ran inside. 'Bet you can't catch me.'

Joey laughed uncertainly. 'Kids today,' he said to no one in particular. 'Looking great, Judith,' he mumbled as she passed him a drink. She gave that giggle again which I thought really let her down.

Harry laughed. 'You cruising my wife again, you dumb schmuck?'

Joey looked down at what he could see of his feet. 'No, no.'

I knew the kids didn't like Joey. He had been bitten by a dog as a boy and the close of those canine jaws had determined his whole life. A life dedicated to revenge. I had seen him in his dog-catcher van. He drove with intense purpose, stopping only to carry out his duties or dust the framed photograph on his dashboard. It was a picture of himself with Vice-President Hubert Humphrey, taken at a whistlestop tour in the '64 election. The VP's train had made an unscheduled halt in

Sassaspaneck and Joey had been the only member of the local administration anyone could get on the phone. I wondered where dog catcher put him on my Chinese list. Stray dogs were number 7, but I wasn't sure about people who spent time with them.

On his day off, Joey shot rats on the waterfront with a rifle. If he was in a bad mood he would just stun them with a BB gun and finish them off with large rocks. The gun fired little plastic pellets and he had once winged the Good Humor Ice Cream man by mistake, but everyone balanced this up with his useful function of keeping down the rodent population.

The men began drinking heavily and the women fussed around them. No one ate the huge steaks which withered on the grill. I went to watch TV in the house but the others wouldn't let me have a say about the channel. After *The Brady Bunch* and *Bewitched* I came out. Only the women were still in the yard. Mother was sitting with Sweetheart. Aunt Bonnie sat on the grass smoking and Judith was sewing on a canvas chair. Judith was in the middle of one of those adult conversations which stops the minute a kid appears.

'Harry won't even read her letters. I mean Pearl—'

Everyone looked at me.

'Where's Father?' I asked.

'The men are dealing with a dangerous smell in the house.' Aunt Bonnie giggled.

'We're doomed, doomed,' intoned my mother in a false Scottish accent. I knew instantly. Drunk, the lot of them. I went in to find my sensible father. In the kitchen Uncle Eddie, Father and Harry were sitting among floorboards.

There was a terrible smell in the room. They had taken up the entire floor and Harry and Father were now taking turns looking under it with a torch. Joey had actually climbed down between the joists and was yelling into the darkness.

'It ain't here. I swear it ain't comin' from here. Ain't nothing here.'

'So anyway,' Father's faint voice pushed itself forward, 'I served under General Ha Ha Splendid Shepherd.'

'Get out of here.'

'No really. Ha Ha Splendid Shepherd. He absolutely adored fighting. Used to plunge into the thick of the action with the cry, "Ha ha, splendid! Lots of fighting and lots of fun." Anyway we were due to attack this particular bridge and we knew the bloody Jerry had called for reinforcements. So you know what he did?'

'What?' slurred Joey.

'Sent them a telegram.'

'Who?' Harry was having trouble following Father's near-mute story.

'The Germans. Ha Ha Shepherd sent the Germans a telegram pretending he was the German colonel, saying don't worry about reinforcements, I've already taken the bridge. So they never came. It was brilliant. Fabulous chap. I remember his first officer was captured and he sent him a pair of wirecutters disguised as a ham bone.'

Harry punched Father on the arm, the way men make friends. 'You served in the war?'

Father tried to stand and salute. 'Certainly did. Royal Horseguards, Major Kane at your service.'

'God damn.' Harry beamed. 'Corporal Shlick, sir.'

The men went off into a World War Two reverie. Through the kitchen door I could see Rocco. He was still sporting my hat and was now lying in a pool of his own devising. He looked at me and chose that moment to emit an explosion of wind so astonishing that it almost lifted him off the parquet, and bounced the hat over one ear. The noise brought Uncle Eddie to the surface.

'Dorothy, do you smell gas? We think we smell gas.'

'I think it's the dog,' I replied.

'The dog!' The men fell about laughing and went back to poking the nether parts of the Schlick house. I stepped over the boards and went and looked at Rocco. By the time I got there he had stopped moving entirely. I knelt down and looked at him. Nothing moved. Not even wind. Under my dark blue cap'n's hat, I was pretty sure he was dead.

It struck me as tricky news. I looked at a small embroidery which advised me to *Look on the Bright Side* and wandered back to the kitchen.

'Mr Schlick,' I began. Father looked over a beer can at me. He was filthy.

'Ah, my lovely daughter Dorothy,' he slurred. 'You know, in our family we only ever send the boys to school but with Dorothy it took ages to make up our minds.' This remark was apparently hilarious. The men fell about, quite literally, with the result that Harry slipped down through the widest gap in the floorboards. He landed next to Joey, who had fallen asleep beside a pipe. Joey's stomach rose and fell like a beached whale mindful of the Japanese hunting fleet. I looked down at Harry. I decided I didn't care if I was rushing the plate.

'Your dog's dead,' I said very clearly. The sober voice among drunks.

He blinked at me. 'What?'

'Your dog. Rocco? He's dead.'

Harry looked at me for a moment and then dug his elbow into Joey. 'Hey, Joey, wake up. My goddamn dog's dead.' Joey blinked back to life for a moment. His greased locks had fallen over his eyes and he couldn't see real well. 'My dog's dead,' repeated Harry.

'I am a dog catcher. I am *the* dog catcher,' replied Joey with what dignity remained. 'If the dog is dead I do not *need* to catch it.' His head fell back on his chest.

'Stupid schmuck,' said Harry, attempting to climb from beneath the floor. 'This is so wrong,' he muttered as Eddie and Father nodded but did nothing. 'So wrong. I am the goddamn Mayor and I should not be lying next to a goddamn dog catcher who won't catch the goddamn dog. Judith!' he bellowed. In seconds she was at his side, followed by the other women. Even Mother had made it to her feet. Harry looked at his wife.

'Judith, the goddamn dog has died and Joey won't catch it. Tell him to catch it. You and he are so goddamn close, you tell him.' It was perhaps not the best way to break the news. To put it mildly, Judith fell apart.

'Don't say that. You don't mean it,' she cried over and over and over. Mascara streamed down her face. Aunt Bonnie patted her on the back and lit a cigarette. Mother decided it was a good time to be helpful and fainted. Father, who had been having something close to a good time, was mortified. He tried to bring Mother round and then he tried to lift her. Meanwhile Harry was in the hall, shaking the clearly deceased Rocco. Sweetheart stood beside him just crying silently. It was mayhem. Father simply could not lift Mother and began to feel faint himself. Aunt Bonnie took him outside to cool off, which left Judith hysterical. Joey woke up and, not knowing what had happened, leaped to Judith's defense.

'What happened, what happened?' he yelled. No one said anything so I said:

'Judith is upset because Harry . . .'

That was as far as I got. Joey heard the words 'Judith', 'upset' and 'Harry', turned around and punched Harry. Judith screamed and for reasons I will never understand grabbed me and began crying on my shoulder. Everything was a little confused after that. In the end it was Uncle Eddie who carried Mother back across the road. Eddie was so strong, it was nothing to him. He salvaged her. We had to go out the back way as no one liked to move the dog. I think Sweetheart helped Mother to bed.

I sat in the Schlicks' sitting room with Judith, waiting for her to calm down. She sobbed for a long time but it dripped right off the plastic covers. When she calmed a little I tried to be helpful.

'I loved that dog,' she said. 'He was my baby.'

'Yes,' I said.

'I don't know how I'm going to say goodbye to him,' she moaned.

We had never stayed anywhere long enough to have a pet so I wasn't sure either.

'Maybe we could have a funeral,' I suggested hesitantly. 'So you could say goodbye. We had one for Father's mum and Mother said it made her feel great.'

'Oh, Dorothy, do you think we could? Would you help me?' I didn't know why she was asking me but I couldn't think why not. I shrugged.

'Sure.'

'You must be such a comfort to your mother. If my Pearl was here she would have helped me.' This notion set her off again. Then Harry came in with a steak on his eye and I decided it was time to go. Back at home I sat up waiting for Father. I guess he had been in the Schlicks' yard all that time. When he finally came in he went straight to his papers in the dining room. I went to talk to him. I had a lot of questions. It had been a very different evening for everyone. Maybe it was a good time to talk.

'Father?' I started.

'Hmm,' he said, not looking up.

'Why did Harry treat Judith like that?' I asked.

'Like what?' His head snapped up. 'Whatever he was doing it is none of our business.'

'But he was hurting her at the barbecue and it wasn't nice. I know everyone had had a lot to drink but . . .' Father looked closely at me.

'What's happened to your accent?'

'Nothing,' I mumbled, trying to remember how to say the word 'nothing'.

'Well, keep it that way. While I am delighted you are having the full American experience I would appreciate it if you left some of the more unpleasant vowels at the front door.' It was a very long sentence for him. He looked back at the table and carefully began to open a new letter from the British Library. I backed away and went out into the front yard. It was obviously not a good time to ask about funerals.

It was still warm out and the cicadas were clicking away in the night air. The Pontiac gleamed in the moonlight. It was so powerful and sleek-looking. I didn't think about it. I went inside and took the keys off the hall table. It was an automatic car. There was nothing to it. I sat on the very edge of the seat, peering over the steering wheel, slipped the car into R for reverse and pulled out into the street. I drove up to the Dapolitos' and past them to the Yacht Club, turned around and went back down to the stop sign. I didn't think about anything. Just drove round and round in circles. Traveling and not arriving.

Chapter Six

I have to be honest and say that I wasn't that keen on Rocco when he was alive. He was really too drippy for a pet. But now he was dead I felt bad. I kept thinking about Sweetheart crying and I wanted to do something to help. Anyway, the funeral had kind of been my idea so I went to the only place I could think of. I had often parked my bike against the window at Torchinsky's Funeral Parlor on Main (*Est. 1928*) while I went to get a piece of pizza from Tony's. Tony didn't want bikes in front of his place because he liked to show off in the window, tossing dough in the air and making it land on the tray. Putting your bike in front of Torchinsky's was okay. It wasn't like Torchinsky's had a big display which you could obscure. They couldn't exactly do embalming or whatever to bring in the customers. The window was done in basic black with a large framed map of the cemeteries in the area marked with their religious denominations. It made it look as if they charged by distance of delivery.

There was organ music playing when I entered but otherwise the place was as quiet as you would expect for the departed. I can't say it was exactly cozy – but it *was* a place of embalming. In my great Chinese order embalmed things were second only to 'Those Belonging to the Emperor'. The store had to be an important place. A leatherette sofa stood against one wall with framed photographs of floral tributes hanging all around. There was a large wooden table with several small boxes on it which Mrs Torchinsky was polishing. She looked up at me as I opened the door.

'So what do you think?'

'About what?'

Mrs Torchinsky held up a miniature coffin complete with brass handles. 'The new oak. I think it looks nice.'

The coffin was maybe ten inches long and three inches wide. It was perfect but I couldn't think what you would use it for.

'It's a little small,' I said.

Mrs Torchinsky laughed. 'It's only for display. Unless maybe you have a dead gerbil. You don't have anything dead, I'm right?'

'No, but I wanted to ask about a small, you know, box. It's for a dog.'

'For a dog?' Mrs Torchinsky shook her head. 'On this we should one day retire.'

The organ music stopped and a scratching sound started behind the curtain. The record had finished. From the next room I could hear rhythmic banging. Maybe someone was trying to get out of one of the oak coffins.

'Builders,' said Mrs Torchinsky. 'Building a new chapel of rest. In our lifetime we should get some rest.' She was a comfortable-looking woman but kind of pinched in at the waist. Her gray hair had been given the general direction of a bun but it had rebelled and hung in wisps all around her plump face. It wasn't a bad thing. It sort of hid the hair which grew on her top lip. She had quite a mustache. I had to remember to ask Sweetheart if Mrs Torchinsky looked like the bearded lady she had talked about. I didn't know how much beard a woman could have. Mother got little hairs on her chin. I knew that, even though she always put the tweezers away if I came in when she was using them. Mrs Torchinsky put down the baby coffin and moved a black cotton drape to put the record back on. From beside the record player she got her coat and hat.

'Ralph!' she called to the back of the store. 'Ralph, I gotta go out and get cookies for the builders.'

A surprisingly loud voice boomed from the back. 'They want cookies they should build a bakery.'

'You got customers.' Mrs Torchinsky put on her coat. 'For a dog.'

'A dog I can do,' yelled the voice. 'A dog would be good. Bite the goddamn builders in the ass. Are you people never going to be finished?'

The question was answered by more banging. Mrs Torchinsky buttoned her coat.

'My husband will see to you.' She turned to go, then turned back. 'I'm sorry for your loss. May the dog rest in peace.' It was very professional. She smiled, pleased with herself. It was fascinating. It made her mustache spread sideways. She left. I waited for a moment until Ralph Torchinsky appeared. He looked like an undertaker. He was dressed like an undertaker. He just didn't talk like one. But the surface picture was great. In his late fifties, he was kind of spooky-looking. He had a slight deformity on his back and you couldn't tell if it was just a stoop or an actual hump. It pushed his bald head down, as if he spent all his time making sure clients stayed below in their graves. He wore fantastically thick spectacles with glass you could have cut from a whiskey tumbler. Maybe he couldn't see into the graves at all. Maybe the stoop and the bad eyes had developed from years of trying to look sympathetic and efficient at the same time, or maybe he had always had it, I don't know. He wore gray striped pants and a tailcoat with an old-fashioned wing-collar shirt. Over the top of his funereal outfit he had a white lab coat. I wished I hadn't come. Maybe he was in the middle of cleaning up some dead person. I was sure I could detect the waft of something chemical about him. Anyway, he looked the part of a funeral man but the voice was bad casting. It was much too loud.

'So you lost your dog?' he bellowed. 'What kind of dog was it?'

'It wasn't actually my . . .'

'I hate this music,' announced Mr Torchinsky loudly. 'Why can't we play anything else? Forty years I've been listening to goddamn organ music. In all those years I never figured out why people want you to be so goddamn quiet in funeral parlors. It's not as though you could wake any of the clients. Band music. That would cheer people up. I love band music. Sousa. There was a man. Come.'

He gestured to the curtained arch which led through to the back of the store. I had suddenly lost my nerve. Seeing a dog dead had been enough. I mean, it had actually been quite interesting but I didn't want to graduate to the real thing. You know, people.

'Mr Torchinsky . . . it's not even my dog and the thing is . . .'

'Come,' he repeated and disappeared out back. I had too many English manners not to do as I was told. Through the cloth arch there was a corridor with several closed doors. Here the dead no doubt lurked, with fixed grins on their lips and formaldehyde up their noses. At the end of the corridor, double doors led into a large room where two workmen were sitting drinking root beer. There were bits of wood and sawdust everywhere.

'Please God no one should die before you finish your goddamn soda,' yelled Mr Torchinsky as we passed by and out a door at the back. The place wasn't what I had expected. Behind the dark store there lay a large open lawn. Beyond it was a substantial glasshouse which stood like a relic of some Victorian era. Mr Torchinsky hurried over the lawn and opened the door. I was right behind him. Heat rose up and hit us as we entered. It was a remarkable place. Far removed from death, it was awash with life. To say that the place contained birds does not begin to do justice to the collection in the interior. It was a Santa's grotto for the ornithologically inclined. There were birds everywhere. Birds of every shape, color, size and flying ability. There were the bombing Biggles types and the quivering victim types. Mr Torchinsky stood surrounded by them. He took a small portion of something and put it on his tongue. A small bird came and sat on his finger and he fed it from his mouth. Now I could see what the white coat was for. A white coat made whiter by bird droppings.

'See this, see this,' called Mr Torchinsky. 'A Hungarian thrush. I have done it, you know, I have done it,' he said, spitting bird food in every direction in his excitement.

Mr Torchinsky began a small dance. He jigged, singing to himself.

'I've done it. I've done it. I will be the person to introduce into the United States every single bird that William Shakespeare ever mentioned. Look at my babies. There are robins, wagtails, skylarks, starlings, hedge sparrows, dunnocks, song-thrushes, missel-thrushes, blackbirds, redwings, my Hungarian thrush, nightingales, goldfinches, siskins, bullfinches, great tits, Dutch tits, dippers, corncrakes, parrot crossbills, house sparrows, cherry birds. Four thousand European songbirds. Think of that. My wife, she has no idea. Such a show I could make before I am too old.

'That time of year thou mayst in me behold,
When yellow leaves, or none, or few do hang
Upon those boughs which shake against the cold,
Bare ruined choirs, where late the sweet birds sang.'

A red bird landed on Mr Torchinsky's bald head and slid off, making him laugh. 'Aren't they wonderful? Even in death there is life. Come, we deal with the dog. Such a sadness when a dog dies. Maybe you should think about birds.'

We went and sat in Mr Torchinsky's office. It looked like any other office except it had several urns on display and a

1968 calendar from the National Association of Morticians highlighting particularly busy times of year – after Christmas, Labor Day, that kind of thing. Framed on the wall was a picture of a large, square house. The one from the painting. I wasn't sure how to explain about Rocco so I started with the picture.

'Is that the Burroughs House?' I asked.

Torchinsky nodded. 'The wrong business I went into. Boots, that was where the money was. The Burroughs they made a fortune out of boots and what did they spend it on? Orangutans and elephants. Boots wasn't enough. John Junior he had to go into showbusiness. That's the old house. I went to work there when I was fifteen. I always liked it best. The new place was too fancy. That,' he tapped the photograph, 'that was a solid house. John Junior built that one to impress his father and you know what his father did?'

I shook my head.

'Died just before it was finished, because life's like that. John Senior, come all the way from Ireland. Made the most beautiful boots and had a daughter who never walked. Poor Phoebe. Ain't life like that too? So then Billie comes along and John Junior he is crazy for her, bam, down comes the old house and up goes the new. Crazy time. I should never have listened to them. So many people were dying those years before the Crash. Everyone thought there was money but it was all falling apart. I was young. John Junior was always looking for an angle. He said to me, "A funeral parlor, now would be a good time for a funeral parlor. I'll set you up." I should have gone into boots. Factories making boots, then I would have made money. Or liquor. Booze was the big money. You heard of Prohibition?'

'No.'

'Made John Junior a lot of dough. The wrong trade I went into. Though death we had plenty of toward the end. People beaten to death in speakeasies, people having "accidents" off the top of skyscrapers. Too much high living. I laid her out, you know.'

'Who?'

'Billie. John Junior's wife. God, she was beautiful, even at the end. Most beautiful thing I ever saw. Here, look.' Mr Torchinsky stooped down some more and reached into a drawer at the bottom of his desk. He rummaged for a moment and then brought out a large paper bag. From inside the bag he carefully removed a magazine and laid it in front of me. It was a copy of *Vogue* from 1925. On the cover a young woman looked out grinning. She was gorgeous. A kind of living poster for what the jazz age wanted to be. She wore a khaki shirt with the sleeves rolled up, a blue-and-green-striped tie and dark pants tucked into knee-high leather riding boots. I guess the outfit might have been considered somewhat shockingly masculine for the time. Billie, however, looked very female and very fabulous. Her short blond hair with its Marcel wave was a feminine full stop to a formidable costume. Beside her, looking calm despite the fame, stood a huge tiger. A banner proclaimed the woman: *Billie Blake, Tiger Tamer*. I suppose it was a cliché of the jazz age really – a 1920s woman, young, blonde, exciting, living life on the edge – but I thought it was thrilling.

'Greatest female cat trainer of all time,' declared Mr Torchinsky. 'And she had some competition then. In her time it was a growing business. I think there were more than fifty animal trainers in the US in the twenties, but Billie carried the flag. Such an instinct the girl had for it.' Mr Torchinsky picked up the magazine and leafed through it tenderly.

'And you knew her?'

'Oh yes, I saw her in the cage many times. So beautiful. It was something to watch. Not that I think her family was pleased. They wanted her to be a nurse, but she couldn't do it. She had this thing about blood. Forgive me, but a nurse who can't deal with blood is like an undertaker who worries about ghosts. I think she graduated and everything but then she had a kind of breakdown. Her father, who was a big noise in bicycle wheels, sent her to California to recuperate. Bicycle wheels, such money in that too. Boots, bicycle wheels, things in factories. Me, I'm an undertaker.' Mr Torchinsky sighed as he looked at the faded, rich people having a good time in the old publication.

'John Junior only saw that magazine and decided to marry Billie. I remember when I met her. When John Junior brought her home to the house.'

After her breakdown, Billie had been packed off to stay with her uncle Lief and his daughter Grace, Grace Gerritsen. Grace was a year younger than Cousin Billie and not anywhere near as beautiful. What she was was tall. 'Statuesque', people said, when they were being polite. She was also fantastically strong. Built like an Olympic rower. It gave her a kind of magnetism a lot of people found attractive. Until Billie arrived, Grace had led a rather solitary life. She was studious and liked to read, especially history. She didn't go out much, but Billie changed all that. The two young women hit it off right away and it didn't take long for Billie to make sure they were the talk of the town. Two independent women with money to spend and the energy to spend it. It was the summer of 1922 when Grace, then seventeen, and eighteen-year-old Billie went to visit Selig Zoo in Los Angeles. There they saw a stuntman wrestle Rajan, a huge four-hundred-pound Bengal tiger. It was the most exciting thing either of them had ever seen.

The stuntman was called Roth and Billie asked him if she could come in the cage with Rajan. People didn't know about wild creatures then, and anyway Billie was legendary for not giving up when she wanted something. She plagued Roth until he relented.

'You have to sign a release form,' said Roth. 'I ain't havin' your friend here crying when Rajan turns you to corned beef.' Billie laughed and signed. She wouldn't let Grace do it. She was like that. Always protecting her. Playing the older one. A small crowd gathered as Roth opened the cage door and let Billie in. Rajan was lying in a corner at the back of the cage. He got to his feet as Billie entered and began to pace round her. Billie stood her ground and let him approach. Grace stood entirely still, watching. The crowd was silent. Then Rajan lowered his head and gently butted Billie on the leg with his forehead. She reached out and petted him. He promptly lay down and fell fast asleep. $350 later, the two women owned a tiger. It was no problem for the zoo. For that money they could get a new tiger and have money left over for

a flock of penguins. Things were different then.

John Junior arrived in California in July of 1925 with two purposes. To do some deals with Hank Forepaugh, owner of the Fantastical Forepaugh-Sells Circus, and to bring home a wife – Billie. By then Billie was quite a name. She had even been in Vogue *magazine. John had never met her but he hated detail. That was what Milton, his money man, was for. John Junior had only been in the entertainment business a couple of years but he was already making a big noise. When he arrived at the Sacramento site where Forepaugh-Sells was currently raking it in, Hank Forepaugh was more than happy to give him the big tour. The two men and Milton emerged from a small side tent. Hank was in full flow.*

'I am telling you, the public cannot get enough of the Ubangis. It is the biggest side-show attraction ever. They are fabulous. From West Africa. French, ain't it? Who knows? Anyhow, there's thirteen of them including Queen Guetika or somethin', and two guys. The rest are women and they are fantastic. They have these lips like saucers. Apparently it's, what do you call it? Tradition. In their culture, you know in Africa, they figure women are beautiful if they have these huge lips. Really. They split 'em open when the girls are babies and stick discs in them. Then they get bigger and bigger discs till they have these flabby lips.'

Milton mopped his brow with an initialed handkerchief. 'Imagine them going down on you. I mean, I was thinking with those lips.'

Forepaugh shrugged. 'What the hell do I know? I don't care. The public can't get enough of 'em. I stick 'em in a side tent and folks can buy fish and unpeeled bananas for a nickel to feed to them. They eat it too. Whole raw fish and unpeeled bananas. If you're interested we could talk.'

'Excuse me. I'll be right back.' Something had caught Milton's eye.

John Junior stepped over the pools of mud round the big top. He was skirting round what he really wanted. Immaculately dressed as ever, and any elephant looking closely at him would have known the truth. John was in musth. He was searching for a mate so hard that he was practically leaving a scent trail. He stayed smooth though.

'What do you hear about Barnum?' he inquired of his fellow promoter.

Hank shook his head. 'Gee, they say he got a mermaid from some Jap fisherman in the Fiji Islands. A genuine preserved mermaid. The real McCoy. That guy gets so many breaks. Imagine that landing in your lap.'

John shook his head. 'Seen it. It's actually the head and upper body of a monkey very carefully sewn on to the tail of a large fish. It's good though. He's making money.'

Hank sniggered. 'Bastard.' He paused and sucked on a large cigar while he contemplated. 'I got a spare monkey. What kind of fish?'

A formidable-looking woman emerged from one of the side tents. She wore a hat so large and so feathered with confidence that it probably could have approached on its own. The woman's hair was pigeon gray and pulled back into a traditional chignon. She wore a black dress. Very long and very proper.

'Mr Forepaugh!' she called in the clipped, forceful manner of the English aristocracy. It was a voice accustomed

115

to calling servants across fierce drafts in large family houses. 'Mr Forepaugh.' Hank sighed and hid his cigar behind his back.

'Mrs Lintz. How delightful. Is everything okay?'

'No, Mr Forepaugh, it is not, as you put it, okay. There is a monkey in that enclosure which is quite clearly unwell.'

'Yeah, oh yeah, the monkey. Don't worry. I have great plans for the monkey. Mrs Lintz, may I introduce John Burroughs Junior? John, this is Mrs William Lintz, she's from England. She takes in sick animals from circuses . . . and stuff.'

'Animals are my hobby and my life, Mr Burroughs. We have a moral duty to see that our animal friends lead a good life,' interrupted Mrs Lintz.

'Indeed.' John tipped his hat toward the elderly woman.

She gave him a small nod and then inquired, 'Would you be the Burroughs of the Burroughs Western Wonder Show of the World with Stupendous New Equine Features?'

'The same,' said John.

Mrs Lintz tutted. 'I went. It only has one horse in it.'

John smiled. 'You don't say? Less work for the animals, eh? Lovely hat, Mrs Lintz.'

Mrs Lintz, unaccustomed to compliments, blushed.

Hank knew a good moment when he saw one and slipped away to his wagon, leaving John with the formidable woman. John could delay no longer.

'Would you care to see the tigers, Mrs Lintz?' He graciously offered her an arm.

Billie and Grace were both at the tiger enclosure. As usual Billie was inside the cage and Grace waited by the door. Billie and Rajan were locked in an embrace which drew *sharp breaths from Mrs Lintz. She and John stood in silence as Billie concluded her workout by opening Rajan's mouth and putting her head in. As she released his jaws and stood up, Rajan's teeth snapped shut. Mrs Lintz gasped.*

'Oh my dear,' she cried, 'isn't that dangerous?' Billie grinned through the bars as Rajan slunk off to a corner.

'Absolutely. Very dangerous.' She leaned closer toward the elderly woman. 'Tigers have really terrible breath.' John laughed as Grace moved to open the cage door and let Billie out. Then she held a small basin for her, checked the temperature of the water and handed her cousin a small towel so she could wash her hands. Mrs Lintz was still somewhat taken aback.

'Don't worry, Mrs Lintz,' Billie chuckled as she splashed water without a thought. 'It's all make-believe with animals. You see, they think you are stronger than they are. It's my business to keep that idea going.' Billie finished wiping her hands and held the towel for Grace to take. The two women smiled at each other as Grace moved to empty the bowl. Billie looked at John. 'So, Mrs Lintz, who's your friend?'

'I do beg your pardon. Miss Blake, may I present John Burroughs Junior.'

Billie cocked her head on one side. 'Of Burroughs Western Wonder Show of the World with Stupendous New Equine Features? I hear it only has one horse in it.'

John smiled. 'Apparently so. I'm new to this line.'

'New? What did you do before you launched into entertainment, Mr Burroughs?'

'Boots. I was in boots.'

Billie smiled. 'Burroughs Boots – The Best Boots Money Can Buy. And now the public stand in line for your shows wearing your boots.'

'I do hope so.'

'Now, Miss Blake,' Mrs Lintz beetled on. 'Your tiger . . .'

'Rajan.'

'Rajan. Is he well cared for by Mr Forepaugh?'

'I care for him, Mrs Lintz,' interrupted Grace. 'He is very happy.'

John looked at her for the first time. 'Happy? Is that a concern? Miss . . .'

Grace looked him in the eye. 'Gerritsen. Grace Gerritsen.'

Mrs Lintz could hardly contain herself. 'Concern! It should be the only concern.'

'I see,' said John, 'and pray how can you tell he is . . . happy?'

Billie smiled. 'Easy, Mr Burroughs: he never tries to eat me.'

It was obviously a passionate subject for Grace. 'Of course we must worry if an animal is happy. Why—'

A fantastic noise erupted from behind the main tent and Milton appeared, running, with his pants halfway down his legs. He was desperately trying to pull them up but this was hindered by the speed with which he was running. Hot on his heels came Forepaugh.

'I'm going to kill you, you prick!' Milton hightailed it round behind Rajan and stood looking through the bars and tugging up his pants as Forepaugh approached. The two men circled round, eyeing each other.

'Look, Forepaugh, I'll make you a deal.'

'You were screwing my wife.'

Milton didn't deny it. 'Must have been a misunderstanding. Listen, we could talk.'

'I am not talking with anyone who is fucking my wife.' By now Mrs Lintz had become quite faint. Grace helped her into the fresh air.

'What do you think?' whispered John to Billie as they watched the stand-off.

'I think he was probably screwing the wife.' Billie eyed the two men dispassionately and whispered matter-of-factly, 'Forepaugh'll kill him.'

'No, I know Milton. They'll cut a deal.' John carried on watching Forepaugh and Milton and spoke out of the side of his mouth. 'I want you to come to New York with me, Miss Blake.'

'Why would I do that, Mr Burroughs?'

'Well, I was thinking, if we're going to get married it would be more convenient if we lived in the same state.'

Grace, Billie, Rajan, Milton and John Junior caught the 8.05 out of Sacramento bound for New York. The porter secured them two first-class compartments for the humans and a boxcar for Rajan. John Junior stopped Milton for a second in the corridor as they boarded.

'So, what deal did you do with Forepaugh?' he asked.

'No problem. I cut him in on the action. There's plenty for everybody and it's so neat.' Milton became sweaty with financial excitement as he removed his notebook from his vest pocket.

'I got it all figured out, John. We buy whole distilleries.'

'What distilleries? They closed them all.'

'They didn't knock 'em down. They just closed 'em. Distilleries, corner saloons. They're closed but someone still 119 owns them and they still have a stock of whiskey. Look, here's an example . . . '

'Forget it, Milton. We are not bootlegging. I want everything above board.'

Milton mopped his brow in aggravation. 'Listen, John, in the last normal year before that splendid law called Prohibition was passed, our fellow citizens consumed two billion gallons of hard liquor. And what are they doing now? Drinking coffee? No, they are waiting for us to come good. They are waiting for us to come through with—'

'No liquor.'

'Did I say liquor?' Milton smiled at his own skill. 'John, would you deny a sick man his medicine? Or a religious man his sacramental wine?'

'Well, I . . . '

'Of course not. So we sell a little medicine, a little church wine.' Milton scanned his notebook for the figures. 'Sacramental wine is very big. Every practicing Jewish family is allowed one gallon per adult per year. The amount of wine a synagogue can get depends on the number of worshippers. Now, I can get you a six-hundred-member synagogue working out of a delicatessen on Upper East Side, five hundred and forty out of a Chinese laundry. All kosher. The Assembly of Hebrew Orthodox Rabbis in America. Nice people. Run by an Irishman called Sullivan.'

John sighed. 'I said above board.'

'Really? Above board? The bearded lady? Snow White's actual dwarves? George Washington's nurse? And you're telling me above board?'

'That's different. Isn't there something else?'

Milton flipped through his papers. 'I was thinking we

could move the factories. You remember boots? You used to make boots?'

'The point, Milton?'

'I just did it as an exercise, but if we close down all the Sassaspaneck factories and move everything south, say Georgia, I figure we can clean up. No unions, cheaper labor. They say the white trash'll do what you tell 'em. We can do a stretch-out. Increase the work but not the money. At the moment we're paying eighteen dollars ninety-one a week per head for forty pair boots. I figure we can go to twenty-three dollars but one hundred pair. Of course, it'll kill the town.'

'Whatever you think, but no bootlegging.' John moved to knock on the door to Billie's compartment and paused. 'So what happened with Forepaugh's wife?'

'Give me a break. She was begging for it. Forepaugh never touches her.'

'But she was a good-looking woman.'

Milton put away his notebook bible. 'Yes, but he hurt his back. Some big fire in Monterey. He had to carry the four-hundred-pound fat lady from the freak show out of the blaze.'

John was impressed. 'Boy, he must like the fat lady.'

'Are you kidding? Do you have any idea of her return at the side-shows? Mind you, some of those side-show dames can be something. I once slept with Barnum's wild lady.'

'Borneo?'

'Nah, Rhode Island.'

'Come on, Milton, I want you to meet the woman I am going to marry. Oh, and Milton?'

'Yeah?'

'Button your pants.'

On arrival, Billie decreed that Burroughs House was plain and that John's sister Phoebe was delightful. Phoebe took to Grace instantly and was soon being wheeled about and cared for by her new friend. On the lawns of Burroughs House, as the sun was setting, John gave Billie her engagement ring.

'Why are you doing this, John?' she asked. 'You hardly know me.'

'I know everything I need to. You are beautiful. You are fearless and clever. I'm rich. I can look after you and together we will raise the most beautiful family.'

It was as good a deal as Billie was ever going to get. So she agreed. They formed a gene pool. In the distant woods a moose sounded his forlorn foghorn. Billie laughed.

'I had always imagined music for this moment, not that terrible noise.'

John smiled. 'Grace would tell you that that is not terrible. It only sounds dreadful to us because we can't hear it with the ears of a moose in love.' That night John began drawing up the plans for the greatest house of love ever built, and Billie lay on Grace's bed and wept and wept.

Torchinsky sighed again and closed the magazine. He looked at the front cover and smoothed the edges with his hand.

'So beautiful. I never laid out anything more beautiful.' It was bizarre. I had come about a dead dog and here I was talking old romance with a humpbacked undertaker married to a woman with a mustache.

'She brought some class to John Junior's shows. Before that he had done nothing but the elephants with a few side-shows. Terrible stuff. Although, I remember I liked the tapdancing goat.'

My head was spinning. Tapdancing goats? The builders had gone back to banging and I decided I ought to get on with business.

'I was wondering about this dog.'

'The dog!' boomed Mr Torchinsky, slapping the table loudly with his hand. 'Of course, the dog. Still dead, still got to deal with it. A big dog or a little dog?' He put the magazine back in the bag and opened the drawer to put it away.

'Well, sort of medium. It wasn't mine. It was Mrs Schlick's.'

'Rocco? Judith's Rocco died?' Completely unexpectedly, tears welled up in his eyes. 'She'll be so sad.'

'Yes. That's why I thought maybe if you had a spare box. A small one, not small like Mrs Torchinsky has in the front, but a medium-small one. A dog-size one. I don't have much money but . . .'

'Of course, a box. No charge. No charge. Poor Rocco. I'll drop something off to Judith.' Mr Torchinsky ushered me out, looking at the floor as he walked. As we got to the door he patted me on the back. 'Come back any time, though God willing next time it will be better news.'

Mrs Torchinsky was just returning with a box of cookies as I left. She smiled at me and her mustache did that spreading thing again. As I collected my bike I could just hear her yelling, 'No charge? No charge? What are we, a charity?'

Having sorted the coffin I thought maybe I should get a card for Judith. Something with flowers and sympathy on. The only place for that was up the other end of town at the Pop Inn, next to Abe's Ice Cream Parlor (*Specialty – the Kitchen Sink – 56 Flavors of Ice Cream Served in a Single Container*). It was the middle of the day and Sassaspaneck wasn't exactly buzzing but as I rode up Main Street I realized I was looking at the place differently. This was a much more exciting town than Father realized. It wasn't about smallpox and Indians. It was about tiger tamers and polar bears walking up to the A&P. It was about beautiful women whom men married off magazine covers and rich men who collected strange creatures and built crazy houses.

The Pop Inn was the coolest place in town. They sold everything a kid could want – Peter, Paul and Mary records, brass peace symbols on leather thongs, posters of Picasso doves, op-art posters and Coke bottles melted into unusual shapes. I liked the Susan Politz Shultz posters best. Especially the ones with pictures of Jonathan Livingston Seagull on them which told you that *Friendship is For Ever*. It was kind of a racy place to go to because it was run by Hubert Thomas and he was the only black man in town. Hubert was the first black person I had ever known to say hello to. He was married to Ingrid, who was a white girl from Iceland. They didn't have any kids but Father was keen to explain what would happen when they did.

Father was always happy to explain everyone's behavior in terms of genetics. I think he was comfortable with that, as it just involved diagrams and showing how

Mother's family input had marred his family's hitherto perfect genetic history. Hubert's potential offspring were the perfect illustration for Father's genetic lectures. The first time we met Hubert and Ingrid, Father took me straight home and did pages of long arrows joining up little black and white bubbles. 'And if you look at this chart, it will show you the percentage chance for what color the children will be in the Thomas household.'

In the event they adopted a kid from Phnom Penh, which rather put paid to all Father's hard work. I think Mother was always uncomfortable with Hubert. Certainly he was a man who liked to speak his mind. After the barbecue Harry had invited my parents to one of his Mayor's Cocktail Parties to which Hubert, as a local store owner, had also been invited. Mother had never been to a party where a black person was drinking instead of serving. Hubert just kept smiling at her until she finally had to speak.

'Uh ... haven't we met before?' she managed to mumble.

'I don't know,' said Hubert earnestly. 'After all, we all look alike.'

Mother never got used to saying 'black' instead of 'Negro' and would describe people as 'white' or 'not white' instead, thinking it sounded more polite. I wonder what Hubert felt like as the only black person there, carrying his label on the outside. He had just put a poster up in the window when I arrived.

Close the Zoo it said in big red letters. Hubert was wearing a pair of flared jeans with a piece of bright orange fabric sewn in a great triangle into the flare. The pants finished early on his hips and there was a gap of black midriff before his sleeveless tank top started. He had short Afro hair and the widest nose I had ever seen. I was fascinated by his nose and looked at it every time I was in the store.

'Hey, Mama,' he called as I came in the door. He lifted his right hand in a laid-back peace symbol.

In the face of such a greeting I still wasn't sure what to do. It made me become rather formal. It brought out my father in me.

'Good afternoon,' I said, nodding curtly and moving to the card display.

Hubert was talking to a young woman. She was not a very big woman, more like a cross between a child and something full-grown. Very thin and not real tall. Like a kind of elf. She had very short, chopped-at black hair held tight with a leather thong round her forehead. She wore a strange collection of brilliantly colored garments. She appeared to have dressed by passing blindfolded through a tie-dye workshop. She was very modern. Really cool. She fitted right in with all the stuff Hubert sold. In fact, she was such a perfect customer for the store she looked like you could order one. Hubert was in full flight about something. He had a lot of opinions, but then you were supposed to.

'You're wrong. The place has to go. It is discrimination against animals. They are being held there against their will.'

The woman shook her head and spoke slowly. She had things to say but there was no hurry. She didn't look as though she could rush at anything. 'That's not why they want to close the zoo. They want to build like some football stadium or something.'

'The place has a bad history. If I had been here forty years ago I would have been a freaking freak show at that place.'

'No way, man. It's not that kind of place. It's like a sanctuary. It's cool.' The young woman shook her head for emphasis and a small bell tinkled on the back of her leather head thong. Hubert was getting worked up.

'Don't tell me no way. Do you know where I am from?'

'I don't know. Like Albany?'

'Not now. I mean in the past.' Hubert stood up proud and tall in his flares. 'I am a Bobangi from the Ubangi – West Africa, the Congo. That place, your zoo, they used to bring the Ubangi over here just for people to stare at their lips.' Hubert banged the counter for emphasis.

The young woman frowned. 'Like why?'

'They had big lips. It was part of their culture. People would buy fish and bananas and come just to watch them eat. It ain't right. Paying money to watch good people eat.'

'It isn't like that now. You should like, come out and see.'

'I ain't takin' part in no oppression. It has got to go.'

I wanted to ask whether the Ubangi men would have had big lips too, or just the women. I tried to imagine Hubert with discs under his wide nose. It must have been quite something. I realized I was staring at him. He raised an eyebrow at me.

'Yes, baby?'

'Just this card, thank you.'

We had Rocco's funeral the next day. Harry dug the grave in their backyard. Mr Torchinsky came out in his pinstripe suit and delivered a plain pine box. He paid his respects to the dog and stood even more humped than usual in the presence of actual death. I wanted to ask him more about Billie and Grace and John Junior and the tigers but I thought maybe it was a bad time. Anyway, he had to go. There had been a pile-up on the thruway and he had a busy afternoon. Uncle Eddie came over and helped Harry put Rocco in the coffin. Then he banged the lid on the box and stood looking solemn with his big hands folded. Aunt Bonnie didn't come. Just Uncle Eddie, me, Harry and Judith. Judith was all in black. Black ski pants and a black mohair sweater with a picture of a white poodle on. The sweater was kind of tight and the embroidered poodle bobbed up and down as she sobbed. She just couldn't stop crying, and I must say I had a tear in my eye. Though for me it wasn't so much the dead dog as the smell. I did feel moved by the occasion but the fact is that somehow Rocco was still with us. There was an acrid odor which pierced through the pine box and was almost unbearable. It was terribly hot and the scent burned the inside of my nose. Judith choked her way through the few words from the Hallmark greeting card I had bought.

> 'When we have love,
> It comes from above.
> You gave me your heart
> And though now we're apart
> You are where you belong
> In God's happy throng.'

'That was so beautiful. Dorothy, did you want to add

something?' she asked when she had finished reading.

The answer was 'not particularly', but there were so few of us I thought I'd better. I cleared my throat.

'Dear Lord, well, you have Rocco now. She—'

'He,' said Harry.

'He was a . . . a . . . poodle. I don't know if you've had a pet before . . . well, of course you have. I know Joseph and Mary had a donkey and that must have died but anyway . . . now you have someone to walk through . . . um . . .' I tried to think of somewhere God might walk with a dog, '. . . the valley of the shadow of death . . . Amen.'

I thought it possibly sounded a little Catholic, but Judith hugged me to her as Uncle Eddie and Harry lowered the box into the ground. Afterwards, Uncle Eddie went back to work and Judith went inside. I followed Harry into his fish place. If he knew about fish I thought maybe he knew about tigers too. Harry set about vigorously cleaning one of the tanks.

'I'm so sorry about your dog,' I started.

'It's bad for Judith, that's all.'

'Still, at least he was happy.'

'Happy?' Harry stopped working and looked at me. I felt flustered. I didn't think suggesting his dog had been happy would be controversial. Grown-ups were funny sometimes.

'I mean here. He must have been happy here.'

'Listen, kid, you don't know what you're talking about. Animals aren't happy. It's not like people. It's all about instinct, that's all. He ate because he was hungry, he went after girl dogs because he was a boy dog, he died because he was old. It's genes and instinct, that's all.' On the wall behind his head, Harry's daughter Pearl grinned out from a picture taken on a beach. I wished I hadn't come in.

'Maybe there was a girl dog he really liked,' I tried.

'We're talking about animals here. Mating is about reproduction. That's all. Happy, unhappy. It doesn't come into it.' Harry stopped his work and went into adult lecture mode. 'London Zoo. They used to have a bear pit, right? In it lived this brown bear. The pit had a large wooden pole in it. The public could buy scraps of food to throw on top of the pole to get the bear to climb up so they could see it above the bars. This bear never climbed on a Tuesday. Now what is that? Was he unhappy on a Tuesday or had he decided that Tuesday was his day off? No. It was simple. Monday was half-price at the zoo and lots of people came. The public spent a lot of time feeding the bear on a Monday so on Tuesday he wasn't hungry.' Harry wiped his hands on a towel and turned back to one of the center tanks.

'Look at this.' He picked up a small crab from the tank and placed it in another. In the corner of the crab's new home sat an octopus. Harry put his face right up to the glass to see what was happening. 'Watch. The assassin of the water tank stalks his victim.'

The crab sat quietly, unconscious of any impending doom. Slowly the octopus made its move. A gruesome shadow appeared over the small crustacean. The shadow seemed to be moving backwards, as if to mislead the prey. Then silently, opening like a parachute, the octopus settled over the crab and began to sink down remorselessly. A horrible tentacle darted out and down, flicking under the victim's shell and turning the crab over, helpless on its back. The tentacles hugged the crab to death and then a great horny bill at the heart of the eight-armed murderer began its fell work.

'Instinct. Survival. See, the aggressive male does better. Food, mating, space. It's his job.'

Chapter Seven

The next day I was sitting on the dock and something was new. I wasn't wearing my cap. The day after Rocco's funeral Judith had come over with it. Mother had gone back to bed and Father was gone on the train. Judith was crying and I didn't want to open the screen door to let her in.

'I brought your hat, Dorothy.' She began weeping again. Through the mist of the gray flyscreen I could see tears dripping off the peak. I opened the door a crack and took the sodden hat but I couldn't wear it. I figured if anything had cooties then it was a captain's hat pulled off a dead poodle. Now I sat on the dock without it. I had spent so long hiding under the hat's brim that I wasn't used to having the sun on my face. I quite liked it. I tilted my head back and felt the worn gray boards under my fingers. I felt different. More grown-up, which was good, because I was building up my nerve. I wanted to go to the zoo, the Burroughs zoo, Billie and Grace's place, but I was scared it wouldn't be what I had imagined. I wanted it to be a place of tigers and tension, bears and bravery. Romance, I wanted it to have romance. I knew it lay just outside town but as it happens I went the long way round on my bike. I didn't realize I could have cut straight over the river and through the Burroughs property.

There was no one at the ticket booth when I arrived. I felt nervous. I don't know what I expected but I knew it mattered to me. I leaned my bike against an old sign advertising the wonders of Geritol and slowly made my way in. The ticket booth was set into a re-creation of a small Tibetan temple. Once you'd paid your money you were supposed to pass through into the temple and then on into the park. The temple was tiny and contained only an ancient relief map of the zoo and a large tiled mosaic of St Francis of Assisi. He was petting some deer while looking warily at a lion which slumbered at his feet. A few of St Francis' face tiles had fallen off and he didn't look at all well. The loud shriek of a peacock heralded my entrance.

The bird was entitled to shriek. He was a fine figure of a peacock. I don't know whether he was giving me the eye or was just generally proud but he presented his full fanned-tailfeather glory to me as I emerged from the temple. Perhaps he had theatrical blood, for as I turned to face him he slowly closed his wide fan and revealed the zoo behind him. Even faded as it then was, it was wonderful. Well, *I* thought so. The place probably wouldn't be allowed now, but no one knew about zoos then. Animal liberation was still a long way down the list. America was only just waking up to blacks and women. Stonewall was still a dream in a silk-stockinged boy's eye.   *133*

Behind the turquoise and emerald shimmer of my shrieking friend stood a large statue of a woman animal tamer holding a tiger at bay. She wore strange men's trousers and a collar and tie permanently pressed in bronze. I knew it. This was the great Billie Blake. Even in bronze she was stunning. I touched her hand, willing her to me. I wanted her to come to life. I wanted to talk to her about great cats and being brave. Behind her a giant carousel of motionless creatures – horses, ostriches, giraffes – waited patiently as their paint peeled. The carousel stood in a small square with four large cages placed one at each corner. They contained animals but I couldn't see what. I didn't go look because a familiar voice made me jump.

'I thought you wouldn't come back,' it said. 'You ran.'

I turned and saw my insect lady from the house. 'Sorry,' I said, always ready to be apologetic, to be English and in the wrong.

'Do you like colors?' she asked.

'I guess.' To be honest it wasn't something I thought you had to have an opinion on.

'How many colors can you see in Mr Honk? The peacock?' I didn't really understand the question. I plumped for an easy one.

'Blue.'

'Really? Just blue?'

'Well, no . . . uhm . . . green, yellow . . . lots,' I said.

She nodded. The woman spoke very quietly, as if she was trying not to take up too much room with her voice. It didn't bother me. I came from a family of partial
134 communicators.

'That's it. Lots of colors,' she said. 'Well then, here's what I don't understand. Say you're a trichromate. Well, you are, 'cause you're a primate. You can make a range of colors out of three basic ones but Mr Honk and dogs and cats, they're dichromates. They only have two basic colors. So why does Mr Honk need all those colors if Mrs Honk doesn't appreciate them?' I couldn't think.

'Maybe it's for us.'

'For us,' she repeated. 'I hope so. Come on.' The woman led the way. She had very thin legs and seemed to walk on the very tips of her toes, making no disturbance in the air. She was still dressed all in brown just like the other day. She probably hadn't noticed that I had changed entirely, what with no hat and no tie. We walked around the outside of the carousel square, past a Spanish-style house and on to a large, formerly white, gazebo-shaped building. It was topped with a white dome and a weather-vane shaped like a pig. The woman opened a door in the side and pushed through some thick, weighted curtaining. I followed her into an intense tropical heat. Plants were growing so thickly inside that the view of the rest of the zoo was entirely obscured. Small cages were dotted about with light bulbs hanging above them, and butterflies flitted above our heads. The woman reached down for a small cage made of mesh net, picked it up and put it on a stool.

'Would you like to see the most remarkable event in the natural world?' she asked, looking straight at me. I supposed that I would. It was not an everyday offer. We bent down to look into the cage together. Inside were a number of leaves on stalks. They appeared to have small pearls on them, some darker than others.

'The darker ones, they're about ready,' she whispered. I looked more closely at the pearls. They were very fine, with delicate ribs running up the side to meet at the top of their small round shapes. In the darkest of them something was moving. Slowly a slit appeared in the pearl. A kind of observation window was being created by whatever lived in there. There was a pause as the creature used the observation slit to check the world out. Then slowly it began, from the inside, to cut a perfect circle off the top of the pearl. It was like watching the smallest can opener in the world at work. As the top came off, small hairs were released from the inside of the round container. Then a head appeared with absurdly large mouthparts. It had no eyes to speak of, but tiny antennae which seemed to take in the world. For a while there was nothing to see but the head, then slowly it began to wave its entire top half and wiggle itself free of the pearl-colored egg. It exerted pressure on the natal leaf and pulled hard to release itself. The creature looked like a brown-headed, naked shrimp. It was not an attractive start in life. The tiny thing was fantastically vulnerable-looking and yet there were no flaws in its determination. Once it was free it turned back to its birthplace. The egg was now empty. A clear, translucent structure. A small rose bowl kept in shape by its ribbed surface. The creature had no sentiment. It proceeded to eat the thing.

'What is it?' I whispered.

'It's not what it is,' the woman replied. 'It's what it will be. That little fellow will turn into the most beautiful owl butterfly. The change from caterpillar to butterfly is one of the most remarkable events in the natural world. Don't you think "chrysalis" is the most beautiful word in the world? Look here.' She pointed to some small brown pods hanging from a branch above my head. 'Inside there the body of a caterpillar is being broken down and gradually an adult formed.'

I looked closely at one of them. It was dressed from much the same wardrobe as the woman, but the thing seemed lifeless. It just hung there. Perhaps it was like the spider. A secret mass of seething emotions. Something fluttered and landed on my shoulder.

'A crimson patch longwing. Look, it has a wing like a bag to catch the air. It would expand like a balloon but it has tiny ligaments inside the wing to stop the upper and lower membranes separating too far. Isn't that brilliant? That one's perfect. You can get crippled butterflies. It's very important that their wings are allowed to expand and dry quickly when they emerge, otherwise they can't fly. Did you know that a leaf-mining moth spends almost its entire life between the upper and lower surfaces of a single leaf?'

I was trying to imagine such a thing but when I looked up the woman was gone. She was weird. Outside the gazebo I could hear whistling so I let myself out and followed the noise. Over in a corner of the park was an old barn. Like the rest of the park, it was halfway between standing up and giving up. The red wooden building was everything I had imagined about America before I came. It screamed life on the prairie, Kansas, the Wild West, bounty hunters and people spitting tobacco. The doors were open and light and hay spilled out in equal quantities. The whistling was coming from inside so that's where I headed. A young woman was sitting at the very top of several bales of hay stacked almost to the roof. She was playing a wooden flute. It was a strange tune which I had never heard before. It wasn't that high-pitched stuff which really only dogs find attractive, but it didn't exactly sound like spring water either. I don't know why I was so drawn to it. I stepped toward the barn, mesmerized. It should have been a magic moment but a cat leaped from the shadows and landed on my shoulder. I shrieked. The young woman looked down and laughed.

'Hello,' she said.

Typically the cat slipped away. Cats never take responsibility. 'Sorry,' I stuttered. 'The cat ... I didn't expect ...'

The woman began climbing down. 'Hey, don't sweat it. Mac is like, evolving. He is reconsidering his life. I mean zoo cat is hard, you know, it's a big responsibility. Also,' she lowered her tone confidentially, 'I do not think he has been the same since his near-death experience. The marabou stork swallowed him whole and Miss Strange had to persuade it to disgorge him.'

I realized it was the woman from the Pop Inn. The one Hubert had been speaking to when I bought Rocco's funeral card. She was young, maybe twenty, but very relaxed for a grown-up. She moved like water in a plastic bag, as if she were almost boneless, and glided to a stop in front of me. Her eyes were wider than seemed possible and she smiled as if that was all she ever did.

'Cosmos,' she said, looking at me with that smile.

'What is?' I asked.

'My name. And you?'

'Dorothy,' I said.

She looked at me. 'Nah. I don't think so.'

No one had ever doubted me on that point before. 'It is. Dorothy. Dorothy Kane,' I said defensively.

'Woah, bad aura. No. No. Dorothy is so wrong. Kane. Sugar. I'm going to call you Sugar.'

A nickname? Someone had given me a nickname? I nearly died of delight.

'Here, help me with this, Sugar.' She tucked a home-made wooden flute into a tie-belt round her middle and moved to shift a large hay bale. I raced to grab the other end. I would have moved the earth for her. It was too heavy but I didn't want Cosmos to know that I thought so.

'Cosmos?' I tried out the name.

'Yes?'

'Who is the . . . uhm . . . brown lady?'

'The brown lady? Oh, Helen. She's like . . .'

A mouse ran out from under the bale. Cosmos gave a strange girly shriek. A Judith sort of noise. It wasn't what I would have expected.

'Damn,' she said, dropping her end of the bale with a shiver. For a brief moment she was less cool than before, then she looked at me and tossed her head with a laugh. The little bell on her head rang and she relaxed back into easy mode. 'Indians used to live here and they were very together. They believed that animals and humans were created as companions, that the animals are our spiritual equals, which is so cool, but I have some kind of block with mice. I'm meditating on it.' I realized I was still

139

holding my end of the heavy bale so I put it down. Cosmos smiled her wide smile at me.

'You want to like, check out the zoo?'

I shrugged, trying to adopt some of her nonchalance. We wandered out of the barn and stood in front of the large doors.

'You haven't been before,' she said, staring at me so intently that I felt she could see right into me, 'so just let it happen to you.' I wasn't at all sure how to do this. Cosmos was wearing a pair of moccasins on her feet. She padded off entirely silently. I took a deep breath before trying to match her Indian footprints. My blue sandals suddenly seemed very noisy.

The once glorious zoological collection had faded rather dramatically by the late 1960s. It certainly wasn't a zoo in the way that we think of them now. It held no pretense of an educational function. The word 'conservation' was never even mentioned. This was old-fashioned family entertainment with Crackerjack concession stands and all-concrete floors because they were the easiest to wash down. Until the place had fallen on financially fallow times, the main response to the death of an exotic animal had been to order another one off the African or Indian shelf.

Most of the buildings were in a kind of pueblo-style architecture. Lots of red brick with small detailed arches on the walls. The park was laid out in a vast rectangle with the carousel square at the heart and cages, pits, buildings and the barn lining the edges. Beyond the carousel stood the butterfly gazebo and beyond that the penguin pool and a small, defunct restaurant which overlooked the Amherst River. Although the animal collection had withered there was still something to see.

There was a pygmy hippo, two Bruijns echidnas, an aye-aye, several tough-looking flamingos, a lowland anoa and a rare Western example of the hog-nosed bat. There was the gentoo penguin, a stubby little fellow with very wide feet which would have been hell to sandal; and any number of Ne Ne geese. It was a strange and eclectic family. We stopped for a minute in front of the South American tapir. It looked like a black pig which had got its head caught in a revolving door. Cosmos squatted down on her haunches to look at it.

'The tapir is so neat. One of the world's most primitive large mammals. If it wanted to it could trace its ancestry back twenty million years.'

Wow, I thought. It's a good job Father isn't a tapir. He'd never finish his project. The sealion pool with its concrete slide was empty, as was the old bear cave, but all the animals left had one thing in common. They all had names. In the farthest corner of the park was an old buffalo.

'Hrotsvitna of Gandersheim.' It wasn't the buffalo's type or species. It was her name. I was amazed. I couldn't even tell it was a girl. Cosmos gave out little pieces of information like gentle smoke signals. 'First known European dramatist. Germany's first poet. A woman. Tenth century.' The buffalo carried on grazing. She didn't seem interested in the weight of her title. Nor did Cloelia, the white rhino.

'Cloelia was seriously cool,' Cosmos assured me. 'She was like, a real star in Rome. She lived in the sixth century which is super long ago and she was taken hostage by the Etruscan King Lars Porsenna during an attack on Rome. Anyhow she escaped and she stole a horse. Then she rode for her life and had to swim this huge river, the Tiber, to get back to the city. Anyway, the Romans were dumb, they gave her back. Can you believe it? But old King Lars was so freaked out by her, you know, impressed with her courage and all, that he freed her and all her fellow hostages.' The rhino grunted as if to confirm the story.

We moved on to Hypatia and Cyril, the polar bears. They were wandering back and forth in their concrete enclosure, shaking their heads and rubbing their sides against the wall. Cosmos leaned against the railing. Cyril stood on the spot and shook his huge, molting body from side to side in the slow rhythm of the deranged.

'Hey, fella,' Cosmos called softly. 'You having a bad day?'

It sure looked like it but it wasn't a subject I felt confident about. This was the whole area of happy and unhappy tigers, brown bears taking Tuesdays off and Rocco not really liking anybody.

'Do you think they have bad days?' I asked cautiously.

'I don't know,' said Cosmos. 'People say that animals are happy in a zoo if the babies play and the adults have babies. I don't know. I mean like, they had babies in the concentration camps and that wasn't too great.'

All the female animals had been named to provide a history of women's achievements. There was Woolf the camel and Tubman the donkey. The boy animals had a different heritage. In the four cages which stood around 142   the carousel were the largest and most dangerous of the creatures. They were all male and each one had been named after a deceased zookeeper.

There was Girling the Gorilla. He was a big fella, named after an inebriated keeper called Edward Girling who was bitten by a cobra at London Zoo in 1852. Then there was a pair of cheetahs called Mr Goss and Mr Kruger. Mr Goss, the seventy-two-year-old parrot keeper at London Zoo, had been trampled to death by a baby elephant called Rostom in 1879.

'He had his leg amputated but he like, died three weeks later. Rostom went to Berlin where two years later he killed another keeper called Kruger.'

A very elderly lion was named after the unfortunate Whittle. 'Late nineteenth century. Whittle worked for something called O'Brian's Menagerie. He wasn't trained as a lion keeper. Got transferred to the lion act at short notice. He liked it, though. Wanted to be famous. In one of his first shows in front of the public he put his head in the lion's mouth. Whittle was not used to lions and, to be fair, probably the lion was not used to him. It closed its jaws.'

Finally, in the fourth cage was Horace, a Bengal tiger just like Rajan from the magazine. This was what Billie would have faced. Through the bars the bright reddish tan of Horace's coat stood out, beautifully marked with dark, almost black, transverse stripes. His underparts, the inner sides of his limbs, his cheeks, and a large spot over each eye were whitish. He was stunning. I tried to imagine opening the cage door and stepping inside. Billie, in her leather boots and tight-fitting pants, adjusting her tie before sticking her head between lethal tiger jaws. Horace, the keeper for whom the tiger was named, had been killed in typical tiger fashion. Horace had been feeding the creature when it seized him by the neck and then let go. There were hardly any external injuries.

'Anyone who knows tigers said it was a mistake. You know – tiger error in the excitement of feeding,' explained Cosmos.

The distinct naming of all these diverse animals gave the zoo a strange sense of being a cross between a serious public place and a personal collection of pets. I was going to ask Cosmos who had named them all when a sound I had heard before cut across the picnic area.

'Cunt!'

A woman stood in the lengthening shadows of the day. A tall woman with a large gray parrot on her right shoulder. I had seen her before. Once outside Milo's Toy Store when she drove by and that first time at the Burroughs House. She waited for us to approach. I had to look up a long way to her face and at first I thought I wasn't seeing well in the fading sun. One side of her face was rather lovely. Well, faded lovely. An elegant woman grown lined with dignity. That side of her, the faded beauty side, she held erect and proud. It was the other side which I stared at. The whole of the right side of her face began at her hairline and then simply fell away. It was as though her face had been made of Plasticine and someone had given it a great yank toward the floor. As if she had strayed too close to the fire. Her eye and her cheek and the right side of her mouth all fought gravity to stay on her face. Her right arm hung limp at her side and she listed over toward it. It meant that the parrot sat at an odd angle all the time.

'Hey,' said Cosmos, unconcerned. 'Hey, Miss Strange, this is Sugar. Sugar, this is Miss Strange.'

Miss Strange. She looked at me and I tried not to look at her. She reached out and pulled my chin up to look her in the eye.

'How do you do?' she said with the slightest Southern twang in her voice. It was an old-fashioned sound with old-fashioned manners.

'Very well,' I stammered. I felt like I was sweating. I didn't know what to say or where to look. 'I've been learning all the names,' I managed.

'Good,' she said. 'Names matter. Did you know that Theodore Roosevelt's son was called Kermit? Kermit Roosevelt. The day he was baptized he was cursed not to follow in his father's footsteps.' She nodded at the parrot and let go of me. 'This is Mr Paton.'

I had got the hang of it. 'How did he die?'

'Killed by Tommy, African elephant, brought back to Plymouth by Prince Alfred, second son of Queen Victoria, on the *Galatea*. They loaded Tommy on the train to London. He wrecked the van and killed Paton.' Miss Strange turned her attention to Cosmos. 'How's the pet corner?'

Cosmos seemed entirely unfazed. 'Pet corner? Oh, yeah. I had like, this vision. I thought we would call it Manitou Manor. Manitou is Algonquin for—'

'Yes, well. I had this vision that we'd open it this week-end, so you'd better get on. Nice to meet you, Sugar.'

'Cunt,' said the parrot. Miss Strange turned to leave.

'Oh.' She stopped and spoke over her shoulder to Cosmos. 'I think the salamander is missing again.'

It was getting late and Cosmos headed back for the barn. The sun was going down and we sat for a moment together on the dropped hay bale.

'I love this time. Listen.' The park was silent apart from the occasional interruption from Mr Honk and the rather distant cry of the timber wolves. 'This is when humans and animals speak the same language. Just think, if we could combine our skills we could overcome anything.' It was quite dark now and the moon had begun to rise.

'The stars will be out soon,' she said. 'You look for seven of them together. They're the Pleiades. The dancing children. A group of Indian children loved to dance. They danced so much that they didn't eat. After a while they floated off to the sky. Now they dance all the time.'

'I have to go now,' I said, though I wasn't sure what for.

'Sure. Hey, you want one of my whistles?' She pulled the hand-carved flute from her belt and handed it to me. 'They use these in the Sudan, you know. To summon the elephants. If the village is in trouble then they all get together and whistle and the elephants come and save them.'

I took the small flute carefully in my hand, thanked her and turned to go.

'Good night, Sugar,' she called. Sugar! I headed for the entrance on a cloud. On the way out I passed a small building next to the barn. Upstairs a light was on. A narrow wooden staircase led the way up and on the wall was pinned a handwritten note. It read:

Remember the dignity
of your womanhood.
Do not appeal,
do not beg,
do not grovel.
Take courage,
join hands,
stand beside us.
Fight with us.
– Christabel Pankhurst

I didn't understand it. I didn't really understand any-
thing. This was the strangest place I had ever been and
these were the strangest people I had ever met. They
were none of them anything to do with me or Mother or
Father or where we'd been or what I expected. I passed
Girling the Gorilla, Mr Whittle, Mr Goss and Mr
Kruger looking out at the still horses on the carousel.
When I got home Harry was watering his front lawn.

'Where you've been, kid?' he called.

'The zoo,' I said.

He snorted. 'Town's gonna close that dump. Should
have happened years ago.'

We looked at each other and I couldn't think of anything so I said, 'The salamander is missing again.' I didn't
exactly know what that was but Harry nodded. It was a
mistake. I should have listened to Father and all his
stories about the war. I didn't know then that I was giving
information to the enemy camp.

Inside, Mother had made me a ready-made meal from
the freezer. She sat at the kitchen table and watched me   *147*

eat it. She hadn't quite cooked it properly but as she rarely did anything culinary I just sucked round the frozen bits. She sat watching me from the edge of a chair. Then she took one of her pills and went back to bed. Like a leaf-mining moth, most of her life was taking place between the upper and lower sheets of a bed. Father was late at work but I didn't feel like driving. I sat up alone and watched Johnny Carson. He was laughing about the news. They kept showing a clip of some man in a tuxedo called Bert Parks who had very unnatural-looking hair. He was standing on a catwalk putting a crown on the new Miss America. I didn't really think she was that pretty. She looked a bit like Mr Parks had bought her somewhere or made her from a Woman Kit. Then suddenly all hell broke loose in the theater. A group called Radical Women stormed the stage and started shouting:

'Miss America is an image that oppresses women.'

They all threw bras, girdles, curlers, false eyelashes, wigs and other things they called 'women's garbage' into a Freedom Trash Can and outside the theater a sheep was crowned Miss America. I wondered if sheep were tame, which would make them third on my Chinese order. Looking at the sheep with the crown on its head, that seemed quite high. I didn't really understand any of it but that was the first time I ever heard of women's liberation.

Chapter Eight

The next morning I was sitting in my usual place on the dock with my Sears, Roebuck catalog. I had taken my sandals off and was wondering whether Mother could be persuaded to get me some quieter shoes. I had just decided to test myself by putting my feet in the water and not worrying that a horseshoe crab might get me when I heard the wailing. It started quite low, from Sweetheart's house, and then it kind of grew. I got up and went round the side of the house. Sweetheart was standing in her front yard, crying and crying. Across the street Judith was screaming and running in demented circles around her lawn. I knew Rocco had only been dead a few days but I still thought it was excessive.

Aunt Bonnie was trying to stop her. Joey had run out of his house and he ran straight at Judith and put out his arms to grab her. She kind of fell into them and was standing with him clinging on to her when Harry and Uncle Eddie came skidding round the corner in the fire engine. All the time the tears were just pouring down Sweetheart's face and she never moved.

'Oh god, Harry, Harry,' she called to her son, but Harry didn't stop. He ran across the lawn, grabbed his wife. Joey was still holding her so without a beat Harry punched Joey to the ground. It seemed to be something they did to each other. Aunt Bonnie pulled Judith away and Uncle Eddie ran up between all of them. I couldn't hear what anyone was saying but I knew it was terrible. After a while Aunt Bonnie came and took Sweetheart home and Harry and Judith went in the house. Uncle Eddie helped Joey up and walked back to the fire truck. As he got up into the driving seat he saw me.

'Hey, kid. Okay?' I nodded. 'Bad news.' He nodded back to the Schlicks' house. 'Harry's kid, Pearl? She's dead.' He shook his head. 'Kids today.'

Uncle Eddie backed the fire truck out of the street and took off. I could still hear Sweetheart crying through her screen door and now Harry had started yelling in his house. That wasn't right. People shouldn't yell when other people are dead. I felt scared. Death seemed to be in the neighborhood. I ran into our house and down the corridor to Mother's room. The door was closed so I raised my hand to knock but I didn't. I couldn't.

I went over to the Dapolitos' to see if I could get something to eat. The house was in the usual uproar. Donna Marie was listening to some records in her room. She had this really fussy room. Her bed had a lace canopy over it and everything was very pink. She was trying on make-up and wanted me to put false eyelashes on. I went downstairs. Eddie Jr was flipping baseball cards in the den but he wouldn't let me have any. Aunt Bonnie had come home and was watching the TV. It was on real loud.

The news broadcast pounding out in color. There had been an anti-war demonstration in one of the Midwest cities. The National Guard had opened fire and Pearl was dead. I had never met her but I had seen enough pictures. Now they had a picture of her on TV. A smiling picture, but she was dead. I kept thinking about Judith screaming and Harry getting so mad. I didn't know what people did after their little girl died. It wasn't what I thought.

'God damn, God damn.' Aunt Bonnie kept saying the same thing over and over, lighting one Virginia Slim from another. A kind of personal smog zone was developing around her as she watched. Then she went in the kitchen to make Sloppy Joes for everyone. I went and watched her. I sat on one of the high stools by the corner bar. Uncle Eddie had made the bar in the kitchen to look like a little Hawaiian drinking place. It was made of bamboo and had a plastic pineapple on top to keep ice in. Cocktail cabinets, full bars, drinks cupboards with ice dispensers, every house had something in those days to dispense alcohol. The Dapolitos' bar had a little refrigerator for Aunt Bonnie's beer and she was in and out of there that afternoon.

'God, Harry loved that kid. He gave her everything he never had.' Aunt Bonnie threw ground beef in a hot frying pan and steam erupted from the cooker. 'Nice house, family. That's what it's about, right, kid? Family. Sixteen she leaves home. Sixteen. I thought Harry was going to die.' She threw tomatoes in the pan and poured a pack of Sloppy Joe mix in from a great height. Red sauce splashed out on the cooker as she stirred. It was lusty cooking such as my mother could never imagine.

'Is that why he's so mad?' I asked.

'Harry's been mad since Billie Blake died.' Aunt Bonnie served up and didn't talk any more. She just shut down into a beer can. I knew I wasn't going to get any more from her for a while but I had a hundred questions. What had Harry to do with Billie Blake? He didn't even like the zoo. How come Pearl left? Could you leave home at sixteen? That was sooner than I thought.

After lunch I was hanging around the front yard when Harry came out and got in his car. I didn't know what to say to him. His daughter was dead. I didn't know about dead. Rocco was the only deceased thing I had ever seen and I really didn't feel that had gone all that well. I wanted to say something but Harry was such a, well, grown-up. It was hard to imagine he had ever had a little girl. I was terribly worried that if I said the wrong thing he would start crying. Grown-ups crying was terrible. Aunt Bonnie was just bringing me a soda when she saw him. She had been drinking a lot so she kind of tripped as she ran over.

'Harry, Harry, geez, Harry.'

Harry looked like his jaw hurt him. 'I have to open the store.'

'No, you don't. Come and have a beer.'

'Listen, I went to war and it didn't stop me getting on with my life. Just because . . . because there's Commies causing trouble . . .' He drove off, leaving Aunt Bonnie standing in the street. It was all very strange. Judith had arranged to take Mother to the Corset Store that day to be fitted with one of the Playtex wonders and no one said anything about canceling.

152   'Do you know about Pearl, Mother?' I asked as she

smoothed her hair for the hundredth time in the hall mirror.

'Go and wash your hands, Dorothy. We're going out to . . . it's arranged, et cetera,' she replied.

Everything was unreal. I remember it seemed completely silent. More silent outside than in my house. There was no wind and even the harbor gave off no sound. I felt like I was drowning. I wanted to run away but I was only ten. Mother stood with her gloves and coat waiting by the front door. Judith honked outside in her Oldsmobile and Mother and I got in as if everything was normal. Nobody really said anything. Since lunch Judith had completely rebuilt her face and her hair. She looked as she always did – taut with make-up – yet possibly a little pale. She didn't say anything but I knew that look. It was the same one Mother got from her pills.

Harry's corset and brassière store was double-fronted, with a door between two bowed plate-glass windows. It had the curious effect of making the display itself appear to have been lifted and separated. Inside was a world of synthetic elastic, the corselette and, to my mind, pain. Harry stood waiting for us with a tape measure round his neck. I didn't know what we were all doing. Judith settled herself on the edge of a leather chair while Harry worked with Mother. Half-mannequins of women's bodies squeezed into a variety of torture garments loomed over me. I suddenly realized why Judith never relaxed when she sat down. She couldn't. Behind the fitting-room curtain Harry worked with his tape measure. Mother was wearing only her stockings and panties but no one seemed to mind.

'You have a fine figure,' said Harry tonelessly while he   *153* measured the depth of Mother's breasts. 'Hard to believe you have had children.'

I looked at Mother stripped down to basics.

'Two. Charles and . . .' She waved in my direction. Harry was right. It was hard to believe that Charles and I were anything to do with her.

'I am so glad you came in.' Harry eyed her chest professionally. 'So many women make the mistake of not having a proper fitting.' Harry swept off into professional patter, his voice on automatic pilot, while his wife sat immobile a few feet away. Mother tried various restraining garments and finally emerged with the beloved eighteen-hour model below her dress. She did look different. Her body seemed more sculpted. Less real. Even more unapproachable.

'Be your turn before you know it,' Harry said to me. Judith didn't move but tears silently began to run down her face. No one could look at her.

'It's a lovely day,' said Mother. 'I think we will walk home. You know it's . . .'

'Yes,' said Harry.

We left him with his silent wife. It was warm out on the sidewalk and Mother seemed a little short of breath. I wasn't surprised. She never really walked anywhere and now she was being suffocated by eighteen-hour rubber. We had to walk past Abe's Ice Cream Parlor to get back so I asked if we could have a sundae. Abe was opening a new barrel of Rocky Road when we came in. There were quite a few people in the store sitting at the small marble tables. I went to order. Beside the list of flavors Abe had put up one of the *Close the Zoo* posters. It was the second one I had seen. I couldn't think why everyone was getting so worked up. I got myself a coffee cone with sprinkles and Mother some rum and raisin in a cup and went to sit down. Mother picked at the ice cream with a small spoon. Even eating dessert she was elegant. The spoon barely touched her lips and there was never any suggestion that her tongue was even remotely involved. The girdle had made her even more upright. She looked fabulous and I was so proud. For a brief moment I thought maybe I could be like her. Maybe it was okay. Suddenly the place went like a Western movie. It was a hot day when any reasonable person might want an ice cream. The swing shutters at the front door parted and Miss Strange walked in. She didn't have Mr Paton with her but instantly the place went completely silent. Everyone stared at her. Abe looked up from cleaning his silver scoop and then made himself busy again.

'Hello, Abe,' she said.

'Miss Strange.'

It was as if she hadn't noticed. 'Vanilla please, no sprinkles.' Abe set about getting her the ice cream while she looked at the poster behind his head. After she'd paid she turned and glanced at everyone in the store. She looked at me and nodded. I knew I should introduce her to Mother. It was the right thing to do. To my eternal shame I looked away and waited till she had gone. We ate our ice cream and went home. Even though the girdle was good for another seventeen hours, Mother went to bed. I felt terrible.

That evening Aunt Bonnie and Uncle Eddie took Donna Marie and Eddie Jr to summer camp. The neighborhood emptied of children. There was just me left and I shouldn't have been there. Pearl never came home. The funeral was held out of town in something approaching national hysteria. The Schlicks' daughter had become a symbol for the anti-war movement and the oppression of government. On the news lots of people were getting very upset and they didn't even know Pearl. I still wasn't really sure what the war was about but I knew you just had to say 'Vietnam' and people got heated on one side or the other. Judith wouldn't talk about Pearl because Harry wouldn't. Sweetheart talked about her but only to Jesus. She was in and out of the impossibly white Methodist church all the time. I guessed it was because Jesus was her friend. She even stopped working as a candy-striper at the hospital.

Then Perry came and she stopped going to church too. Perry was three and he was Pearl's son. Well, he was, but Sweetheart seemed to be the only person who knew it. After the funeral he arrived at La Guardia Airport with a big label on the front of his coat that said *Perry Schlick, 2 Cherry Blossom Gardens, Sassaspaneck.*

He was a seriously cute kid with huge eyes and a great smile. You would think Harry and Judith would have welcomed him with open arms, but there was a problem. Perry was black. He was illegitimate too, and I don't know which was the bigger problem. Pearl had told them about him but as they hadn't seen their daughter for four years they had never met their grandson. She had told them the father was a Negro but Harry had said, 'That's just another thing she's saying to deliberately upset us.'

Perry came at a bad time. It was the summer of the election and for the first time Harry was being challenged in his re-election for mayor. I couldn't see how it would make a difference but, apparently, what he didn't need was 'some black bastard turning up, claiming to be a relation'.

To be fair, Harry did give it a try. He collected Perry from the airport. I mean the kid was three, you couldn't leave him there. I think when Harry went to meet him, he was still hoping that somehow the strong white genes of the Schlick family would have overridden anything black. I don't think Father had helped.

'Theoretically, Harry, if you look at this chart, it is possible that the child could be china white.'

But he wasn't. Whatever light you looked at the kid in, he was black all right. Now, in the world of nature, if any creature is going to show compassion then it is most likely to show it to a member of its own species. But not with Harry. Harry did not regard Perry as his own because Perry didn't look right. Judith didn't get a say. Harry tried to send the kid back to the Midwest but there was no one there who could take him and the airline refused. So Harry brought him to Cherry Blossom Gardens. He arrived back banging doors and left the three-year-old in the car. There was a lot more shouting.

'He is not coming in the house, Judith. Do you have any idea what this could do to me?'

'She didn't do it on purpose.'

'I don't want to talk about Pearl.'

Then Sweetheart got the kid out of the back seat and took him to her house. Harry never said anything about it. He just launched himself into his campaign with terrifying vengeance. Looking back, I think he thought Perry was his daughter's final Democratic ploy. Anyway,

I guess it pushed him over the edge.

It seems incredible now that Harry thought what he did was okay, that he could get away with it, but that was then. Things were changing right across the US but the tide was only just lapping at the feet of Sassaspaneck. Since the passing of the Civil Rights Act in 1964, forcing the desegregation of the public schools, there had been a lot more talk about black rights. In Sassaspaneck it was all theory because we only had Hubert, a few Poles and some Italians down by the railway station.

After Perry came, Sweetheart didn't open the door to anyone and no one ever saw Judith. Things were getting worse at home. Mother spent all her time in bed eating pecans out of a bowl. I did try to sit with her sometimes but then Father would bring home something from the drugstore for her and she would send me out.

'Go on, darling, you're getting fat. Go and run outside, play some . . . thing.'

And they would fight.

'I am not staying in this hellhole for another moment,' Mother would begin.

'There isn't any more money,' Father would whisper.

'I'm telling you, Charles, I will leave.'

I ran a lot. Round and round the house. Sometimes I ran all afternoon and was still running when Father got home from work. He would go straight in and sit at the dining-room table. He had a large wood-and-crystal drinks tantalus which his father had given him, and he would put that in front of him. He kept the key in his pocket and if I heard it in the tantalus lock then I knew there would be no speaking to him. We had stopped even pretending to have dinner. Mother had gone mad in the A&P one day. Alfonso had persuaded her to try Italian food and she had bought the fixings for spaghetti. When Father got home it was on the table.

'What the hell is this?' he whispered.

'It's spaghetti,' said Mother. 'Charles, I wanted to . . .'

Father looked at the meal. I thought he would be pleased. I couldn't remember the last time Mother had made an effort. Instead he said, 'I don't want any foreign food,' and then did something quite extraordinary. He picked the spaghetti up and threw the plate at the ceiling. Italian food and china came raining down. No one said anything. Father didn't like change. He didn't want anything different. He would rather not have anything at all. Mother went to her room. She didn't bother after that. Father just sat in his chair under a great red stain and drank his whiskey.

I didn't really mind. I developed my own routine. Lunch I sometimes got at the Dapolitos' or made myself, and I had dinner every night at Walchinsky's Hot Dog Stand. I took a dollar from Mother's purse and went on my bike. The stand was across the street from the school. It had been there for ever. It wasn't some temporary thing. It was a regular building but with a pagoda roof. Green Chinese tiles which curved up into the back of a dragon. Not exactly hot-dog-like but I thought it was impressive. Frank Walchinsky Jr was the second Frank in charge. He had left school at sixteen when his father had had a heart attack while bowling what would have been a perfect game. Frank Jr just left his homeroom, walked across the street from school and put an apron on. I liked him. He was a big bratwurst of a man with a brilliantly red face. He made my dog for me himself every night.

'Hey, kid, how you doing today?' he would call as I arrived on my bike.

'I'm good, Junior. Real good,' I would reply. Everyone called him Junior even though he was as old as Harry. You know, maybe fifty. Old.

Junior threw some onions on the grill and smacked them down with his egg slice. 'So what do you know?'

'I know that there's never going to be a better shortstop than Bud Harrelson.'

'Amen. So did you think of a new name for the stand?' he asked.

A McDonald's had opened in town and Frank had decided he needed to update his business. We had been talking and I said he needed a snappier name than Walchinsky's Hot Dog Stand.

'How about Frank's Franks?' I said. 'And you could have a slogan; *Be Frank – Frank's Franks Are Best.*'

Frank screwed his eyes up and looked at me. 'A slogan? Like on a button?' I nodded. 'I like that. Yeah, I like that. Buttons. Rockefeller, he's got buttons. See.' He held up a campaign button which read *We Want Rocky*. It was like a lot of American politics – simple and to the point. Frank shook his head in amazement at the idea. 'We could have buttons,' he repeated.

If it was raining or business was slow, Junior would let me sit inside behind the counter and eat my supper. I would sit next to him while he cut up onions, tears streaming down his face. Inside the stand, on the wall, Frank had black and white photographs from the opening

of the hot-dog stand. There were balloons and ribbons

and everyone was dressed up. At the back of the picture was an elephant wearing a sequinned coat and a top hat.

'Only hot-dog stand in America designed by an architect and opened by an elephant,' Junior would say. Then he would put down his knife and go through the people posing from the past. 'That's Mr Burroughs, everyone called him John Junior; Sweetheart and her son Harry; my father; Billie Blake; and that's Grace carrying Phoebe. Used to bring her down here all the time.'

I knew Grace from the magazine and the others were starting to be familiar too.

'Phoebe. She had a wheelchair.'

'John Junior's sister. Frail as a bird. She had polio when she was a kid. It didn't matter how much money John Junior made, he couldn't make her better. Then Grace came along. You never saw two people happier together. Grace would carry her everywhere. Everybody said she was Phoebe's legs and Phoebe was her heart. That's how come Pop got the stand. Phoebe wanted a hot dog so Grace got John to build her a hot-dog stand.' Junior wiped his sweaty red face with a towel and sat down.

'You been out to the house?' I nodded and he smiled. 'What a place. Took three years and every builder in the county to build it. Of course, it didn't help that Billie kept changing her mind. She was a gal. She had been to Europe once and she wanted all of it in one building. She used to sit drawing pictures of houses and driving John crazy. "Billie," he would say, "you can have what you want but you have to decide on one style." In the end I think it was a little wacky. The front was that place in Venice – the Doge's Palace, I never been – and the tower from Madison

Square Garden in New York. And big. Thirty bedrooms, fourteen baths, plus kitchens, pantries and servants' quarters. People came from Paris to do the plaster on the walls, they got chairs handmade in Florence, floors from South America, artists to paint ceilings, wood walls from Italy. You should see the organ in the tower gallery. Four thousand pipes. Fifty grand. I don't think anybody ever played it. I was only little but there was money then. The parties my dad used to cook for. But it couldn't last. There wasn't the money to make it last. One time Billie wanted a gondola so John Junior gets a gondolier too. You know the Dapolitos? That was Eddie's father, the gondolier. I think it's why he still lives by the water.'

So that was my life. Walchinsky's in the evening, driving at night, and the zoo during the day. I was learning a lot at the zoo. Cosmos gave me jobs to do and the insect woman, Helen, let me in for free. I already knew that when the rear ends of female baboons went red and swollen they weren't sick, just in estrous. That meant they wanted mating. I also knew that the books said Girling the Gorilla was supposed to be mainly foliverous. That meant he was supposed to like leaves and stems and things from plants, but you got nowhere with him unless you gave him spaghetti with tomato sauce. He wasn't like Father, he loved it. Girling was also scared of the plastic dividers in ice-cube trays. Miss Strange didn't know why but he would back off as soon as she produced one.

I didn't see a lot of Miss Strange. She kept in the office when the zoo was open. Cosmos had done a great job on the pets corner – Manitou Manor – and for a while a few families even came. The kids loved Cosmos. She would sit on a bale of hay, tooting her flute, while they fed the goats and stroked the rabbits. The angora rabbit had babies and I spent for ever holding them. They were just the same color as their mom.

'That's genetics,' I told Cosmos with ten-year-old knowing.

She looked at the bunnies. 'Yeah, neat. Aren't mothers just the most? They are like ... everything. The Algonquin believe that Gluskap made the whole world from the body of his mother.'

I found that hard. Everybody had these weird ideas about mothers. I was sure you couldn't make anything out of mine. Not even sweat.

If Cosmos wasn't telling stories then she was whistling, and if she wasn't whistling she was carving new whistles and giving them away. She also made a thing out of old sewer pipes for us to crawl through and feel what it was like to be prairie dogs. None of this could really hide the fact that the place was falling down, but I loved it. I became kind of a mini-know-all, standing in front of the polar bears declaring to all and sundry:

'The girl is Hypatia. She was far out. She was like, a scientist, mathematician and philosopher. In her time she was the leading intellectual of Alexandria. She taught philosophy, geometry, astronomy and algebra at the university. She invented the astrolabe and the planisphere. Anyhow she had this really powerful philosophy about scientific rationalism. That you could sit and figure everything out. Well, Cyril, the boy? He hated that. He was like, this big Christian, which was really new then. It was like, the fourth century and Cyril was Patriarch of all Alexandria but I mean if he was going to have that job then I think he could have had like a better name. So Cyril hates her because she's so smart, and he gets this mob of monks to drag her from her chariot, strip her naked and torture her to death by slicing her flesh from her bones with shells and sharpened flints.'

People were sometimes impressed. It was thrilling. Then the campaign over the zoo heated up and folks started feeling uncomfortable about coming. There was a rally in the town, a Meet the Candidates event in front of Torchinsky's Funeral Parlor where both parties, the Republicans and the Democrats, announced their mayoral tickets. Harry, as the incumbent, was announced first. He began his speech with a sure-fire winner.

'How about them Senators?' The Sassaspaneck Senators, the high-school football team, had had a very good year. The crowd went wild, waving red and blue banners and tossing fake boaters in the air. 'Was that some season or what?' More cheering. Everyone in the crowd could have run a touchdown themselves. Judith sat at the back, perched on a chair from Torchinsky's. She had a fixed smile on her face which only make-up remover could shift. She never said a word. She didn't clap or cheer either. Just sat. It was kind of spooky.

'When I was quarterback for the Senators, people used to ask me what I felt, and I told them: pride. I was proud to be from Sassaspaneck. Proud to be quarterback for the best high-school team in the county. And I'm still proud. The Senators represent everything that is good about this town. They are young, talented men and they are winners. And we need to reward that. I have been your mayor for four years now and I am going to spend the next four years giving this town a place to show off our pride. At my own expense I have commissioned architect's plans for a new Senator stadium. It will be the latest, the greatest and the most modern stadium in the state.'

'Where you gonna put it, Harry? In your yard?' came a cry from the crowd. Harry laughed and held up a map of the town.

'Right here.' He pointed to the zoo. 'If elected I will close the zoo. I think we all agree that the place has become a health hazard and it has had its day. I say, let's clean up this town. Close the zoo. The Senator stadium is the future.' Abe and Hubert surprised themselves by cheering together. So that was it. Harry's close-the-zoo platform. Then the Democrats had their turn. The local party gave the announcement the usual build-up and then declared:

'The Democratic candidate for Mayor of Sassaspaneck is Joey Amorato!'

To be honest, the place didn't exactly erupt. There was more of a murmur which went through the crowd.

'The dog catcher?'

'They chose the dog catcher?'

'Do they mean Joey?'

'I didn't even know he was a Democrat.'

I don't know why, but Joey had decided that 1968 was his year to stand tall. Maybe everybody knew that Harry was unbeatable so they let Joey stand as a token. Whatever, little Joey came out fighting.

'Hey. I'm Joey Amorato and I don't just know you, I know your dogs!' As an opening line in a fierce campaign it probably lacked something.   *165*

'What about the stadium, Joey?' called Tony from the door of his pizza parlor.

Already Joey was into tricky territory. In his time at Sassaspaneck High, Joey had never been on a single sports team. Everybody knew this. He had always been on the chubby, unfit side. Indeed, it was his inability to run which had led to him being bitten by a dog in the first place.

'I think there are more important things in this town,' he began.

'Like the zoo? You gonna come out for the zoo 'cause you like dogs?' shouted someone, and everyone laughed. It was not an auspicious start. Harry laughed loudest of all. Joey stood on the platform looking at him. Judith, seated between them, didn't move a muscle. The two men had very different agendas. Harry wanted to close the zoo but Joey didn't care about that. He wanted to close out Harry. The zoo was about to get caught in the middle and so was I.

One night I had slipped out to drive the car as usual. It was always the same time. I would watch TV till a commercial came on with a deep man's voice.

'It's ten o'clock,' he would say like he was Orson Welles. 'Do you know where your children are?' It was delivered in such a way as to suggest you might also know where some other people's children were. Father would have been sitting at the tantalus for some time by then, so he never noticed me leave. I drove very slowly because even on my fruit box I couldn't see real well. Down to the Yacht Club entrance and round and back to the stop sign. Then I had to back up to avoid going on to Amherst, which

I figured, as it was a main road, probably wasn't allowed.

That night I had tried a little spying, but it hadn't gone well. The neighborhood was very tense since Perry had arrived. Uncle Eddie had sided with Sweetheart.

'You can't turn away any kid,' he said, almost raising his voice.

But Aunt Bonnie said the kid ought to go. That it was upsetting Judith. I couldn't figure it out because Aunt Bonnie liked kids. She said it was all about family. I parked the car for a while and went round the back of the Dapolito place. Maybe Aunt Bonnie was having ice cream. In the backyard I could just see her lying on Eddie Jr's trampoline. I knew she was in estrous because she had a very red bottom and Harry was mating her. When I looked across the yard to the edge of the water I could see that Joey was watching, which I didn't think was nice. I ran back to the car.

I don't know why but it made me feel panicked so I shot the car into reverse and pulled straight out on to Amherst. There seemed to be cars coming from every direction and I drove kind of wildly down the road. I didn't know what the hell was going on. Mating, that was about reproduction, but Aunt Bonnie already had kids. She had kids and then she sent them away for the summer. Harry had a kid who he didn't want to talk about and now she was dead but *her* kid was here and Harry didn't want him. Perry was family. How could you not want family? And why was Joey watching? It wasn't nice. I knew it wasn't nice. I thought he liked Judith more than he was supposed to, but why was he watching Aunt Bonnie? Nothing made any sense. I don't know how long I was gone. Maybe a half-hour, because I couldn't find any place to turn around. I would keep seeing a good space, then lose my nerve and pass it. When I got back, I turned the car round at the end of the street and pulled up outside Sweetheart's house kind of shaking. Karen Carpenter was singing to me on the radio but it didn't help.

Sweetheart's front door was open and I could hear that she and Harry were arguing. I could see them half lit through the screen door. Sweetheart was holding Perry and Harry was trying to grab the kid off of her.

'You know what it did to me. Don't do this again,' he was yelling.

'It is not his fault,' said Sweetheart, clinging on to Perry, who was crying. Harry made a grab for the kid.

'I am not going to let this ruin my life.'

I was just about to pull off home but the next thing I knew, Sweetheart ran out with Perry in her arms and got in the car.

'Hurry up! Drive! Drive!'

Harry came storming out of the house and ran at the car so I just floored it. We hit Amherst so fast the car fish-tailed round the corner. This was new. This was real driving. I had people in the car. Passengers. I pulled on the huge steering wheel to try and sit up more and see more while still pressing the accelerator. I knew to stay on the right-hand side of the road but I didn't know how to get anyplace except the bit of Amherst which I had just tried, and I really didn't know anyplace off Amherst except the zoo. Perry was crying and Sweetheart was trying to comfort him.

'Where are you going?' she asked.

'The zoo,' I said.

It was as if she expected it. 'Yes. Good.'

When we got there it was completely dark. I knew my way around so it wasn't a problem. I opened the car door for Sweetheart and kind of held her by the elbow. She had Perry in her arms and she just let me guide her like I knew what I was doing. I liked that. Like Father leading Mother across the road. What was strange was that I didn't need to. She knew exactly where we were going. As usual the place was wide open so we wandered in through the Tibetan ticket booth. It should have been like one of my silent spy moments but we all jumped when the fire siren went and the timber wolves began to howl. It woke Mr Honk up. He fanned his feathers at me. I'd have liked to show Perry how handsome he was but it would have to wait. Sweetheart had started making very still crying sounds and I didn't know what to do. I mean, she was too old to cry.

'It's real good you're not wearing a hat,' I tried. 'Queen Sammuramat, she's the ostrich, she's taken to attacking anyone wearing a hat. Do you know about Queen Sammuramat? She ruled Assyria for forty-two years. She irrigated the whole of Babylon and led military campaigns as far as India.'

Maybe it wasn't appropriate but it was all I could think of. I don't think I had ever thought about what Cosmos, Helen and Miss Strange did when the zoo was closed. I just presumed they would be there, and that night they were. The lights were on in the food store. Miss Strange was sitting with Sappho, the female orangutan. Sappho had a big flat face like she had swallowed a Frisbee, a neat beard and a sad expression. Actually everyone looked serious. There was a discussion going on between Cosmos and Miss Strange. The orangutan seemed to be taking an active part, or at least a more active role than Helen. As usual, Helen, all-brown Helen, was curled up in a corner so that I didn't notice her at first.

They couldn't have been expecting us but when Miss Strange saw Sweetheart she stood up. Mr Paton was perched on her shoulder but he didn't move or speak. I'm sure I hadn't thought about what would happen but I know it surprised me.

'Hello, Sugar,' said Miss Strange as if I had never snubbed her in the ice-cream store. Perry had fallen asleep and without a word Miss Strange shook out her coat on a hay bale. Then she took Perry from Sweetheart's arms and laid him on the warm coat. She didn't say a word but led Sweetheart to sit down. I would have thought there were a million questions but she didn't mention how late it was or ask how we came to be there. Miss Strange took out a handkerchief and gently wiped away Sweetheart's tears.

'I need your help again,' said Sweetheart.

'Of course,' said Miss Strange. 'I'm glad you came, Sweetheart. We have a problem and I need your advice.' I went and sat with Cosmos. It was confusing. I didn't even know Miss Strange knew Sweetheart. 'We've had some news. You remember Artemesia?'

Sweetheart nodded. 'Oh, bless her. Didn't you lend her to a circus?'

'I did. It's folded and they want us to take her back.'

'Will you?'

'I thought about it. I don't know if we can deal with her. It's been thirty years.'

'You'd learn again.'

'Do you think so? They might close the zoo before I can find out.'

Sweetheart and Miss Strange talked like two old ladies who had met for a gossip. Cosmos sat back on a hay bale, whittling slowly at a new flute with her knife, while Helen sat entirely still. An exercise in camouflage. Mr Paton climbed down from his perch on Miss Strange. He carefully walked a short distance and collected some pieces of straw. He returned with a beakful, which he laid at Miss Strange's feet. Then he climbed back up beside her head, settled on the sloping shoulder and very quietly leaned forward to stroke her deformed cheek. Miss Strange looked at the bird.

'It's getting cold. Let's all go up to the house. Sugar, do you have to go home?' she asked gruffly.

'No,' I said, not really sure. Miss Strange shrugged and picked up Perry. As she did she stroked his cheek and held him close. I had never seen Miss Strange be soft with anyone. We walked up to the big house.

Every time I went to the Burroughs House I remember being amazed. It was a fairy-tale place where extraordinary people in an unreal time had played out their lives. Our little band of women, the abandoned boy and an orangutan crunched up the circular drive to the front marble steps. In the still moonlight we climbed the five steps to three high arches supported by Greek goddesses which heralded the front door. A front door carved from twelve-foot-high pieces of maple into Roman panels.

The library seemed to be the only room in regular use now. It didn't have dust sheets on the furniture and there were signs that people still lived there. Cosmos lit a fire in a fireplace you could live in while Sweetheart and Miss Strange settled Perry on a sofa. Cosmos went to get some more wood.

'Helen,' said Miss Strange. 'Some cocoa.' They went out, Helen silently fluttering behind the height and strength of Miss Strange. Sweetheart and I were left alone by the fire with Perry sleeping. He slept without a trouble in the world. I guess he didn't know who did or didn't want him. Sweetheart sat down in a chair and I sat on the floor beside her. I didn't say anything. I didn't want to draw attention to myself in case I was made to go. After a time Sweetheart got up and began wandering around the room. She picked up small objects from the library shelves and looked at them. After a while she stopped in front of a sepia photograph in a silver frame. When she spoke I don't think she was really talking to me. She just stood looking at the picture. Billie and John Junior smiled back at her from inside the shining frame.

'This was the room where I was interviewed. I never thought anyone would give me a job again. John needed a secretary. He was doing so many shows then, and there was the business. He left Billie to choose. She was quite fussy.' Sweetheart laughed to herself. 'She didn't want anyone too good-looking and she didn't want a man because any man who was willing to be a secretary had to be a . . . Well, anyway, I was last on the list. Come all the way from South Carolina. I was twenty-eight. I had great secretarial skills but no references. Billie was just getting to this when Grace slipped in the back of the room. She stood there by the door.

'"You say you have ten years of experience?" said Billie.

'"Yes," I replied.

'"Yet you don't have one recent employer who will vouch for you?"

'"No." And I looked her straight in the eye. "You see, I am not married and I have a son. He's eight. I used to keep it quiet and then when anyone found out I usually got fired. I got tired of living a lie. I can't do it and I don't think it's good for my son. I don't want him to grow up that way. So I came to New York. I hear you have a more liberal attitude." For all her gusto I don't think she knew what to say or do. She was a Catholic at heart, you know. She kind of stumbled.

'"Yes, well, uh . . . Miss . . . uh . . ."

'"Schlick."

'"We'll have to . . ."

'And Grace spoke up from the door. I can still hear her. "Hire you. We'll have to hire you. You're hired. Welcome to Burroughs House, Miss Schlick." She saved me and Harry and now Harry won't . . .'

'Harry lived here?'

'Oh yes. John fussed so over him. He bought Harry a little tuxedo for parties. There was a miniature railway cart which ran from the cellars right into the house and behind John's chair at the dining table. Harry used to work the car and serve the champagne. John loved that. He left me to arrange everything. Used to call me his sweetheart. And the house was always full of people. Rich people, friends of rich people, and crazy people from the shows. Emile Pallenberg was always trouble if he came. He had a troupe of bears who had been trained to roller-skate and bicycle and insisted on doing it across the terrace. Then there was Patrick Culpeper from the New United Monster Shows who arrived with an entire tribe of Zulus just as we were sitting down to lunch, and Colonel Edgar Daniel Boone and Miss Carlotta came with their lions one Christmas Eve. Nothing was strange then. Everyone just got on with being who they needed to be. There was John's Uncle Robert, who refused to sit down at dinners but rode round the table on his giant tortoise Rotumah, wearing a top hat and waving a lettuce leaf on a stick in front of its mouth. John had bought Rotumah from Lord Rothschild, the Honorable Walter, for one hundred fifty dollars. It was Uncle Robert's second tortoise. He said the first one died from sexual over-excitation, but as he was a lone male everyone thought it was either unlikely or peculiar. Uncle Robert would go round and round the table telling stories about Africa.'

'*So Joseph Tompson's making his way across the highlands, totally uncharted, and a group of these warriors, the Masai, get after him.*' *Uncle Robert paused in his story to shake a lettuce leaf at Rotumah and get him moving. The tortoise lumbered forward. 'Well, Tompson hightails off on his horse and they catch him. He stands there facing them in their tribal paint, terrifying, and Tompson is shaking so much his false teeth fall out in his hand. Bingo. The natives think he is magic and start worshipping this man who can take all his teeth out.'*

174

John Junior laughed and nodded. 'Magic, that's what holds them. I once got given a very nice woman because I convinced the chief that my hurricane lamp was really a piece of star fallen to earth.'

'John and I are thinking of going to Africa. Aren't we, John?' called Billie.

'Absolutely.'

'You'll love it, my dear,' replied the tortoise-supported Robert. 'All you have to remember is to keep the spirits up, the bowels open, and wear flannel next to the skin.'

It was a heady time. There were the parties, where for three days cars swept continuously up the circular drive, to be met by John and Billie on the front marble steps and then passed on into Sweetheart's care. Everyone came. Not the old money, but the new stuff, with all sorts of people from every walk. Prominent industrialists, politicians, celebrities – Alfred Smith and James J. Walker; the Governor and Mayor of New York; Florenz Ziegfield and his wife, also called Billie; Bernard McFadden, the body builder; Lord Cranworth, the African explorer; and people from the boot-legging business which by now kept the Burroughs enterprise afloat. Billie and John had their portrait taken to mark their engagement. She looked almost coy as she posed, all in fur despite the summer heat. A sepia picture showing a white leopard coat with beaver collar, leopard hat and single red rose exposed at her bosom. Her hands hidden in a matching fur muff. John standing beside her – tall and bursting from his waistcoat with pride and affluence. At the engagement party everyone got presents. Sweetheart was told to slip a $100 bill under everyone's plate and Harry was allowed to sit at the table.

'This wine comes direct from France,' beamed John, serving endless banned claret. 'Well, it swings by a relay station. The French island of Miquelon, off the Canadian coast? I have Bill McCoy's word that it's genuine,' he boasted, smiling at Billie. 'Did you know there's some Prohibition crazy trying to rewrite the Bible? Ain't that right, Phoebe?'

Phoebe smiled. 'Dr Charles . . . Something. He wants to remove all references to wine. So Jesus will turn water into a cake of raisins.'

Sweetheart did not sit.

'More eland, anyone?' she would ask while Grace, as usual, devoted herself entirely to Phoebe. She would allow no one else to help her and more often than not carried her rather than put her in the wheelchair.

'What do you reckon to Harding, John? Gonna be President?' called a guest.

'No way. Poor old Warren hasn't a Chinaman's chance.' Everyone nodded. John was the oracle. The wine flowed.

During dessert, Unus, the Upside-Down, Gravity-Defying, Equilibristic Wonder of the World, stood on the table to entertain. His real name was Franz Furtner of Vienna. Like the guests, he wore tails, but also had a top hat and white gloves. Sweetheart arranged a lighted globe on the center of the table and turned out the lights. Unus waited till he had everyone's full attention. Then he put the forefinger of his right hand on the globe, near the Antarctic, and went up into a handstand. Well, a fingerstand.

'Isn't that incredible?' whispered Phoebe.

'Yeah,' said Grace. 'Most of us can't even stand on our feet.' At which point Uncle Robert fell off Rotumah, rather
 underscoring the point.

It didn't all go brilliantly. Edith Clifford, whose act included gulping razorblades, a huge pair of scissors and a sawblade, did not appear. She had been rehearsing a new finale where she placed the tip of a bayonet blade in her mouth and lowered the hilt into the barrel of a small hand-held cannon. The blast had unfortunately jammed the blade down her throat.

After supper Toto, the elephant, was brought to the front door. A thick strip of leather studded with silver beads went across his forehead, almost over his eyes, with a loop over the crown of his head, one below the chin and one behind his ears, all fastened with vast brass rings. He was accompanied by a steam calliope – an organ fixed into a red wooden wagon frame trimmed in cream and gold. Two evil-looking jesters in pointed shoes and hats held the oval open frame surrounding the steam pipes. It played as Toto led the way.

John had presents for the women in his life. First there was Phoebe, then Billie, and finally Grace. Grace carried the emaciated Phoebe round to the terrace overlooking the river.

'These columns? All antique,' John called to his guests. 'Ninety-one of them. Mostly eleventh-century. They're all mounted on brick pedestals of varying heights and then covered with cast stone to make them the same height.'

The courtyard, with its rhythmic repetition of arches and columns, was a natural theater. Its inlaid-mosaic doorframes, antique columns, wall fountains, statues, friezes, medallions, cartouches, bronze doors and loggia walls acted as splendid sounding boards. Everyone sat down and waited as Sweetheart brought out Phoebe's gift. A small, slim woman appeared on the terrace. Phoebe gasped and Grace looked at her anxiously.

'It's Doris Humphrey.'

Sweetheart made the introduction. 'Ladies and gentlemen, we are privileged to have with us Miss Doris Humphrey, pioneer of the American modern dance and an innovator in technique, choreography and theory of dance movement. Tonight she will present one of her famous music visualiz-ations. Water Study *incorporates her theory of fall and recovery as the key to human movement and uses only non-musical rhythms – waves, natural human breath and pulse rhythms.' Sweetheart sat down and Doris danced. Phoebe was nearly beside herself. She clutched Grace's hand as the elegant Doris swayed low to the ground and then recovered.*

'It's the arc between two deaths,' whispered Phoebe, who longed to dance.

It was a curious, silent performance. Doris constantly held the moment between motionless balance and a falling im-balance where she seemed incapable of recovery. She understood that every movement a dancer makes away from the center of gravity has to be followed by a compensating readjustment to restore balance and prevent uncontrolled falling; the more extreme and exciting the controlled fall attempted by the dancer, the more vigorous must be the re-covery. The arc between two deaths.

As her wedding present from John, Billie got a theater. Not just any theater, but the eighteenth-century interior of a theater from the castle at Asolo near Venice, which John had had shipped and reassembled.

'It's the only original . . . what was it, Milton?'

'Baroque.'

'. . . baroque theater in the United States.' It was

178 gorgeous. The audience consisted of three rows of galleries in an oval shape with three hundred velvet seats. The ornate décor included portrait medallions of Dante and Petrarch.

'Who are they?' asked Billie.

'I haven't the faintest idea,' said John. 'Dead, I guess. Sure haven't heard from them.'

Professor Heckler's World Famous Trained Flea Circus was the first act and the last. There had been a problem in rehearsal and the fleas had not been troopers. The show had not gone on and the fleas had abandoned the stage for the auditorium. The seats were infested.

Grace carried Phoebe out laughing and excited. 'Theater. It's an old Greek word meaning "to see".'

'I didn't know we were going to feel it as well,' chortled Billie, scratching all over. 'Come on now, John, what does Grace get?'

John stood, his feet spread wide. A colossus in his empire.

'Grace? Why, Grace gets romance. Here.'

Around the corner of the main house walked Sweetheart's young son, Harry. He was leading the most beautiful female elephant. The boy looked fit to bust with pride as he gently held her by a giant ear. The great pachyderm was soft with the boy. She walked with the gentlest tread on huge cushioned feet. The noblest of creatures, she had a slight smile about her which suggested she had seen a mirror and knew she looked ridiculous. Her gray skin was almost entirely obscured by her costume. A vast blanket with a hundred thousand hand-sewn sequins had been draped over her. Above her head the blanket had been molded up into the head and body of a swan. It was Lillian Gish in an ill-advised musical. It was over the top. It was terrible but Grace was in love.

'For Toto. A mate for Toto.'

John shrugged as if it was nothing. 'Oh well, you keep going on about animals being lonely and whatnot. So there you go. She's called Ellen.'

The day after the engagement party Billie started packing her trunks for her honeymoon to Africa. Huge patterned boxes with inner drawers and hanging space were filled with her finest clothes. Across the bed lay a flowing silk gown shaded in purples and blues.

'That's beautiful,' said Grace, stroking the rich silk while Sweetheart helped fold endless garments in tissue paper.

Billie held the gown against herself and danced across the room.

'I shall wear this for cocktails at the foot of Mount Kilimanjaro. Elephants will wander by in single file as a lion roars under the stars. Come with us, Grace. Doesn't it sound romantic?'

I was drifting off to sleep when Miss Strange and Helen came in with the cocoa and Cosmos returned to build up the fire. Sweetheart put a coat over me. She stroked my cheek and I wanted to cry.

'I don't know why, but she reminds me of Phoebe.'

'Poor kid, she seems kind of lost.'

I went to sleep dreaming that Miss Strange carried me in her arms. I lay sure and still as she gathered me up. We laughed and wondered together at the animals as her strong arms held me up to see. I was home. I was safe.

When I awoke the women were all talking about the elephant.

'I don't see why it's like, a problem,' said Cosmos,

emphasizing each word with a cut of her knife on a new flute.

Miss Strange was firm. 'Cosmos, we cannot deal with Artemesia. We don't have the facilities.'

I was having trouble following. 'Who's Artemesia?' I asked sleepily.

Miss Strange looked at me, sorry that I had no education. 'First known woman sea captain. Fifth century.'

'No,' I said. 'I meant, what kind of animal?'

'An elephant. The most beautiful elephant,' replied Sweetheart with a smile I had not seen before. 'Ellen and Toto's baby.'

'But it's the most blessed thing that could ever happen to the zoo,' persisted Cosmos. 'Touch an elephant and you receive enlightenment. Buddha himself was born into the body of an elephant in an elephant trainer's family. On the night of his birth, an elephant entered the dreams of Buddha's mother, Queen Mahamaya, and Gautama Buddha was thus born patient, strong, meek and unforgetful.'

'Did emperors have elephants?' I asked, already agog at the thought of this romantic creature.

'Have them?' said Cosmos. 'They adored them.'

Miss Strange was unmoved by emperors' feelings or otherwise. 'That is all very well but this is upstate New York, not India. We can't do it. The elephant would need a huge reinforced outdoor paddock. We don't have anything like that.'

'So we'll make one,' insisted Cosmos.

Miss Strange shook her head. 'We couldn't do it. We couldn't afford the labor.'

'We can make it ourselves.'

'You don't know what you're talking about. This is not some pets corner we need.'

'Where did we used to keep her?' inquired Sweetheart, frowning.

'Up by the restaurant,' sighed Miss Strange. 'But I don't think those fences would keep her now. It's hopeless.'

Sweetheart nodded. 'She was lovely.'

Until then I had kept quiet, but the second I heard about Artemesia I knew I wanted the elephant to come. I wanted to receive enlightenment.

'Why doesn't Cosmos whistle for help?' I suggested. I looked at Cosmos. 'You said your whistles brought help.' The women looked at me. I think everyone thought I was overtired. It's what grown-ups decide about kids who have said too much. Everyone, that is, except Cosmos. She leaped to her feet and held her small flute aloft.

'Yes! Yes!' she cried. 'Sugar's right. If you're in trouble and you whistle then the elephants will come to save you. The elephant will come to save us. The elephant will come.' She put the flute to her lips. It wasn't even a finished one but the sound carried clearly in the night air. Cosmos began marching round and round the library, whistling her strange tune from the Sudan.

'Come on, Helen,' she called between pipings. 'Come on, Sugar, Miss Strange.'

'Cosmos, for goodness' sake! This is ridiculous,' called Miss Strange.

But Cosmos was not listening. She threw open the french windows to the garden and marched out. Slowly we followed, Miss Strange with Mr Paton on her shoulder and carrying Perry, Sweetheart followed by Sappho, the orangutan, and me. At last even Helen uncurled herself and very slowly came to see what was happening. A curious collection of womanhood. In the moonlight Cosmos was our Pied Piper. We followed her as she led us across to the zoo and up into the corner field. There she began pacing out the paddock, calling out encouragement to us to join in and dance. Sweetheart started to laugh and began marching behind her. Mr Paton began his own tune and the orang clapped along. Then Miss Strange and I tagged on behind and we marched, laughing, under the moon. Putting her arms around a sagging post, Helen clung on tight, and watched as Cosmos spread her arms into the light.

'We shall make a *gajapatti* – an abode of elephants,' she cried. 'And we know that it is written: "The form under which Buddha will descend to the earth for the last time will be that of a beautiful young white elephant, open-jawed, with a head the color of cochineal, with tusks shining like silver sparkling with gems, covered with a splendid netting of gold, perfect in its organs and limbs, and majestic in appearance."'

'Cunt,' said Mr Paton.

Chapter Nine

I guess it was a good summer for an elephant to come because it was so damn hot. Like Africa. It was as hot in Sassaspaneck as I thought Africa ought to be. After the night Perry came to the zoo no one ever discussed again whether Artemesia ought to come. At least I don't think so. We just kind of got on with it. Not that it didn't mean problems. The old elephant enclosure now belonged to Hrotsvitna, the buffalo. It was up in the far corner by the river. The first thing to do was to move her. There was general agreement that whatever Artemesia would stand for after a life in the circus, it wasn't living with a buffalo. So Europe's first dramatist got moved in with Tubman, the liberating donkey. It wasn't ideal but everyone was having to make sacrifices.

In the morning light we stood and looked at the field. The old fencing was not long for this world. Most of the posts had rotted over the years. Hrotsvitna had apparently stayed put through inertia rather than restraint. Not for her the stampeding dashes of her forefathers. An elephant would be a different matter. Perry, who had a three-year-old's notion of calm, took a running leap at a fence support and it clattered to the ground.

'She can't just wander around,' said Miss Strange. 'Artemesia. She can't just wander around.'

'How big is she?' I asked. I wanted to be helpful but I didn't like to admit that my knowledge only ran to the fact that 'E is for Elephant'. Helen sucked on her lip for a moment before speaking.

'Full-grown. I guess she must be maybe four tons, about ten foot tall.'

I couldn't imagine such a creature. All I could think was that she would make a good basketball player. It was totally outside my previous city-dwelling experience.

'All the old fencing round the perimeter of the field will have to go,' tutted Miss Strange. 'I really think we should . . .'

Sweetheart rubbed her hands as if clearing them for action. 'Get started then. Come on, let's not give up before we've begun. Plenty to do.'

The field wasn't huge – maybe half an acre – but as the workforce consisted of four women, a ten-year-old, a small boy and an orangutan, it was a tall enough order. The zoo had no money for outside help. If it was going to happen we would have to make it. The heat had made the field dusty. As Cosmos and Miss Strange dug up the old posts, swirls of dry earth clouded round them.

'It will all have to go,' sighed Miss Strange as she leaned on her shovel and looked at yet another yard of metal wire and wood-stumps. Sappho leaned on a post, casually waiting for work to resume. Mr Paton sat beside her, keeping a weather eye on the proceedings. Sappho had turned out to be handy in stacking up the old wood as it came out of the ground. She took the heavy stuff while I shifted all the light, rotting bits. A large bonfire was slowly building in the heart of the field. The sun beat down unhelpfully. Sweetheart sweated in her corset while she handed out cups of Kool Aid. She was too old to do any of the physical labor. Besides, she had to watch Perry. He was having a fabulous time. At three, almost anything would amuse him. He would spend hours playing with a branch. Stroking the ground with it to cause yet more dust, or roaring around with it raised as a gun. Had his peace-loving mother survived she might not have been best pleased. For Perry, life was for kicking and roaring. He and Sweetheart had moved into a room in the big house. Neither Judith nor Harry had been near the place in a week. While Cosmos and Miss Strange heaved and cleared, Helen watched, wrapped in herself. After a while, perhaps stirred by all the activity, she got up and went to the barn for a little. She came back with a large wooden tray and a saw.

'Helen, will you help? There isn't much time,' called Miss Strange.

Helen nodded and slowly began cutting holes in the tray.

'Sandwich?' asked Sweetheart, producing a large plate of baloney on rye. Everyone stopped for a moment and sat down to eat amongst all the mess. Sweetheart sat in the middle, upright with the plate on her lap. Perry flopped down and leaned into her, molding his little body to hers while he munched. We were filthy. Miss Strange sighed. She did a lot of that at the moment.

'It looks good,' said Sweetheart encouragingly.

'The town doesn't want elephants. They don't want us at all.'

Sweetheart would not be swayed. 'Well, we'll make them. You know, Cosmos, the first time John Junior brought Toto home, no one in Sassaspaneck, or anywhere else for that matter, thought it was a good idea. He got letters, people came round saying it was dangerous to have a bull elephant around and Toto ought to go back to Africa. Well, John got mad. Now, in those days part of the Burroughs estate was still farmed. The fields ran alongside the Amherst Railway tracks where trains ran to the city. He placed Toto in the corner of a field next to the tracks, along with his keeper, dressed in oriental clothing, and a plow. A regular horse-type plow. Every day he would get the keeper to attach Toto to the plow and they would pretend to do a little work. Hundreds of people on the railway saw this every day. It didn't take long for questions to begin flooding in from every kind of passer-by, farmers, engineers, the New York Agricultural Society. John held a meeting and invited anyone interested to come. The attendants were enthralled.

'"We've seen your elephant plowing. Is it a profitable animal in the field?"

'"How much can it plow in one day?"

'"How much can it pull?"

'"Will it become 'generally useful' on the farm, adapting to other chores?"

'"How much does an elephant cost?"

' "How much does it eat?"

'To all the questions, John claimed to not really know. He said that he wouldn't recommend the use of an elephant and that really it was a very bad idea for a farm. No one listened. Everyone thought that John Junior had the Midas touch. That he must be keeping the answers to himself for a reason.

' "Where do you buy one?" they said.

'The answer, of course, was right here. John sold twenty elephants that duly went off to make a nuisance of themselves on previously successful properties. After that no one complained.'

Miss Strange shook her head. 'It was a long time ago. Even if we get it cleared, I don't know that we can get the new fence in place before Artemesia comes. She's due next Tuesday.'

'Yes, we will.' The bell on Cosmos's head rang several times as she sprang back up to work, still eating. I had never seen her so excited, and that was saying something. Helen too looked quite close to animated. The brown of her clothes blended perfectly with the earth she sat on but her face had changed. It was brighter somehow. The decision to accept Artemesia seemed to have made Helen, as much as Helen could, come to life. Well, at least she was spending time with us. She read a lot, sometimes out loud as we worked. I tucked in to another sandwich.

'These are good,' I said, always thrilled to have fresh food made for me.

'If it doesn't work out with Artemesia we can always have elephant steak, eh, Sweetheart?'

I was shocked at Miss Strange. 'You can't really eat elephant, can you?'

'Sure.' Miss Strange passed half her sandwich to Sappho, who fed some to Mr Paton. 'After the Franco-Prussian War, the people of Paris ate the whole of their zoological collection. They didn't have any other food. They had elephant sausages, camel steaks.'

Sweetheart stood up, unable to get comfortable on the ground. Perry flopped over and lay in the dirt.

'Eland, I remember, that was quite nice. Tender.' Sweetheart answered my frown. 'Kind of antelope.' I didn't like the subject of eating any of them so I changed tack. It was a diplomatic skill I had learned from Father.

'Did Sappho always live in the house?' I asked as the orang helped herself to another sandwich. 'I mean, wasn't she in the zoo?'

Miss Strange nodded. 'For a while. She had a partner, Jacob. He escaped one night by unraveling the wire netting of his cage in the ape house. Once he was free, he smashed the skylight with a potted plant and escaped.'

Sweetheart laughed. 'He built a nest of twigs in a nearby lime tree. Everyone was so impressed.'

'Instinct will like, out,' nodded Cosmos.

Miss Strange snorted. 'Instinct! What did you expect? That he should think, Hey, I'm free, I think I'll go to a nightclub? Of course he went up into a goddamn tree. Had to get him down with a fire extinguisher. When he died she seemed happier to be out than in.' Helen sat sanding the holes she had cut in her large wooden tray. 'Helen, we have less than a week, what are you doing?'

Helen nodded and stared resolutely at her masterpiece.

She spoke quietly but with great purpose. 'I'm trying to recreate eating in the bush. I've been reading about animals getting bored. I thought if we put this tray with the holes in it on a high pole, and then put fruit on it, Artemesia has to learn to push the pole so that the fruit rolls around and falls through the holes.'

Sweetheart looked puzzled. 'Then what?'

Helen shrank back as if she had gone too far. 'She can eat it.'

'What the hell is the point of that?' barked Miss Strange.

'Can't we just give her the food?' I asked.

Helen put the tray down and retreated into a corner. There was an uncomfortable silence till Cosmos picked it up in triumph.

'I think it's so cool.' She looked through one of the cut holes. 'I mean like, boredom, right? I mean, wouldn't you like, get bored? You know, confined and everything? Artemesia, this like, giant creature, she's like, in solitary confinement. She needs stuff to do.'

'She's just had thirty years in the circus doing two shows a day,' said Miss Strange.

Sweetheart nodded. 'She'll be tired.'

'If you'd spent thirty years of your life tightrope-waltzing to an accordion player, I should think you'd need a rest, not some annoying tray.' Miss Strange stood up and blocked the sun from me.

Every new nugget of information about the impending arrival made my eyes go wider and wider.

'She can tightrope-walk? She's ten foot tall and she can tightrope-walk?'

Miss Strange knocked back her drink and gave half a smile. I was sitting on the good side of her face and it looked almost nice, but I was wrong. It was one of those grown-up, fed-up-but-trying-to-be-patient smiles. 'Yes, our Artemesia is the Parading Pachyderm. If we're very lucky she will arrive with her own tutu.'

'Maybe we should put a tightrope up so she feels at home when she comes. Do you think she might show us? I mean, I've never seen . . .' I never finished my hesitant suggestion.

Miss Strange banged her hands together abruptly. 'Is it just me or does anyone else realize that we have a great deal to do? For God's sake. I am breaking my back to give this godforsaken creature a home and all we talk about is tightropes and boredom? Who cares? What else are you going to give it? A TV?'

'Can they watch TV?' I was probably not being helpful. 'Do animals get bored?'

Miss Strange snapped out her answer. She was getting irritable. 'Bored? You'll be asking if they fall in love next. They are not stupid like us. Animals do everything for a reason. They mate to reproduce. To increase the genetic stock. They don't get bored and they don't get sentimental. Isn't that right, Helen?'

Miss Strange sounded like Harry. I didn't like it. Pinned for an answer, Helen mumbled, 'I don't think we should anthropomorphize animals.'

Cosmos smiled at Helen. 'We'd be lucky if we could do it with you.'

'You didn't used to feel like that,' said Sweetheart, looking straight at Miss Strange. Miss Strange looked at me and picked up her shovel. She started digging with renewed energy.

'What's anthropo . . .?' I was having trouble following.

'Don't make animals more important than people,' Miss Strange replied as she attacked the earth. 'A brown bear may be nice to look at but it's never going to do anything useful. It is not going to compose Beethoven's Ninth.'

Sweetheart stared at Miss Strange. 'Neither are you.'

Everyone was getting a little warm. 'Oh come on, Sweetheart, you'll be having the animals go to church on Sunday next. What do you say, Sweetheart? Will there be bugs in heaven?'

Cosmos interrupted. 'Even the humblest can aspire to enlightenment.'

Miss Strange shot back at her, 'Yeah, and any asshole with money can become President.'

'Buddha believed anyone can make the quest for enlightenment. Anyone can find nirvana – absolute truth.'

'And what is that?' demanded Miss Strange.

'Buddha doesn't say.'

'How mean of him.'

'Because it escapes definition.'

'That's a neat trick.'

Sweetheart was quietly adamant. 'You only need Jesus.'

'I think believing in Jesus is like being invited to a fancy-dress party,' said Helen. Everyone looked at her. 'Well, it's nothing but worry. You know, what if you go dressed as Marie Antoinette and no one else bothered? They just turned up in shorts. Before the party no one knows, and with Jesus lots of people have gone off to the party but no one has ever come back and told you what you should wear. If you see what I mean.'

It was the longest speech I had ever heard her say with so many people present. Sweetheart nodded her head.

'I don't know about all that. I just know that Jesus holds me up.'

I looked at the old woman. I knew it was one of Harry's corsets which held her up, but in that moment I wanted to believe. I wanted Jesus to be my friend mainly because I couldn't bear for Sweetheart to be disappointed.

'And don't start with me about me being related to Sappho and all that.' The orang looked at Sweetheart and passed her a cookie. Certainly they didn't have a family resemblance.

'You believe what you like. I don't believe in any of it.' Miss Strange sweated but never stopped working. She seemed angry now, the way grown-ups can suddenly turn when you don't expect it.

'Judaism, Confucianism, Buddhism, Christianity, Islam – ridiculous. All that divine inspiration transmitted from a male power to males for their benefit. Five patriarchal systems providing clarity, certainty, a synthesized worldview. They're just soap powders. Different ways of washing yourself whiter than white with different advertising slogans. Islam – *There is no God but God*.'

Sweetheart shook her head. 'Don't be so bitter.' But Miss Strange was on a roll.

'And Jehovah said to Jesus, "I am the Lord your God and thou shalt have none other gods before me." Why did he say that if he *is* the only god? Was there competition?

Why did he need to say it? Do you think other gods were setting up shop? I tell you, if I die I ain't going to heaven. It'll be some asshole place run by a bunch of Apostles. Goddamn men in beards who abandoned their families, sitting arguing and talking about fishing.'

Cosmos came into the discussion from left field. 'The Sumerians worshipped the Great Goddess, Inanna. She had a lap of honey, a vulva like a boat of heaven and bounty poured forth from her womb so generously that every lettuce in the land was to be honored as the Lady's pubic hair.'

Sweetheart put down her sandwich. The mention of lettuce had been too much. I didn't understand a lot of the conversation but I was so glad to be there. I felt grown-up, valued, important. We were talking about important things. Cosmos went back to digging while Helen sat down with yet another book. She had raided the library in the big house. When we weren't working in the field Helen and I spent a lot of time in the library. There was every kind of animal book you could imagine. We had found a whole stack about elephants. I think by then I was building a strange image of the arriving creature. I knew that she would be big, so big that fence posts couldn't hold her back, that she could tightrope-walk and that she would never forget anything. Helen wasn't really helping. She read out quietly from an ancient tome:

'"1844 ... Charles Knight ... The surgeon Sir Everard Home, who carried out an exhaustive anatomical examination of the elephant's ear, maintained that its structure precluded the animal from having any appreciation of music."'

I nodded, not sure what to make of it. 'I guess that's TV out.'

'"Elephant herds consist of up to four generations of females and young, immature males. The herd has a dominance hierarchy based on age, with knowledge passing from mother to child to grandchild."'

'She'll probably remember.' Cosmos called out to Miss Strange. 'You know, Artemesia. Being here, I mean. She might even remember you. It's true about their memories. Doesn't it say in that book, Helen?'

'They never forget. A calf was once knocked over by a train in Assam. The mother elephant waited until the train came the next day and then she put her weight against it and derailed it.'

'Can't you find something useful in there?' snapped Miss Strange. 'We're not having a herd, I'm not going to play her music and she ain't playing on the train tracks.'

Helen sucked hard on her lip and turned the page. 'The average bull consumes one hundred twenty-five pounds of hay per day.'

'Great. Something else we hadn't thought of.' Miss Strange heaved another post from the ground. For her age she was remarkably strong. From the left side she looked incredibly powerful and perfect.

Perry was running around tracing circles in the dust with a twig. He tripped over nothing at all and crashed to the ground, grazing his knee. Sweetheart scooped him up and held him close. She rocked her great-grandson while Cosmos and Miss Strange dug, Helen read and I tried to be helpful. We were a strange group. It was very hot and we all looked terrible. I was fairly sure that Mother would feel we were not making the most of ourselves. Not that we had time. There were problems to deal with.

A dog began attacking some of the smaller creatures at night. There were two geese who lived at Manitou Manor. A gander called Troilus and his mate Cressida. Two nights after we started work on the elephant run, Cressida got savaged by the unknown dog. In the morning we found Troilus standing silently beside her partly eaten body. Troilus was inconsolable. He hunched his body and hung his head. His eyes looked sunken and he seemed to cry pain and distress. It made Cosmos cry but Miss Strange shrugged.

'Zoo's so damn good, animals are trying to get in,' she said. She said she would call Joey to get the dog but I don't think it made the goose feel better. It just hung around looking terrible, which didn't exactly help. When you are busy what you don't need is a depressed bird getting in the way all the time. Once the fencing was clear the next difficulty loomed at us. Something had to take the place of the old wood and we were running out of time. Building a fence strong enough for an elephant was no mean feat. This was a creature who could use her trunk like a forklift truck. A mammal with the strength of fifty men. One evening I rode home on my bike past the big house. I loved to watch the sun turn it golden in the evening light. Down by the river, the railway track trudged its useless miles along the bank and across the water. Miles and miles of metal lying silent. I was thinking about tightrope-walking so I got off my trusty steed and had a go on the track. Rusty with disuse, it still did not flinch when I bounced up and down on it doing my circus-elephant impression. The old track was strong and usable. I just wasn't sure how.

On my way back I stopped at the A&P. Mother had asked me to get her more pecans. She never asked me why I took all day doing it. It was a good excuse to stop at the store. We were going to need a heck of a lot of fruit at the zoo when Artemesia came and I figured Alfonso would help. When I came round the apple display I saw that Harry was talking to him. Harry was holding a roll of the *Close the Zoo* posters and he was almost jabbing them at Alfonso.

'I need your support here, Alfonso.'

Alfonso picked up an apple to shine as if his life depended on it. 'Look, Harry, I know you want the stadium and I've always voted for you before. You're a good man and I know you've had troubles . . .'

'Alfonso?' I interrupted. I couldn't bear it if he took a poster. I had to talk to him first. He looked relieved. A man at home with avocados and oranges did not want to dabble in politics.

'Hello, Dorothy, come for your pecans? Beautiful thing, the pecan. Member of the walnut family and native to these United States. The ones we have in today are from Indiana and . . .'

Harry lost his cool. 'I don't give a damn about your stupid nuts.'

'Oh, you should. They are a native product and . . .'

Harry took his posters and left. Alfonso watched him go and handed me the polished apple he had been holding.

'I think he needs more fiber,' he said.

I nodded. It was a fruit-and-vegetable kind of approach. 'He's mad all the time now.'

Alfonso shook his head. 'It's a shame. He used to be such a nice kid but he had a tough time.' It was hard to imagine Harry having a tough time. 'Growing up at the zoo and his mom not married. I think it was okay till Billie died. He thought he should have saved her. After that there was Miss Strange and all. He sure did get teased at school. Then he went away to war and he came back so tough. Pearl was good but when she went there was nothing left to soften the edges. It's a shame.'

I wanted to ask about Harry and Billie but someone came in for potatoes and Alfonso swept off on a short root-vegetable lecture. I got the pecans and went home. When I got back Mother was waiting. I used to dream about her waiting for me, standing there with milk and cookies and a solicitous word about my day, but this was the wrong day. I didn't want to see her when I was sweaty. When I was thinking about Harry being teased. When I had been digging and pulling and generally doing things which were probably bad for your nails. I knew she wouldn't approve and it was terribly important to me just then not to hear that. She didn't seem to notice much about me at all. I gave her the pecans.

'Dorothy, I've got you something. A present, you know, you said . . . a few things, et cetera.' She spoke with the quietness of Father which we all used in the house.

She produced a box. The box I had longed for, from the Sears, Roebuck Company. It was my shorts and matching T-shirts. I went as red as if I had been supplied with something risqué from an erotica collection. The clothing mattered terribly and yet I couldn't tell her. There was a

moment when we might have actually said something to

each other but that time I spoiled it. I took the box without saying a word, went into my room and shut the door. I wanted to put the clothes on privately. They mattered too much for an audience.

The next morning I looked fabulous. No Joan of Arc in newly polished armor could have been more confident of her appearance. In knee-length royal blue shorts and matching T-shirt, I was fit for battle. I led my herd at the zoo round to the old track. I was unstoppable.

'If we can break up the old track, we can dig it in and make the enclosure. It's very strong.'

Miss Strange eyed me and nodded. It was a great idea. Cosmos clapped her hands.

'Ganesh has answered our call.'

'Ganesh?' inquired Sweetheart.

'Don't start her off,' sighed Miss Strange, but Cosmos had moved on.

'He's the Hindu god with the head of an elephant – the remover of all obstacles and bringer of good fortune. He is on our side. We can achieve all.'

'Right ... yes ... so,' said Miss Strange. 'Just one thing. How much do you think each piece of track weighs?'

We all looked at the slumbering lengths.

'A lot,' I said as a ballpark figure.

Miss Strange nodded at Cosmos. 'So, do you think you could get your Ganesh to come up with something to get the track from here to the field?'

Miss Strange went to finish clearing the old wood and get the bonfire started. Cosmos and I were to try and see if any of the track could be shifted from the old sleepers. *199*

I think Miss Strange was just trying to keep me out of the way. Helen drifted off to the butterfly house. Sweetheart and Perry kept the drinks coming. I was glad of a little time with Cosmos. After all the discussion, I had spent the night trying to have a vision from Jesus and nothing had happened. I thought maybe Buddha was a good second option.

'So, Cosmos, you worship this Buddha?'

'Oh no, Buddha is not a god. He's a Great Teacher whose doctrines and example each individual may follow on the road to enlightenment. You know, trying to ascend to higher levels of being. He was a real guy – Siddhartha Gautama. "Buddha" is just a title. It means awakened or enlightened one. He was a prince. Son of the rulers of the kingdom of the Sakyas. When he was sixteen, he married his cousin, Princess Yasodhara. They lived in this fabulous luxury palace. Then when he was twenty-nine he realized that all human life is suffering. That, you know, everyone has to die. So he gave up the palace, left his wife and infant son and went looking for the truth.'

'He left his wife and son?'

'He wanted to find the four noble truths.'

'I don't think he should have left his kid.'

'That's not like, the point, Sugar.'

But I thought it was typical. Leave the princess at home to do all the work. I went off Buddha in an instant. Why couldn't his wife have gone to find the four noble truths? At least they could have made it a family trip. I didn't think Buddha would be my friend either but I did think of Gabriel over at the Mobil station. He was my

friend. He had a religious kind of name and he had a tow-truck. At lunch I biked over to the garage to see if he would help. I was beginning to judge the businesses in town by whether they had a *Close the Zoo* poster or not. There were a lot of them around but not at the gas station. I figured it would be okay.

'Hey, Gabriel,' I called casually, popping a wheelie on my bike in the forecourt.

'Yo, Professor.' Gabriel thought I was real smart ever since I had read his draft letter. I forget how I asked him. I don't think it was too subtle. Something along the lines of 'You wanna come help with an elephant? You'd need a truck.'

He'd shrugged and mumbled something which sounded like 'Okay.'

You couldn't tell with Gabriel how much had gone in. I wasn't sure he would turn up so I didn't say anything to the others.

We were all just helping to finish piling up the bonfire when Gabriel arrived in the tow-truck. It was a huge white machine with *Jacobson's Garage* painted on the side. It had ridiculously massive tires and a crane at the back. Off the school bus and behind the wheel of his massive machine mover, Gabriel looked impressive, even to me. Helen was reading quietly to us when he arrived and I don't think she really noticed him at first.

'"Once a bull is mature it will enter a state of musth once a year. The word is Urdu for 'intoxicated'. During musth, a young bull is drunk with only one thought – to pick fights and seek females in estrous. It can be a dangerous time. A fully mature bull has the strength of around seventy men."'

Gabriel slipped from his truck and grabbed one of the last posts from Miss Strange. He tossed it on the top of the fire with barely a muscle ripple. Unaware, Helen ploughed on.

' "The bull advertises his condition with a striding walk showing off his tremendous size, strength and confidence." '

Gabriel grinned at all of us and moved to his truck. He walked led entirely by his hips. A loose open walk which advertised all that he had to offer. Sweat ran down his forehead and his arms as he walked. He was just eighteen but a strong scent of male and grease pervaded the air. If the Army could see him now they would definitely have to rethink that 4F status.

' "The bull's temporal glands, above and behind his eyes, swell and release a thick fluid which flows down the side of his head. Everything about him tells you that the bull is a swaggering male on heat. One bull can produce as much as a liter of ejaculate. A single jet of elephant sperm from the four-foot-long penis can provide enough protein to feed a forty-foot-high anthill for a year." '

For Helen it was straightforward scientific fact, but everyone was entirely silent as she looked up. Gabriel leaned against the Jacobson's logo on his truck, muscles bulging against muscles. Muscles where there shouldn't ought to be muscles. Muscles on top of muscles. He wore breathtakingly tight jeans, a white T-shirt and a large pair of work boots. He smiled and he sweated. No doubt we were a strange sight. Five females with their mouths wide open and not speaking. Instinctively I understood a great deal at that moment. These were the moist moments in life which Mother always guarded against. Certainly I knew that it was a bad time for Harry to show up.

The election was in full swing. You couldn't drive through town without a loudspeaker on someone's car yelling, 'Stick with Schlick' or 'Say hello to your own Joe'. The whole of Sassaspaneck had become addicted to Styrofoam boaters. The men wore them at rakish angles proclaiming their Democratic or Republican fervor. The women were less comfortable with their hats and perched them on top of carefully constructed coiffures. It made them look less confident about the whole thing. As if the hat and the political affiliation had landed when they weren't looking. Harry swept into the zoo sitting on the back of a convertible Caddy. Blue balloons trailed from every piece of chrome. He stood up as the car came to a halt. Football hero Harry liked to be the center of female attention. Arriving when everyone's focus was entirely on young Gabriel probably didn't help how it went.

'Thank you, thank you. Hello, people.'

The people said nothing. Harry leaped down, leaving his entourage ready to move out at a moment's notice. I didn't know what he was going to do. The general form was to shake a lot of hands and then kiss babies. I didn't think anyone would really want to shake hands. Perry was out of the question and Gabriel probably didn't have the brain to have an opinion. Harry was smiling but he seemed rather nervous. He looked beyond us to the bonfire.

'Burning the place down, eh? Great! Save us a lot of trouble.'

Miss Strange looked at him. 'Where are your manners, Harry? Good afternoon.'

He almost blushed. 'Sure, right, good afternoon. Uh, Miss Strange, have you seen the plans for the new football stadium? Going to look mighty fine.'

Miss Strange looked straight at him. 'Forget it, Harry. You are not building anything here.'

Harry smiled and tutted at the same time. 'It's over but you won't let go, will you? I am talking about building a future for the young people of this town and all you want to do is cling on to the past. Hanging on till some bastard animal gets you too.'

Little Perry grabbed at Harry's pants and pulled. 'Balloon,' he said. Harry ignored him. He was in full speech mode and would not be swayed.

'This place is nothing now but a health hazard. A hazard which the people of Sassaspaneck will not tolerate. I have therefore been in touch with the county health authority, who will be sending an inspector. An inspector who will no doubt find, as I do, that this place is no longer fit to remain open. Can't even keep the animals in any more, can you?'

Miss Strange's head snapped up. 'What do you mean?'

'I hear one of them is missing. I hear there is a salamander gone AWOL.'

I wanted to die. I knew it was my fault. I had told Harry about the salamander. I was the traitor in their midst. Everyone was going to hate me.

'How do you know that?' demanded Miss Strange.

'I told him,' I whispered. Harry looked at me triumphantly.

'It disappears all the time,' interrupted Cosmos. 'It comes back. It's like, a free spirit.'

'Balloon,' said Perry again, looking at the car.

Harry smiled a mayoral smile and got back in the car. Sweetheart moved toward her son.

'Harry, your grandson wants a balloon.' Harry's smile faltered a little as he leaned right down to his mother. He spoke in a forced whisper.

'He is not my grandson. You are showing me up. You shouldn't even be here. You don't need to be here. Get in the car and come home.' Sweetheart didn't move. Harry, surrounded by his entourage, was getting a little un-comfortable. 'Look, we can talk about the boy. Find him some place.'

Sweetheart looked at her son and stepped back. Perry ran to her and she held him close. Harry shrugged and stood up in his chariot. He left. As he did a balloon flew loose from the car and Cosmos caught it. Perry got his balloon. No one mentioned the inspector coming. We just got on with the work.

That evening I had to have dinner with Mother and Father, which was in itself quite unusual. With the General Amherst Restaurant out of action since the fire, we had no choice but to go to the diner on Palmer, which was not quite so refined. It was my parents' wedding anniversary. All I kept thinking was that if it was my wedding anniversary then I wouldn't take my kid. Outside the diner, I could see people driving by with the now-familiar boaters on their heads. The town was close to excitement.

I had a lot in my head by then from the zoo and I was desperate to talk. I wanted to discuss religion and the origins of the world and whether your hair stayed the same after you were dead. I thought that would interest Mother. She sometimes had days when she couldn't do a thing with her hair, and that would be a very bad day to die on. Mother made me have melon. I think she thought it had vitamins in it like a vegetable. She also had the melon but that was all. I don't think she could really eat in the new eighteen-hour girdle. It didn't look like there was room. Besides, she didn't like the restaurant. She didn't say anything but we all knew it wasn't good enough. When Mother disapproved she just withdrew. I know now how much the prescription drugs didn't help with that, but in those days it was okay. We had a bathroom cabinet full of the stuff. They let Mother slip from us slowly but surely.

As usual, Father and I carried the can for conversation. He steadily drank martinis while I was allowed one kids' cocktail called a Shirley Temple and a pitcher of water. Father had always taught me and Charles to have suitable topics for the table but I don't think any of mine were entirely successful.

'What have you been doing with your time, Dorothy?' my father inquired, his whisper making it sound as if there might be some intrigue.

'I'm helping at the zoo.'

'Zoo?'

'Yes. We're getting ready for Artemesia.'

'I see,' he said, although he didn't at all. 'And who is Artemesia?'

'She was the first known woman sea captain. She commanded a whole fleet at the Battle of Marathon and she was so devastating and brilliant that the Athenians put a huge bounty on her head. She survived the Persian Wars, and I mean thousands of others died, but then she threw herself off a cliff when she fell in love with a much younger man and he rejected her. Don't you think that's a shame? I mean just because he was younger than her didn't mean they couldn't fall in love, don't you think?'

It was not a good subject. It involved discussing emotions, which is what we did worst. I had come to realize that it was a British thing. That's why they go out in the midday sun. If you lay in a cool room you might have to think about how you feel. I realized I had lost my parents entirely. Father swallowed hard.

'I had a letter from Charles this morning. He is doing very well,' he segued. I polished off the melon and took a gulp of my Shirley Temple.

'How come Charles goes away to school and I don't? You know that Plato says that the state which doesn't train and educate its women like its men only trains its right arm. Do you think that's right?'

'Who told you that?' It was Mother's only contribution to the festivities.

'Miss Strange.'

Father looked hard at me. 'Miss Strange? I really think perhaps you shouldn't go to that zoo. I really can't have you coming up with these . . .' Father's voice rose almost to audible. I think he had had quite a lot of martinis because he lashed his arm out for emphasis and the jug of water smashed on to the floor. We went home in silence. Father was thirteenth on my list – the one who broke the water pitcher.

That night I stayed up late watching *The Johnny*

Carson Show on my own. I wondered if I could talk Father into color TV but I didn't know if he would see that as a trichromate I needed it. Mother had retired long before, but Father sat drinking carefully and steadily. It was very refined. For every drink he would remove the key to the tantalus from his pocket and unlock the top. Then he would remove the bottle and carefully pour himself a measure. The bottle then went back and was once more locked into place. It was very neat and very steady. He had given up on his project. A letter from the British Museum had put paid to that. It seemed that Elizabeth I had never visited Ickenham. The *ER* signature at the Ickenham Arms had almost certainly belonged to an Edmund Rossiter, a brush salesman who had passed through in 1598 with a bag of samples and a flourishing signature. The discovery seemed to have done him in.

When Carson was finished I put Father to bed. The bottle in the tantalus was empty but still locked away. He lay staring at the wall. I didn't change him or anything. I didn't like to. I just loosened his tie. He lay there, immaculately dressed, intoxicated but not in musth. I took his shoes off and took them to the kitchen to polish. I thought if he had clean shoes in the morning he might forget about the zoo. He did, but the shoes had nothing to do with it. The next morning Mother was gone and she didn't come back.

Chapter Ten

I was pretty sure that Mother left because I was so different. I knew I was from the way she used to look at me. I wasn't the little girl she had dreamed about. I didn't want any of the things she did. I didn't even like the smells she did. The perfumes and the powders in her room made me feel like I was drowning. Yet when she had gone I went into the bedroom and sat on the bed sniffing the air. I looked at myself in the mirror and willed myself to be like other little girls. With friends my own age and dolls and a giggling laugh. That's what Mother wanted. That was why she left. Because I didn't laugh right. I tried to talk to Father but he was slipping from me too. He didn't want to tell me anything.

'She's gone back to England. You'll see her there.'

'When?'

'I don't know.'

'Is she not well? Did I say something?'

'It's all right, Dorothy. It will be all right.'

But it wouldn't. If she could have gone to a shop to get another daughter I thought she would have. One in the right shade. Maybe I was a Dixie cup kid. Father went to work. I was used to being on my own but now it felt strange. Since we had arrived in America and gone to the house Mother hated, she had spent almost all her time in her room, but at least I knew where she was. Now I was adrift and to blame. I didn't know what to do with myself. Even the zoo didn't seem like a good idea. I went up to the Burroughs House, the house of love, and let myself in. I don't think anyone ever locked anywhere then. The others were all working out in the field and the place was completely still. The house was huge and there were plenty of rooms I had never explored. I stood in the vast entrance hall looking up at the chandelier. What would it be like growing up in such a place? Mother would have been happy here. She could have swept down the stairs at night in some elegant gown, ready for some elegant dinner. She wouldn't even have had to know where the kitchen was. Father waiting for her in black tie and tails. Smiling at her. Loving her. Maybe I could have had a gray dress with pearls, like Phoebe in the painting, and Grace would have loved me. Mother would have loved me. I looked down at my beloved shorts and T-shirt and knew I had been a disappointment. Would always be a disappointment.

Beyond the Polar Room, where Helen and I had first watched spiders spinning emotional turmoil, lay a set of elaborate double doors. I had never really noticed them before as they had always been closed. Now the right-hand door stood ajar and drew me down the room. There were no lights on but the morning sunlight drifted through the colored glass from the garden. I stepped across a rainbow and looked through the open door. Inside was what must have been the largest room in the house. Acres of wooden floor stretched out under shuttered windows. There was no furniture but across the ceiling dancers from countries around the world tripped the light fantastic in a mosaic of painted movement. Thin shafts of light penetrated the wood shutters, giving the floor an irregular striped pattern over which moved Joey Amorato. Joey, the dog catcher, was dancing. He was not an athletic man but he moved over the floor with a ballroom dancer's grace, holding an invisible partner close in his arms. It was an elegant soirée for one. I slid my back down the wall and sat watching. In the half-light, the brown dog-catcher's uniform with the embossed name of the town across the back was the garb of a cavalry officer. Joey's short, podgy figure was Fred Astaire and Gene Kelly in one. Soaring music from a string quartet rose as . . . Joey saw me and tripped.

'Sorry. I'm sorry. Geez,' he said, stopping in the middle of the room. 'I came for Miss Strange. She called me . . . about a dog. I came about a dog. Something with a goose. There was no one here.'

'They're all up at the field. There's an elephant coming,' I said. We stood looking at each other. I don't know who felt more awkward. 'I liked to see you dance,' I said.

Joey blushed furiously. He was mortified.

'Oh, that's not dancing. Not real dancing. I don't. This place ain't for people like me.' Joey was very embarrassed. I think he thought the only answer was to go grown-up.

It was what he did with everybody. There was a streak of officialdom in him which came out all the time. I don't think Joey knew how to just be himself. He was a town official through and through. He pulled his belly in above his belt and marched heavily over toward the wall where I was sitting.

'What are you doing here, anyhow? You shouldn't be here on your own. Does your mother know you're here?' I half expected him to whip out a notebook and take down a statement.

'My mother left,' I said. This stopped him for a moment.

'Left? Like departed?' I nodded. 'Yes, well, that ain't good. That ain't good at all.' He paused. 'Sorry, kid. She was a beautiful woman,' he added, as if she were dead. Small particles of dust drifted in the strips of light. 'I came about a dog,' he repeated before falling into another awkward silence. Maybe the mention of the dog reminded me of the sad goose, I don't know. Whatever it was, I burst into tears. I don't know which one of us was more embarrassed. Joey looked away and then slid down the wall to sit beside me on the floor. We didn't touch but he sat close as though he meant to comfort me.

'She left your dad, huh?'

I hadn't thought about that. I supposed perhaps she had. I had only thought about Mother leaving me. Maybe it was the anniversary dinner. The food hadn't been anywhere near good enough but also I had talked too much. No one in our family ever talked that much or about such things, life and death and that. But maybe she hadn't just left me.

'It could just be temporary. Your mother might just be getting some air.' We sat for a long time in silence. I didn't think Mother was getting air. I don't think she really approved of the stuff. After a while Joey cleared his throat. 'I read that sometimes couples, good couples, couples that were meant, get a rainbow bridge between them. Sometimes it's an instant one, from the minute they meet, and sometimes it kind of grows. I mean something invisible. I never had that. Do you think your folks did?'

I thought for a minute. I didn't think so. I liked the idea of it but I was sure Mother and Father never had it. Harry and Judith didn't have it, and I didn't ever remember seeing Uncle Eddie look at Aunt Bonnie that way. I wiped my nose on my sleeve.

'I don't think so.'

'No. It's rare, real rare. Mr Burroughs thought he had it with Billie but I don't know. You couldn't tell with Billie. I don't think it counts unless both people feel it. They had a wedding like it was there but I don't know.'

'Did you know Billie then?'

'Sure.'

'Did you ever see that rainbow thing?' I asked.

'You don't see it. You kind of feel it. You been to the pool here in the house?' I shook my head. 'Fantastic piece of work. Lots of Indian stuff. Sometimes they used to let us swim there after school. Grace always took Phoebe. There was nothing of Phoebe. Even I could have lifted her and I was little when I was a kid.' Joey was quite little now but I didn't say anything.

'Grace used to pick her up in her arms and carefully carry her down the marble steps into the water. Phoebe would move her arms and legs while Grace lapped the water on to Phoebe's shoulders. There was this picture of an ocean on the ceiling and Phoebe would stretch out flat, staring up at it.'

The indoor pool was new. It was to be the last building John Junior added to the Burroughs House. As with every architectural detail, the marble room was beautiful, if a little overwhelming. It owed its inspiration to the Raj. All around in minute mosaic detail, the god Vishnu floated on the cosmic ocean, dreaming his cosmic dreams. Grace liked this room best of all, for here Phoebe was free.

She lifted her weak friend into her arms and carefully carried her down the marble steps into the water. She laid her gently on the surface and watched Phoebe take new life. Phoebe's frail and unsure frame became usable and strong. Phoebe stared up at the cosmic ocean above her head.

'Look, Grace, we are not in our world. We are somewhere else. We are free,' mouthed Phoebe to the Indian god.

Grace placed both her hands under Phoebe's back and began to slowly swirl her in the water. Billie watched from the side in silence. It was a display of tenderness such as she had never been subject to. This was love. Not lust or sensible arrangement or reproduction or any of the other reasons why the men and women she knew clubbed together, but honest love. It hurt to watch it. For those three it was to be a final quiet moment. Not that anyone could have predicted it. Not that anyone would have taken the time.

They still felt like winners. Winners for ever. When they got back to the main house they heard the news that Milton was dead. He had made one deal too far. It took all the steady part of their lives away. Milton might have been a crook but he had been a sensible one. Now the kids had no parent to tell them off when they went over the top. John didn't know he couldn't manage by himself. He wasn't grown-up enough. Sweetheart tried but it was too big a job and maybe it was too late.

Joey sighed. 'I remember watching Grace and Phoebe in the water. Billie didn't swim but sometimes she would watch from the side in silence. I think maybe she was jealous. Maybe we all were. But that was that thing, that rainbow bridge.'

'Did you go to the wedding? Billie and John Junior's?' I asked.

'Yeah. I mean, I was just a kid but I danced with Billie and Grace and Sweetheart. I was only eight. What a party. Mr Burroughs, he never did nothing small. The shows he did. I think that summer it was the big Joan of Arc stuff. They had like a thousand performers, hundreds of soldiers on horses, forty elephants and a real fire at the end. When they took it to London they needed *four* ocean liners. That was something because P. T. Barnum only needed three for his and he was some showman. Anyway, lots of the acts came. It was a heck of a party. Even the elephants got dressed up. What the hell were they called?' Joey sat and thought.

Ellen and Toto, Grace's elephant couple, had been given new costumes for the event. They were dressed as bride and groom. Ellen had a full veil and a bunch of roses while Toto wore a bow tie, a silk-lined cape and a top hat. Grace didn't like it.

She thought it was wrong to dress them up like that, but it made Phoebe smile. John had bought an orchestromelchor for the occasion. It was a huge musical instrument which on its own could give the full effect of an orchestra for five miles.

'I think they won't like the music. It's very loud. I don't want it to upset them.' Grace fretted over the elephants all day. No one else did. Everyone else was too drunk. It really was a day of carnival without end. Two hundred and fifty people turned up and six hundred bottles of champagne went down. The guest list was quite extraordinary. Quite a lot of John's shows had closed ahead of paper. This meant they returned to Sassaspaneck before the end of their posted season. John didn't mind the losses. He was busy organizing the biggest show ever, to blow Barnum out of the water.

The Flying Vazquez Family arrived to add their dimension to Jeanne d'Arc's demise. They drove around in a converted potato truck, yet somehow they looked like glamour. Italian-looking boys who hardly took a breath before they had rigged a rehearsal harness up in the trees by the bird house. Here they spent their hours on the triple somersault. Endless shouts of 'Hup, hup, hey!' as the youngest Vazquez swung back and forth, up to sixty miles per hour, before flipping three times and flinging himself out into the arms of his oldest brother.

As Grace carried Phoebe to the ceremony, physical perfection was spinning over their heads. It was the strangest mix of people. Midgets, giants and the Fiji Cannibals headed for the temporary altar built on the lawn. Mabel Willebrandt, the Deputy Attorney General for the last eight years, was there. She had caused a great scandal when she adopted a baby girl after she got divorced. Then there was Lord Delamere, a man happy to take someone else's money.

'I am telling you, ostriches have been my downfall,' he announced to Captain Adam H. Bogardus, Champion Wing Shot of America. 'I was just on the verge of making a fortune out of the wretched birds' feathers for hats when motoring took off. Absolutely scattered the chances of feathers as finance.'

It was a time of peacocks and champagne. Of lingering looks between men and their best friends' wives. So many people being spoiled and badly behaved. Africa loomed large in much conversation as the tamer of John's menagerie wandered about for the ceremony.

'Do you remember Denis Finch Hatton? I heard a marvelous story about him the other day. There he was, deep in bush, hundreds of miles from anywhere, when he saw a sweaty native running after him with a cleft stick. The boy only had a telegram for him. It had come all the way from London in relays. Anyway, old Denis read the telegram and it said, "Do you know Gervase Pippin-Linpole's address?" Do you know what he sent back as an answer? "Yes." Isn't that brilliant?'

John was like a small child. Heady with excitement. Only Sweetheart kept cool and got everything going. She stayed sober for Harry because Harry needed her.

'You must start the ceremony now, John,' she counseled.

'Yes, yes, I will, but look at this. Look at this wedding present.' He stood in front of a small table made from a curious wood. 'It's not wood at all.' He whispered his delight like a small boy with a dirty magazine. 'It's made entirely from coprolites. Do you know what they are? Fossilized saurian feces.' His voice boomed out his appreciation. 'It's a

table made from old shit and no one will know. Isn't that perfect? Isn't it the most perfect thing? And look at these –
candlesticks made from the vertebrae of an ichthyosaurus.'

Everything was about wonder. About the extremes of experience, of human and of animal life. On that day you could have searched the ends of the earth for a rarer experience. It was unreal and it could not survive. Mme Yucca, the Female Hercules – the Strongest Woman on Earth, Handsome, Modest and Genteel, in the Costume of the Parlor She Performs Feats of Strength Never Attempted by Any Other Man or Woman – carried Billie on a carved chair out to the lawn. She looked like a white goddess emerging from the house. She had on her tiger-training uniform but everything was in white linen – the pants, the shirt, her neat tie – and all finished off with knee-high white leather boots. It was Billie's own way of dressing for a wedding.

John looked more somber in his dark suit, but his waistcoat was white silk with buttons made from the bones of an alligator. The orchestromelchor struck up as Ellen and Toto took up their places either side of the altar. As the priest began his rites Billie looked to Grace, but she was too busy making sure the animals were okay. She still thought the music was too loud. It wasn't actually the music which caused the commotion. It was Mlle Zazel, the Human Cannonball. She was supposed to perform as the climax to the wedding vows. She had her trick down to a fine art. She was a small woman who stood on a circular platform within the tube of her cannon. The bottom of the small circle was attached to a heavy spring. As the tension in the spring was released, a light gunpowder charge was set off and she would sail off to land in a large net some seven feet away. Unfortunately, that day

218

some wag had interfered with the quantity of gunpowder.

As the ceremony concluded, John kissed Billie and Mlle Zazel flew over their heads with no apparent intention of stopping. She narrowly missed joining the Vazquez Family on a permanent basis and continued on over to the conservatory. It was the loud crash of glass which finally sent Ellen and Toto running off in separate directions. Grace, unsure who to follow, seemed to set off in both ways at once. John laughed and laughed, sure and confident in his domain. The animal world was his to command. With Billie secured to his side, he felt very powerful. More cocktails were gulped as the crowd moved to see his final gift to Billie.

Rajan, her beloved Rajan, stood in the most magnificent new, round enclosure. It was the perfect setting for this most perfect of Bengal tigers. His massive striped head stared out at the wedding party from behind the bars. Grace, having ushered Ellen and Toto to their own enclosure, pushed Phoebe to the front of the crowd so she could see. Billie, immaculate in her white, stepped up to the cage door.

'Hello, my old friend,' she said quietly to the giant beast. 'Have you got a new home?' She spoke gently to the four hundred pounds of muscle. Through the bars the bright color of Rajan's coat stood out. He was stunning. Billie moved to unlock the door. John suddenly became nervous. He had never been nervous before, but Billie had never been his wife before.

'Don't you need your whip?' he called.

Billie smiled at him. 'You have to balance fear and respect, John. A beaten child has only fear.' Then, just as she was about to open the door, she leaned toward her new husband and whispered, 'I'm pregnant.'

Before John could say a word, Billie stepped into the cage   219 and locked the door behind her. She faced the tiger square on as Rajan padded as far from her as possible. Billie moved slowly, reaching her hand out gently toward the top of its head. She had done this a hundred times. The drunken crowd was completely silent. This slender bride in white matched against one of Nature's furies. It was good entertainment, till the tiger spoiled it. He must have wound the muscles in his legs like the spring in Mlle Zazel's cannon. One minute he was standing there and the next he was on Billie. Grace was the only person who moved. Without thinking she was in the cage and on the back of the tiger. Somehow, by surprise or luck, she managed to release Billie from its grasp. Blood ran from Billie's arm, a scarlet cloak across her white wedding wear. Finally John was able to move, and he pulled his wife from the cage, but now the tiger turned to Grace. Grace inched her way round the cage toward the door. The tiger was playing with her. At first it seemed it was going to let her go. Then, as she approached the door, it reached out with one massive paw. The rip into her flesh started at the top of the right side of her head. It tore through her skin, from her hair down her temple and across her cheek. The destruction had no end as the claws reached her shoulder and then down, shredding, tearing, slicing, destroying her right arm and hand. The right side of Grace's body pulled for ever down and down. A single shot from Captain Bogardus finished the horror. The tiger was dead.

As the tiger slumped to the floor Phoebe rose in her chair, trying to reach Grace. As she did so her body pitched forward and then back. For a moment Phoebe moved like a dancer. She was beautiful, poised between dropping and recovery, between balance and uncontrolled falling. An arc of death. Then, finally, she slumped into young Harry's arms and she was gone.

Joey sat completely still in the empty room as the people of the past moved around us. At last I asked him:

'How come you were there, Joey?'

'I was Harry's best friend.'

Chapter Eleven

Joey and I parted in the house with some awkwardness. I don't know who was more embarrassed by the unexpected encounter. To be honest it had probably been a little too intimate for both of us. He went off to look for Miss Strange and get 'dog details' while I went to find the others. I was pretty sure Joey and I could rely on each other never to mention our conversation again.

It had been a revelation, though. Miss Strange was Grace. She had been beautiful. She had turned from Grace to Strange. I thought about seeing her in the ice-cream store and I wanted to die right then and there. I had no place on any list of any kind.

When I arrived at the field everyone was busy getting ready for Artemesia. Something extraordinary was in the air. Happiness was filling the place, and it seemed to be contagious because it wasn't just the humans. The sun shone under the clearest blue sky and as soon as I came in the gate I knew things were good. Right at the entrance

Girling the Gorilla greeted everyone with his particular song. It was a happy sound, somewhere between dog whining and human singing. He would munch on an apple and when Cosmos came to feed him he put his arm round her and sang even louder. Sweetheart and Perry couldn't stop laughing at the bonobo chimps. They played endless solitary games of blind man's bluff. The small chimps would cover their eyes with a leaf, or their fingers or arm, and stagger about the climbing frame.

I knew then that I never wanted to leave there. This was my family now. This was where I would find my rainbow bridge. I tried to put Mother out of my mind. She wasn't well. I couldn't bear to be in the house. There was a new quiet. A silent drowning. I just stayed at the zoo where we were busy. We were getting on with the job. Doing what women do best – working by instinct. Cosmos said it was the best way.

'There's a lot more to instinct like, than men think, you know,' she explained to anyone who would listen. 'Women's intuition is like, excellent. I mean, imagine you're in space, okay?, and this like, meteorite or whatever is coming at you, then your problem is A, the meteorite, right? Now the answer to getting out of the way may be D, but you don't have time to go A then B then C therefore D. What you need is the intuition which tells you D right away.' Cosmos said it was a special strength in women. Anyhow, it was that summer.

We worked all day preparing and digging the holes for the new enclosure. Around lunch, Gabriel arrived with the Jacobson's tow-truck. He had come most days. He would lash three or four of the metal rails together and haul them over the field. There we put them in upright about every two foot or so. Gabriel didn't say much but we couldn't have done it without him. We needed that much brutal strength on our side. He worked for a while without a word and then, as he turned to go, he just said the one word, 'Welding,' and was gone. Not one of the world's great communicators. We didn't pay that much attention to him because a strange thing had started to happen.

Women, other women from the town, had begun turning up. Now you have to remember the Sassaspaneck Zoo wasn't exactly the local hotspot. But Harry talked about the zoo all the time in his electioneering and I guess it put the place in people's minds. Or maybe they just heard about our building work. I don't know. Anyhow, at first there was just a couple of onlookers and then gradually more and more women came. Usually around lunchtime. Some would bring sandwiches and just sit and watch us work. Cosmos said we were becoming the zoo's most successful exhibit. But soon others were helping out a little or getting drinks for the workers. No one said anything about it but the workforce just kind of grew. I think after a while everyone had heard about the elephant coming, and all those women who normally sat home or went to the store wanted to see. There was Hubert Thomas's wife Ingrid, and Doreen Angelletta whose husband Tony ran the pizza parlor, and even Mrs Torchinsky stopped her coffin-polishing to come over. I don't know why. Maybe it was just something so out of the ordinary. The whole town must have been getting dusty because no one seemed to be home doing housework any more. Ganesh was providing for us big-time.

Perry was in heaven. He was such a cute kid. He'd been hidden out at the big house and at the zoo, so no one in town had really met him before. He was kind of a clown and made all the women laugh all the time. All day he raced around from one new game to another. Then he would suddenly plump down on the lap of one of the women and go straight to sleep. They loved him but there was never any talk about his grandparents or his mom. Me and Perry were about the only kids in town. Everyone old enough had gone to camp. Maybe we were a novelty.

Time was running out so we worked even harder. Miss Strange was in charge although no one ever said so. No one said much of anything. We worked when she worked and stopped when she did. This curious half-woman led the way. Artemesia was due on the Tuesday and it was Sunday when Joey and I had had our talk. It was that same evening that Aunt Bonnie and Judith pitched up. They hadn't come to help. Judith looked real thin. Thin like Aunt Bonnie, not corset-thin. She was dressed as coordinated as ever but somehow it wasn't working. She still had insanely high heels on but her mountain of hair had suffered something of an avalanche down one side. Everything about her looked a little untucked. Miss Strange kind of started when she saw Judith. Aunt Bonnie was sort of leading her. It sure didn't look like she wanted to be here. Miss Strange moved forward and I thought for a minute she was going to kiss Judith hello but she didn't.

'You haven't been,' she said quietly. Troilus, the widowed goose, began making little whimpering noises. I don't think he wanted the distraction from his grief. It should have been his moment.

'I can't drive. Really, I can't drive.' Judith never looked at Miss Strange. She just kept looking at the ground. This was not the Welcome Wagon woman I had first met. She didn't have any bounce in her at all. I doubted she would ever carry a green cake again.

'I drove her over. She's a little shaky.' Aunt Bonnie dragged the life out of a cigarette and looked at the morose goose. I don't think she was much for animals but it's not often you look at a goose and think instantly of therapy rather than stuffing. Aunt Bonnie looked away and rather stiffly patted Judith on the arm. She talked to her like one of her kids late with a book report.

'Go on. Get it over with.'

Judith looked everywhere except at Miss Strange. I had got so used to Miss Strange's face that I never noticed it any more. That's just how she was. Now Judith seemed to make all of us look at the disfigured right side just because she wouldn't. It was horrible. Judith obviously had a short speech prepared but her heart wasn't in it. She just said it like she had learned it for school.

'Harry asked me to come. He will win, you know. He wants the stadium. The town needs a stadium.'

Miss Strange wasn't taking any nonsense. 'That's not why Harry wants to close the zoo and you know it.'

Judith was beginning to falter. 'Everyone will vote for him and you'll have to go. If you can't do it for the town then at least do it . . . for the family. I still own the land.'

'You and Helen own the land. This is your history, Judith. What are you doing? Honey, I . . .' It would be a stretch to call Miss Strange soft, but she did have kind of a soft look on her face with Judith. She moved toward her as Sweetheart strolled over from the house with Perry on her hip. Judith looked up at her grandson for a second and then trailed off with:

'You can't win.'

There was no conviction in her voice. The other women from town had started to arrive for the day and everyone stood around looking at her. After she finished speaking there was silence. Troilus took the moment to shuffle forward. Whether he wanted sympathy or simply couldn't stand any more from some unseen injury, he chose to put his head on Judith's knee. Apart from his whimpering it was very quiet.

Aunt Bonnie dragged on her Virginia Slim. You could hear the air sucking through the menthol. Troilus sobbed. Finally Aunt Bonnie asked, 'What's wrong with the goose?' Miss Strange didn't say so I volunteered.

'A dog killed its mate. It's . . . sad.' I looked at Miss Strange. I didn't know if that was okay. If a goose could be sad. It didn't matter because Judith burst into tears. Then all the women did what women do. They cooed and clucked and someone went to make iced tea. Miss Strange and Cosmos kind of stood on the outside of it all then they went back to work in the field. Judith could hardly contain herself. She was worse than the goose. They howled together. Sappho, the orangutan, who had been sitting in a corner, looked away in disgust. It was then that Joey arrived at the field in his full dog-catcher regalia. Judith saw him show up and howled even louder. I felt sorry for him. He was obviously having a day of females crying.

'I came about the dog,' he said. The women all looked at him. 'Miss Strange called me.' Judith sobbed on. Troilus, having found a soulmate in sorrow, hung over Judith's knee, abject with grief. Joey shuffled his small feet on the ground, stepping first toward Judith and then away.

'Oh God, Judith, don't cry. I'll get the dog. No goose-killing dog is going to last in this neighborhood. Judith!' Joey ineffectually reached out a plump arm toward woman and bird and I saw then that he had it – the rainbow bridge, for Judith. I think everyone saw it because suddenly everyone was very busy with their work. Mortified by his day, Joey began frantically pacing out the yard. He paused for a moment in his deliberation, gave a kind of contained nod in Judith's direction and turned to me.

'Are you able to tell me when exactly this crime had its perpetration? Do you have any leads as to possible dog species involvement?'

They were probably good questions but I wasn't the person to answer them. I had no idea.

'Don't you worry, young woman.' He came quite close to patting me on the head but stopped in time for both of us. 'I'll get the varmint,' and I was sure he would. Troilus had not allowed anyone near the body of his deceased partner, but he made way for Joey's official examination. Joey examined the neck for teethmarks and checked everywhere for footprints. He was very thorough. All the time Judith sat watching him with Troilus draped inconsolably across her knee.

Some two hours later, Judith was still seated on a hay bale outside the barn. Sweetheart was organizing snacks and Aunt Bonnie had taken over playing with Perry. The two of them were having a wonderful time. Aunt Bonnie had hung up an old tire in the barn and she and Perry couldn't stop laughing. They were playing at being monkeys and kept pretending to pick bugs off each other.

'Ugh, ugh.' Aunt Bonnie came towards Perry like Girling the Gorilla. He shrieked with laughter and swung out of the way on his tire. Judith's face leaked tears. I don't think she would have had the energy to go unless someone had carried her out. I guess with her kids at camp Aunt Bonnie didn't really have a reason to go home. Anyhow, they both stayed.

It was the hottest and probably the hardest day. The uprights for the enclosure were all dug in now. There were just the crossbars left to do. The women humped and heaved the last of the track pieces into the places they would eventually go. Everyone was waiting for Gabriel to come back. He returned in his truck. He was wearing tight white jeans, a white singlet and no shoes. He leaped down from the cab like some knight from his white horse. It was ridiculous.

'God almighty, look at those muscles,' whispered Mrs Torchinsky through her mustache.

'I may work all day,' answered Ingrid, who had been ready to quit.

They weren't alone. All the women went quite gooey. Stupid, I thought. From the back of his truck Gabriel took down a big gas tank, some piping and a large metal mask. He smiled at everyone, aware of his performance, and then began calling out instructions. While the women heaved and held the solid metal, he began to weld the crosspieces into place. In his white sleeveless T-shirt and with that glass and metal mask with blue and purple sparks flying around him he looked like a god. An un-obtainable god. All afternoon long he gave off this incredible aura. The women worked harder and harder. Women who had never done anything manual without rubber gloves and a Brillo pad lifted metal into place and stood under a shower of sparks.

Up at the barn, Joey continued with his job, examining every nook and cranny of the crime scene. A couple of times Miss Strange had passed by the barn but she and Judith never said a word to each other. I think Miss Strange wanted to but Judith just looked away. By night-fall, the enclosure was nearly finished. After a sandwich lunch Sweetheart had moved on to organizing dinner. Doreen Angelletta had called Tony at the pizza parlor and Sweetheart had been to collect. There was pizza for everybody in the barn. It was getting dark now and maybe twenty or more women had got together for the food.

There probably hadn't been a gathering of women in the town like this for years. Certainly it was the first one with a disconsolate goose present. Judith sat silently, matching her body language to the drooping bird. They were in hell together. Out in the field, the sparks from Gabriel's work continued to splinter the air.

'God, he's gorgeous,' announced Mrs Torchinsky, looking out through the barn doors. 'And I seen a lot of fellas.'

'Yeah, but they've mostly been dead,' laughed Ingrid from behind a piece of Sicilian.

Aunt Bonnie sat on a bale with Perry. She was playing some counting game with him. They kept laughing. It seemed weird to me that she was so good with kids and yet she sent her own away for the summer. I'd have stayed with her.

'You be a horse again, Aunt Bonnie,' he cried as the game moved on. In the distance the fire siren sounded but no one moved or even counted the blasts.

'I haven't worked this hard since I gave birth to the twins,' grinned Doreen Angelletta.

Sweetheart handed out drinks in Dixie cups. I kept thinking how my Mother would enjoy that. The Dixie cups.

Doreen sighed. 'I think I'm in love,' she declared as Joey passed by outside. There was a general shriek of disbelief.

'With Joey Amorato?'

'Ergh, you'd never get the dog hairs off your clothes. Ain't that right, Judith?'

'How you ever chose between him and Harry I'll never know.'

Everyone laughed. Doreen was chanting through a crack in the barn door. 'Gabriel, oh Gabriel!'

'What's the matter, Doreen? Ain't your Tony coming up with the goods?' called one of the women.

'Sure,' said Doreen. 'Once a year on New Year's Eve after Guy Lombardo's been on the TV. God forbid that Lombardo man ever dies, my married life will be over.'

'New Year's Eve, you're lucky,' said another woman. 'The only person who touches me is my hairdresser.'

Helen slipped in through the barn doors. When she saw how many people there were she tried to leave again but Miss Strange gently grabbed her arm and moved her into a corner.

'I lit the fire,' Helen said quietly and curled away.

Cosmos was explaining one of her theories to a few of the women. She clutched a piece of paper earnestly as she spoke.

'You see, you have to find your place in the cosmos. Like, it might not be here.'

I nodded. 'You mustn't be an Et cetera,' I said, which I thought was the worst on my list.

'For God's sake, Cosmos, you do talk some talk sometimes,' said Doreen.

'It's like important. You have to find your place in the Great Scheme,' said Cosmos.

'And is this your place?' asked Mrs Torchinsky to the soft and gentle young woman. I expected a spiritual reply but Cosmos shook her head.

'Nah, I ran out of money on the Greyhound bus just past the zoo. It's cool. I have to be here for a while before I move on.'

Doreen moved on to a subject everyone could relate to.

'I think Troilus has fallen in love with Judith,' she called cheerfully.

Judith looked at the floor. Maybe she didn't even hear. She had stopped crying but she had sunk so far into herself that afternoon that there seemed no getting her back. There was hay on her once-perfect clothes and her mask of make-up had begun to fade away. I thought she looked prettier than before.

'Just lucky, huh, Judith?' laughed Ingrid. 'There's a hunk in the field and you get the thunderbolt from a Christmas dinner.'

Miss Strange looked tired but I think in her own way

she was trying to get through to Judith. She looked straight at her.

'Don't be ridiculous. Animals do not love.'

I didn't like the idea of this. 'Mr Paton loves you,' I said and I knew it was true. He was sitting on her shoulder, stroking the indented side of her face.

'That's not love,' replied Miss Strange, getting mad. 'I'm just his meal ticket.'

Cosmos thought for a moment. 'I think we don't want animals to have emotion because then we wouldn't know how to treat them. Anyway, if they have no emotion it makes you feel, like, better than them. More than them. But they feel stuff. Did you ever see anything more passionate than the excitement of a dog going for a walk?'

Miss Strange snorted. 'That's not passion. It's about gratification.'

Cosmos tried again. 'It's not like humans do emotion real well. They can't always express what they're feeling.'

Doreen was trying to follow. 'Yeah, but they do express it, right? That's what makes it different. At least people, what do you call it, communicate.'

'Not always,' said Mrs Torchinsky, who lived among the departed. Cosmos's focus was absolute. She was not distracted.

'If someone from another country didn't speak English and you couldn't talk to them, does that mean they don't feel anything? I mean we speak the same language and . . . Ingrid, try and find one word for what you feel right now. Better yet, what I am feeling or Sweetheart.'

Ingrid looked bewildered. 'I don't know. Of course, I don't know.'

'No you don't. Can anyone understand the inner land-scape of anyone else's life? Do you know what someone else is feeling? Presuming that animals lack feeling is just an excuse for treating them badly.'

Mrs Torchinsky was adamant. 'We are not like animals.'

'No, we're not like animals, we are animals,' replied Cosmos.

Doreen looked out the door again at Gabriel.

'Of course, some men are more animal than others.'

Mrs Torchinsky laughed. 'I'm sure you have a point, Cosmos, but I can't worry about this. I can't spend Sundays wondering if the chicken on my table was depressed. How could you tell anyway? Bad posture?'

The women started laughing and Sappho clapped along with delight.

'Yeah, Cosmos, tell us, do chickens have pecking orders?'

'Do penguins have bad days?'

Cosmos smiled. 'Did you ever see two herons court-ing?' she asked. 'They wrap their long necks around each other and reach such a pitch of emotion that I could have wished to be a heron so I might experience it.'

Miss Strange tutted. 'Heron love. Love! Why do women talk about it all the time? It's no wonder men think we're lame-brained.'

Mrs Torchinsky produced several bottles of red wine and some fresh cups while the discussion continued.

'Men don't know about love,' declared Ingrid. 'All they worry about is size and performance.'

As the subject of size had often come up in many of the *234* women's minds in relation to Ingrid's husband Hubert from the Pop Inn, this gave them pause. He was the only black man in town and even I knew there were rumors about what that meant.

'That's not true,' declared Doreen, defensive of her Tony.

'All right,' cried Ingrid, getting excited. 'What is the difference between men and women?'

'The size of your bowling ball,' volunteered Doreen, and everyone laughed. The women sat and talked and drank. It didn't take long for them to get on to the subject of sex. Miss Strange was getting slightly slurred.

'Camels have very civil breeding methods although otherwise they are rather bad-tempered and I do not recommend them for a pet. If a female in the camel pack . . . sounds like a cigarette . . . anyway, if the female goes into heat then the males won't fight for her. They just line up single file and in an orderly fashion to "service" her. When they're done, they get off and go back to the end of the line.'

Cosmos was getting annoyed. 'Yes, but none of this means animals can't love.'

'Oh, stop bringing love into it,' snapped Miss Strange so sharply that Mr Paton removed himself to the other end of the hay bale. Cosmos would not be swayed.

'Animals love their babies.'

Helen surprised everyone by joining in. 'The female Asian diadem butterfly will guard her eggs by standing over them. Sometimes, if the eggs don't hatch, she will do it till she dies. Her rooted corpse standing watch over her offspring.'

'Is that love?' I wanted to know.

'A butterfly will do that?' said Sweetheart so quietly we almost didn't hear. 'That's more than Judith will do for Perry.' Perry had fallen asleep with his body molded to Aunt Bonnie. There was a terrible silence, broken by Joey appearing at the door.

How Joey ever thought he could run for office I'll never know. At any rate he couldn't deal with the crowd of women who turned their attention to him. He didn't really have much to say. He tried to pull his substantial stomach in a little and smoothed back his hair. He blushed as he spoke.

'Oh, yes, hello. Miss Strange. Uh, Judith.' He looked and smiled at the floor in the direction of Judith. 'I have located the entrance manner of the perpetrator and I think if I stay here the night then I could bring the matter to a useful conclusion. What I am saying is that I think the dog will come back and I could——'

Outside the roar of an engine brought everyone to silence. The thud of heavy boots was followed by the banging open of both the double barn doors. There stood the whole of Sassaspaneck Fire Brigade. Defenders of the town and husbands to every one of the women sitting inside. The men were filthy with soot and smoke. At the center of the group stood Harry. In his fireman's braces, filthy T-shirt and heavy boots, he looked macho in the way that men believe women admire. He eyed the group of seated women. Not one of them felt comfortable. There wasn't a woman in the room Harry hadn't seen naked and bulging in his corset store and he knew it. A dangerous priest who might forget the secrecy of confession. He

stripped them down with his eyes and then wandered over

to Joey. Harry was considerably taller. He stood un-comfortably close to the little man and looked down at him.

'Well, well, an election rally for the Democrats, eh, Mr Amorato? Cornering the female vote? I think you might be wasting your time, eh, men? I think you'll find the ladies will be good enough to vote sensibly with a little guidance from their husbands.'

'I wasn't . . . I was here to . . .' Joey stumbled over every word.

Harry patted him on the head and dismissed him with a wave. 'No need to explain.' I thought Joey was going to try and punch him again. Instead he just hitched his pants up over and over.

Miss Strange stood up. 'Hello, Harry. Thought maybe you had forgotten your way out here. Been a long time.'

Harry pulled himself up tall but a flash of a little boy crossed his face. 'Don't start with me, Miss Strange.' Harry clenched his jaw and turned back to Joey, to safer ground. 'Pity you couldn't join us on our little outing just now, Joey. Oh sorry, I forgot, too short for the brigade, aren't you?'

'I have asthma. You know I have asthma.'

Harry smiled around at his chums. 'Sure, of course. Still, I expect it was a man's work cutting up those pizzas for the ladies.' Harry moved in on Joey. He reached out and snapped his finger's at Joey's bow tie. 'My, you look good tonight. I always forget what a fine uniform that is.'

'I'm here on official business,' stammered Joey, step-ping back a little. He seemed to shrink even smaller as Harry rounded on him.

'Official business,' repeated Harry. 'Dog catcher to the zoo, huh? Not really a man's job is it, Joey? Animals?

Furry animals? I mean, look at all these women. Much more their line, don't you think?' Harry turned back to his brigade for approval. The men were grinning.

Joey pulled himself up as tall as possible. 'Don't do this to me, Harry. You always do this to me. I have a job to do.'

'No!' Harry stepped back in mock surprise. 'What are you catching today, Joey? A dangerous poodle? A pest of a pooch? A schnauzer with a problem home?'

Joey was sweating now. He eyed all the men watching him and then said with as much dignity as he could muster, 'A dog killed a goose.' Harry laughed.

'May the good Lord save us in our beds. And to think we were fighting a fire while all this was going on. Saving homes while our women were busy finding other things to do.' Harry dismissed Joey from his mind and turned to the silent women. 'Now then, ladies, we men are hungry. We drove past our homes and there was no one there. That can't be right, can it, Judith? Judith?'

Judith said nothing. She sat so hunched now she could look at no one. 'Judith, get up!' barked Harry. His face twitched a little as she failed to move. Very aware that everyone in town was watching, he hissed at her.

'I am talking to you. Now get up.' Harry moved to the hay bale where Judith was sitting and put his hand on the back of her neck the way he had at the barbecue.

Joey stepped toward him. 'She's not feeling good.'

'She can do that at home.' Harry's hand closed a little tighter. Everyone was silent. 'Come on,' he insisted.

Miss Strange's voice was quiet but clear. 'That's how the tiger holds its prey, isn't it, Harry? You remember?'

Nobody moved. It was Aunt Bonnie who broke the moment.

'Stop it, Harry. Leave her alone.' Harry dropped his hand and looked at her. His jaw was doing overtime clenching and unclenching. Then he looked at Uncle Eddie who was standing in the middle of the brigade.

'You gonna let your wife talk to me like that, Eddie?'

Eddie shuffled his feet but didn't speak. Aunt Bonnie stood up holding Perry in her arms. 'I think you should go now, and perhaps you would like to take your grandson with you.' She didn't yell but it felt the same. Harry looked at the sleeping black child.

Harry spoke quietly through clenched teeth. 'That kid is nothing to do with me and you know it.'

Aunt Bonnie stood right in front of him and held Perry out in her arms.

Harry stood his ground for a moment, moving his huge jaw backwards and forwards.

'He's Pearl's child,' she said.

Harry spat out words under his breath. 'Pearl is dead and he should be too.'

There was silence followed by a general shuffling. I didn't understand why but slowly the women began moving toward the door. Doreen leaned over to Sweetheart as she left. 'Bring Perry into town. You don't have to hide him out here. Bring him.'

Joey stood to one side, trying to look official, but his uniform just didn't cut the same kind of ice as the firemen's. Gradually the women paired up with their men and moved off. Everyone except Aunt Bonnie and Judith. Judith didn't move at all. She just began to weep. Quietly at first and then louder and louder. Harry stood still watching everyone depart. He looked at Aunt Bonnie like he would kill her. He didn't move but just kind of barked. 'Come on, Judith.'

The only response was more sobbing and a low wailing. Faced by such emotion, Harry did what my father would have done. Nothing at all. Uncle Eddie never said anything. Harry stood his ground, looking at his distraught wife, then he turned on Miss Strange.

'This is your doing, you goddamn bitch. If it's the last thing I ever do I will shut you down. You and your fucking animals.' He turned and was gone. Uncle Eddie stood for a moment and then followed.

Joey moved to Judith. He sat down beside her but obviously didn't know what to do. Awkwardly he began patting her on the shoulder.

'I know, I know. Rocco. You lost a lovely dog.'

We sat for a while but then it got a little cold in the barn and everyone, including Troilus, the goose, Sappho and Mr Paton, moved up to the house. I know Joey wanted to come but he stayed in the barn.

'I'll wait for the dog. Judith? I'm here if you need me.' Judith didn't say anything but at least she had stopped crying. Her hair had quite fallen down to her shoulders now but she didn't seem to notice. She just followed along with the rest of us, the orangutan and the devoted Troilus. Up at the house, Cosmos sat on the floor in a yoga position while Helen, Judith, the goose, Aunt Bonnie, Miss Strange and I settled round the library fire.

It was Sweetheart who got the drinks out. She had sur-

prising energy for someone her age.

'Time for one of John's settlers, I think,' she said, mixing something in a big silver shaker. No one was feeling too good but Sweetheart seemed determined to cheer everyone up.

'Helen, did I ever tell you about that time Grace and Billie got stopped in the Packard by a motorcycle cop?'

'Yes,' said Helen quietly, but Sweetheart plowed on. She was enjoying the company. Maybe it was like old times in the house.

'Well, Billie had been shopping for her final items to prepare for the big trip to Africa. She and Grace were heading home in the Packard when they got pulled over by a motorcycle cop. Billie was driving but Grace got out to talk to him. He wouldn't be pacified. They had been breaking the speed limit and he wanted to talk to Billie. When he got over to the car Billie was sitting with her leg pulled up on the seat. Peeping below her skirt you could just see a silver flask tucked into her garter belt.

' "What's in the flask, ma'am?" demanded the officer, pushing his hat back on his head.

'Billie smiled. "Oh, you don't want to worry about that. It's just a sample."

' "I think you had better let me be the judge of that." The officer held out his hand. Billie shrugged and coyly removed the flask from the top of her leg. She handed it to the officer and winked at Grace. The officer, rigorously doing his duty, flipped open the lid and took a huge gulp. He paused for a moment and then spat all over the ground. Billie smiled.

' "I said it was a sample. I just didn't say it was a urine

sample." Billie had peed in the flask while Grace was doing the talking.'

Miss Strange smiled, sipping her drink. 'I forgot. Phoebe laughed so. She touched my face and she laughed so.'

Everyone drank quietly for a while and it was nice. But grown-ups are so funny about drink. It didn't happen fast but slowly things began to get a little out of hand. It had gone rather quiet. Miss Strange hadn't said anything for ages until she suddenly exploded with:

'Harry's a son of a shit.'

'He was a nice kid.' Sweetheart defended her son. 'You loved him. You know he's still angry. He blames this place for killing Billie and he always will. They teased him at school, you know they did. Living out here . . .'

'Yeah, with crazy ladies.'

'I didn't say that.'

'Living with Miss *Strange*.'

Sweetheart sighed. 'It was my fault. He hated me not being married.'

Miss Strange sat looking into her glass. 'Nothing was the same after Phoebe died. The record had been playing so fast till then and suddenly everything slowed down. I never even saw Phoebe buried.'

'Down by the river.'

'I know.'

'Billie never came out after that. She lay on that vast canopied bed of hers surrounded by all those cabin trunks we'd packed. Trunks going nowhere. Her arm mended fairly quickly but she never went near the tigers again. She never went to any of the animals. I think she couldn't believe that one of her beloved creatures would turn on her. It changed everything. She had lost all her power. The only person she allowed in her room, the only person she could stand to see, was Harry. Harry helped bandage her arm. I made plates of food for her but she would only let Harry bring them in. He read to her and I know he looked the other way when she injected herself with morphine and more morphine. For a while John Junior tried to get in but it was hopeless. He tried everything. Remember the team of elephants from England who played cricket? It was pouring with rain and he stood outside Billie's window all dressed in white.'

'Billie!' he called up to the window. 'Billie, watch this!'

A young bull bowled the ball to John's bat and he lashed out at it. The mud took the earth from under his feet and John fell at the wicket. He looked up at the house he had built for his beloved Billie. He looked at her window and saw Harry. The son he now longed for. Maybe a son would make it all right. Billie was pregnant.

John scoured the land for a key to his wife's heart. There was Lord Byron, the educated pig that John had procured at great expense. He stood pathetically in the hall outside Billie's room and called to her about his porcine purchase.

'Listen, Billie, I can ask it anything.' John turned to the pig. 'Now then, Lord Byron, how much is four plus two?' There was a silence followed by six pawings on the ground with a small trotter. John applauded enthusiastically and made the noise of a marching band with his mouth.

'Isn't that great? If you come out I can show you

the finale. He can select a US flag from a box of banners and wave it at the crowd.'

But there was no response. He brought her maps of the corners of the earth. From Singapore, Lapland and Peru, anywhere that they might travel and forget.

Grace was in the county hospital for months. No one thought she would live but somehow she pulled through. Well, what was left of her pulled through. She was a scary sight and she knew it. It was months before she returned one night in the dark to the Burroughs House. She too had declined all visitors. Harry wrote her. He thought it would help his beloved Billie if he could persuade Grace to return, but the letters lay unanswered.

Grace came back because she had nowhere else to go. The house was silent when she returned. Her limping footsteps echoed on the marble floor in the hall. She found John Junior in the study. The place was littered with old bottles of Jack Daniel's. John sat on the floor with maps of Africa spread out before him.

'Gracie, Gracie,' he called without getting up. 'Grace has returned to the house of death.'

'How are you, John?'

'How am I? I am terrible. My great balloon adventure is a disaster. Have a drink?'

'No, thank you.'

'Mind if I have yours?'

John poured another belt and went back to his maps.

'W. D. Boyce, remember him? Chicago newspapers, asshole, more money than sense, so he asks me to go in on the American Balloonograph Expedition, the great American Balloonograph Expedition. He was supposed to bring back

right? That would be worth money. Maybe even a side-show. So he gets out there with his balloon and some of my money and he inflates his damn balloon and attaches the movie camera to it which he is going to operate from the ground. Now, it's very windy so he doesn't want the balloon to fly away. He ties it to a mule. A mule, for Christ's sake. Well, you know what's going to happen. One heavy gust of wind, it seizes the balloon and the goddamn animal. Apparently the mule brayed miserably before disappearing into the clouds and never being seen again. That is because Boyce is an asshole. Milton would never have allowed it. Sweetheart is quite annoyed. I keep wondering what some poor native is going to think when a mule suddenly lands on his head in the middle of nowhere.'

John began to roar with laughter as Grace moved forward into the light. She had been so beautiful but now she was like two sides of a coin. From the left she still looked young and lovely. From the right she had turned in an instant into a harridan. Her face, still livid with the fresh scars, clung on to her bones for dear life, but it was an impossible battle. Everything on the right was pulled down by gravity and injury. She was her own freak show.

John turned a table lamp to look at her. He pulled her quite roughly to him and ran his fingers over the grooves and welts that had once been her face.

'So you're home but I don't know you. My wife won't know me and I don't know you . . . Miss . . . Strange. Shall we make money from you, Miss Strange, shall we exhibit you?'

Grace began to cry. Softly, tears spilling unbidden from her torn and damaged eye. John pulled his handkerchief from his pocket and wiped them.

'Milton would have loved you. He liked anything different. Those fat-lip Ubangi women, Anna, that giant woman with the mustache, the Fiji cannibals. He would have loved you.'

Grace began to sob. John Junior took her in his arms. He rocked and rocked her until at last he laid her down on the carpet. He moved the light to see only her damaged side and then he made love to her.

The autumn of the great stock market crash, Billie delivered her child. Grace too was pregnant by then but the house was silent about it. John Junior only slept with Grace that one time and after that he didn't much talk to her or anyone. He kept spending money right up to the end and the house was still host to some strange characters. Sweetheart did her best to keep control but really it was impossible.

It was the morning that the temple from India arrived that Helen was born. Sweetheart was dealing with eighty tons of stone, shipped like a giant jigsaw in 250 crates, which had been deposited on the lawn. The crates were accompanied by an almost equal number of Indian artisans whom no one could communicate with. The noise and babble meant no one heard Billie's cries as she produced her beautiful daughter. She called her Helen for Helen of Troy and handed her over to Harry.

'I can't do babies,' she said, and turned her head to the wall.

Harry brought the child down to find its father. He carried the baby carefully and walked with slow precision to the dining room. John Junior and Jack Riddell, a soldier turned ivory poacher, were in there, taking it in turns to jump the huge table on horseback without disturbing the crockery.

'She's come,' said Harry, holding the child out.

'I didn't order it. Get out. Give her to Sweetheart,'
snapped John and moved his horse for another attack.

Billie didn't live long enough to see Grace's child. She
knew about it but she didn't seem to care. One morning,
shortly after Helen's birth, she just got up and went and
drowned herself in the pool. Harry found her. It was Harry
who brought her out. John had the place drained and locked.
Sweetheart made all the arrangements. John gave everything
to Grace and left for Africa. He never came back. Three
weeks later Grace gave birth to Judith, defender of the people.
No one even mentioned that Ellen and Toto had also been
delivered of a daughter. Sweetheart named her Artemesia.

The past swirled around us and the drink flowed. Too
much drink flowed. After a while Miss Strange started
making speeches. I had never seen her so worked up. The
more she drank the more speeches she made.

'No, I'm angry,' announced Miss Strange, standing up
to make her point. 'We'll beat him. You see, we . . .' her
withered arm moved to include us all, '. . . are Amazons.
It's from the Greek *a*, meaning "without", and *mazos*,
meaning "breast". Which is particularly suitable for me.
I am without my breast here, you see.'

She opened her shirt. The right side of her chest was a
mass of scar tissue. There was no bulge. She didn't need
one of Harry's corsets. All those years later it still looked
painful. Red and raw, and yet it seemed to me to be so
very female. She didn't need a breast. She was strong like
some great fighter. She wasn't trying to be anyone but
herself and I thought it was the most wonderful thing. I
wanted to hug her. Wanted to have her enfold me to her   *247*

side in a way Mother never did. No one said anything. Embarrassed, I moved away and climbed up the stairs to the balcony above the room.

'Did you know,' she continued, her shirt draped loose about her, 'that it was a woman dressed as an Amazon who led the attack in the storming of the Bastille? Théroigne de Méricourt – a most gifted singer who trained in London and Naples. It was women who led the bread march to Versailles. And the assault on the Tuileries. Théroigne commanded a battalion of Amazons. The women of the French Revolution knew what they were doing,' boomed Miss Strange out the window, where Gabriel could still be seen working in the distance. 'The women stormed the National Assembly and the bishop shouted, "Order!" and do you know what the women shouted? "We don't give a fuck for your order!"'

Miss Strange began to sing.

> 'My country, 'tis of thee
> Land of grape juice and tea,
> Of thee I sing.
> Land where we all have tried
> To break the laws and lied!
> From every mountainside
> The bootlegs spring . . .'

Cosmos was also somewhat the worse for wear. She had wandered off from the entrance hall and returned dragging a large cabin trunk. 'Look what I found.'

'Africa!' cried Miss Strange. 'We shall all go to Africa.' She poured herself another drink as Aunt Bonnie came back from putting Perry to bed. Sweetheart looked exhausted. She sat next to Judith on two of the French reproduction chairs. Judith had stopped crying and just sat stroking Troilus. Aunt Bonnie set to knocking back the wine. Helen sat on the stairs with Sappho and watched.

'It's the real McCoy. I met him once, you know, smelled of salt water.' Miss Strange nodded to herself. 'Here in the house, I met him with Billie and Phoebe.

> 'Oh, we don't give a damn
> For our old Uncle Sam.
> Way, oh, whiskey and gin!
> Lend us a hand
> When we stand in to land.
> Just give us time
> To run the rum in!

'I think the greatest elephant keeper of all time was Mary Sparks. You remember her, Sweetheart? She died while she was working at the Ringling farm in Wiliston, Florida. One of the bulls knocked her down and stomped her. It was a shame because she had a great trained-goat act and was a hell of a giraffe jockey.'

Up on the balcony, I sat down at the ivory keys of the Aeolian organ which hardly anyone had ever played. Downstairs, Cosmos was starting to dress up.

'Look at these.' Cosmos had opened the trunk and was pulling out the contents. It held the most beautiful dresses and ornaments, all ready for a wondrous journey. A staggering array of silks and satins. A parade of feminine frippery from another age. Cosmos tried on hats and scarves, necklaces and bangles, the accessories of a wealthy woman. From the bottom of the trunk, folded in tissue paper, she pulled out a gown of the palest blue and purple silk. The shimmering colors blended from one to another in a rainbow spectrum. It was stunning. Cosmos held it to her and began to dance across the room. The gown flowed with a Ginger Rogers life of its own, its hem brushing the women as Cosmos flew past. Miss Strange began humming some air or other and Sweetheart began to join in. At last Cosmos came to a halt in front of Helen. The others stopped humming and Cosmos looked down at her squatting friend. Cosmos made a slight bow and put out her hand to raise Helen to her feet.

She stood as if she had been mesmerized by the dance. In her brown cardigan, brown corduroy pants and brown shirt she seemed an unlikely candidate for a princess's ball, but that is what transformation scenes are about. Cosmos moved the dress to rest on Helen's shoulders. Miss Strange moved toward Helen and slowly she and Sweetheart began to remove her clothes. Helen didn't move, and soon all her garments lay in a single brown pile on the floor. Completely naked she looked a different woman. Not all curled up and cocooned but rather lovely. Like one of the statues in the garden. She wasn't young any more but she was still pale and perfect. An untouched woman. Cosmos and Miss Strange took the extraordinary gown and lifted it into the air. It seemed to float by magic over Helen's naked form and down across her shoulders. She was swathed in silk. Butterfly colors rained down on her and she was beautiful. A great wave of material attached to the wrists and up under the arms hung down like expectant wings. The dress reached almost to the floor and in her bare feet Helen looked like one of her beloved floating fancies. The dress seemed to intoxicate her. She began to run slowly and then faster round the huge, square entrance hall. I understood it. I knew how clothes could change a person. I knew I had grown up since donning my T-shirt and shorts. From my haircut to my knee-high pants, I had become myself.

I began to play the one tune I knew on the organ. A little Beethoven emerged from the pipes and slowly the others began to dance. Faster and faster. At last I was doing it right.

'Spread your wings, Helen, or you won't survive,' called Miss Strange as she opened the front door and released Helen to the air. She ran across the lawns, past the windows of the house and on to the field, raising her arms so that she seemed ready to take flight. The bonfire roared now and the field was lit in oranges and reds. Gabriel stood watching the blaze as Helen appeared before him. I don't think she saw him at first. She was too busy with her own release. Round and round the fire she danced, like a blue morpho butterfly attracted to the light. She grew taller and more majestic as we watched. Gabriel had no choice. He moved toward her. In the dark there was no age difference between them. I knew now what would happen. She would do her courtship dance until he showed interest. Then she would hold her wings ready for him to land alongside her and spread his scent. They would tap each other with their antennae and remain locked for moments or maybe hours. It was the way of the butterfly.

The women all stayed at the window in silence but I couldn't watch. It wasn't for me to see. I felt a great choking in my chest. Something was happening that was about more than grown-ups having sex. I didn't understand. I wanted my mother back but I knew she wouldn't come. Even if she had it wouldn't have been right. I wanted to know where I was in the cosmos but I didn't actually know what that meant. I felt terribly confused and alone. I slipped away, meaning to go home. That's how I was at the gate when they arrived. Despite all the preparation it was kind of a shock. We weren't really ready for Artemesia, and we certainly weren't ready for her to bring family.

Chapter Twelve

We had talked a lot about size. I mean to do with the elephants. We had probably built the world's strongest enclosure out of the old train tracks but I still don't think we were ready. Well, I wasn't. I stood there watching three men unload the elephants from a large truck. Artemesia came first. The truck had rough slats as a walkway for her to come out of the vehicle so her feet were kind of at my eye level. At least it's what I noticed first. This massive animal walked almost silently. The only noise came from the creaking wood as she swayed down toward me with incredibly precise footsteps. A silent walk with the track of her hind legs coming to rest precisely in the spoor of the front. Her sole spread out to take weight at each step. It was slow and deliberate. As she lifted her foot I could see the cracks and ridges underneath. Like the grip on a great pair of sneakers. Then her foot would descend again, its built-in shock absorber of fatty fibrous tissue cushioning the impact. It was so neat.

Her feet had shiny round toenails. A smart lady out for the evening. She could have followed a dance card on the floor, this elegant, shimmying thing. So slow and precise and so silent.

As she got closer I moved up to her legs. They were tall, straight columns which supported her massive bulk, and she was big. I expected the vast expanse of gnarled skin. I knew from Helen's reading that she was a pachydermata. It came from *pachys*, meaning 'thick' and *derma*, 'skin', but I didn't know so much of it would be so soft. A great deal of it was like upholstered leather – a patchwork quilt. I reached out, completely unafraid. Her sides were prickly to feel – covered in short, stiff hairs. I moved my hand toward her head. She was mostly coarse and grainy to touch but some places were pliable and spongy, like around the loose baggy pants above her back legs. Endless rivers of wrinkles stretched above my head. A great Ordnance Survey of life across leather skin. The lines almost made grill marks across her sides and flanks, but it was at her head that I fell in love.

Artemesia looked at me. She had a constant, shy smile. There was not a wicked bone in her body. Mother would have said that the hair all round her mouth and chin looked like it needed plucking, but I loved it. It was a full and fearless growth. Her eyes seemed small for the size of her head and they had long lashes Judith would kill for. Soft brown eyes fringed with lashes as long as a hand. Her ears, the shape of Africa, flapped slightly in the warm night air. At the outer margins of her ears you could just see vast rivers of blood vessels surging with her life. Inside her ears and around her mouth, her skin was paper thin and delicate. I reached up to touch her face and she bent down to help me. I put my hand behind her ears and felt a place as soft and cool and smooth as silk. Something happened in my stomach. I didn't know, but I suspected it was my first encounter with sheer passion.

The other elephant was smaller. A lot smaller. Maybe three foot tall and just a few months old. I couldn't tell. I mean, baby or not, she still must have weighed two hundred pounds. She was just as beautiful but maybe a little fatter. The mini-Jumbo was covered in soft baby fuzz and had a hunched, shuffling gait. Her skin was really too big for her body. She looked as though she had been dressed in an oversize gray Babygro. It bagged and sagged around her haunches. The baby was less delicate in her movements. She thumped out of the truck, treading on and tripping over her trunk. Although the two had made the journey together she hurried to greet Artemesia. The baby put down her head as she ran to the larger elephant and they both began to make low rumbles at each other. They gently used the tips of their trunks to snake over each other's heads, fondling, feeling and smelling tenderly. Then the baby snuggled close to her mother, put her trunk in her mouth and sucked at it like a baby with a thumb. She stood under the protective umbrella of Artemesia's great body – like a child hiding in Mother's skirts. I had never seen such open affection.

'You signing for these?' The delivery man thrust a clipboard at me.

'I shouldn't really . . .'

'It's late. You work here?'

'Sort of.'

The man was getting irritable. He still had an ostrich to get to New Jersey. 'Come on, son, just sign.' So I did. Son, I quite liked that. The man handed me a delivery note and he and his friends pushed off in the truck. I watched them go. It was a little daunting. I had only been going home and suddenly I had taken charge of two elephants. I looked at them. I needed to get Miss Strange, or maybe not her as she was drunk. Maybe Helen, or maybe not her as she was busy. I needed to do something. Artemesia and child looked at me.

'Stay,' I said with as much authority as I could muster. I raised my right hand to emphasize the order and turned back to the house. I walked off purposefully but when I turned to look, Artemesia and her child were right behind me. So much for me being in charge. We got to the big lawn and I didn't know what to do next. The elephants seemed quite happy to let me decide. I didn't feel I could leave them so I threw a stone at the window and Miss Strange appeared. We must have been a curious sight. A small kid in shorts standing between two giants fresh from the circus.

Miss Strange and Cosmos came out. They weren't walking too straight. Sweetheart followed a little behind. As they approached across the lawn Artemesia went a little funny. She moved slightly toward Miss Strange and then she stopped. Suddenly she began to make deep rumbling noises in her chest. Then she lifted her trunk and gave a vast trumpeting sound. She began to flap her ears, spin and turn, and matter spilled out of her at every end. She peed and defecated while tears seemed to stream down the side of her head. Miss Strange watched and laughed. At last Artemesia calmed and walked on again. She reached out her wet trunk and gently put it round Miss Strange's shoulders. Miss Strange patted it and smiled.

'I'm pleased to see you too, Artemesia.'

It was a greeting of two old friends. The strangest greeting I had ever seen but heartfelt none the less.

'There's two, I'm afraid,' I said.

'I'm glad to hear it. I thought my eyes had gone.'

I handed Miss Strange the paperwork from the driver. She looked at it without focusing and handed it on to Sweetheart. Miss Strange went back to stroking her old friend. Sweetheart looked at the papers.

'So, Artemesia, you have a daughter.' She turned to the slightly smaller creature. 'Welcome . . .' She checked for the name. 'Betsy? Hmm, we'll think about that. Now where the hell are we going to put you?'

The enclosure wasn't ready. Wouldn't be ready for at least another day. It was Sweetheart who thought of the swimming pool. Miss Strange went kind of funny. She was drunk so there was no reason in it.

'We are not using the pool. I am not going in there.'

'It would be perfect,' argued Sweetheart. 'They'll be fine for the night. It's empty, it's strong, we can wash it down easily.'

'Forget it.'

'What else do you suggest?'

The argument was going strong when Helen drifted up from the field. She had a strange faraway look in her eye and a small tear in her dress. The dress flowed behind, loosening itself on her shoulders so that they stood out milky white in the night sky. She smiled and ran with her arms outstretched toward the elephants. When she reached Artemesia she hugged her.

'They need to go in the old pool,' said Sweetheart, trying to get everyone shifted. 'There isn't anywhere else.'

Helen was not herself. She didn't look like herself and she sure didn't act like it. 'Come on,' she shouted. Helen never shouted and now she led the way, Pied-Piper-like, turning to make us march to the old marble pool.

The place had been shut up for years and the lights came on with fizzy reluctance but it was perfect. There was no water now but the shallow steps down into the basin made it easy to get the elephants in. The solid marble and mosaicked walls would easily hold them until the enclosure was done. Miss Strange was stiff as we moved to get Artemesia and Betsy happy.

'Come on,' said Helen again.

'I don't want to be in here. I don't think they should be in here,' replied Miss Strange. She looked sweaty and tired, the alcohol beginning to wane.

Helen continued to work with confidence. She and Cosmos got bales from the barn while Sweetheart and I tried to find a drinking bucket. Miss Strange sat at the side and watched. It was weird to see Helen take over. You would have thought that these creatures were too big for a woman who lived in the land of the winged insect.

Artemesia and Betsy stood head to head in the middle of the empty pool while all the activity went on around them. Occasionally they would reach their trunks to each other's mouth, then entwine them, sniffing each other's face and body, appearing to sample breath and saliva, then

Artemesia would give a low rumble and they would stand still again. Miss Strange sat on the side of the diving board, looking down to where once the water had been.

'They never said anything about two. Did they say anything to you, Sugar?' I shook my head.

Helen didn't sit for a second. She was unstoppable. She shifted hay, pulled the hose and gave it to Sappho to fill the bucket we'd found. Sweetheart went to check on Perry in the house. When she came back Perry was awake and sitting up in her arms. Aunt Bonnie, Judith and the goose drifted in behind.

'Elephants!' Perry cried at the sight of them. 'Look, Great-Grandma, Aunt Bonnie, elephants!' He jumped down and ran towards the steps.

'Perry!' Sweetheart called in panic.

'It's okay,' said Miss Strange. She had gone very quiet. The drink had left her subdued. She picked Perry up and moved down the steps with him. She gave a slight shudder and then moved toward the two new inmates.

'I like elephants,' announced Perry, and reached out to hug Betsy, who seemed to hug him back. 'Why are they so wrinkled? Great-Grandma is wrinkled.'

Sweetheart laughed. 'So I am, thank you, Perry.'

'It helps them to keep cool,' explained Miss Strange, stroking the gnarled but delicate skin. 'See, there's more skin to get wet. The cracks hold on to the water and keep it longer in the bright sun.'

'Isn't it wonderful!' Helen seemed almost intoxicated as she danced around the bottom of the pool.

'They can't really stay here,' said Miss Strange. 'I don't think the enclosure will hold both of them.'

Helen jigged about. 'Of course they can. Do you know, Perry, if it wasn't for stupid people then elephants would probably be the most successful species on earth. They or their ancient relatives have lived everywhere from deserts to rainforests to glaciers.'

'They can live here,' agreed Perry. 'Look at the ears, look how big they are!' he cried.

Helen smiled and reached up to touch one. 'You know, it is said that in Ethiopia the elephants link themselves four or five together into a sort of raft and, holding up their heads to serve as sails, are carried on the waves to the better pastures of Arabia.'

Cosmos left her hay preparations and jumped down beside Miss Strange. 'Come on, Sugar, Perry, Helen, hold my hand, let's duck under them. It's good luck. Come on, Sweetheart.'

Sweetheart laughed. 'They're too big for me.'

'Nothing is as big as it looks,' cried Cosmos, trying to get all of us to join hands. 'We increase the size of things in our minds. I don't believe it is as far to Africa as we think it is.'

'Yes, come on.' Helen and Cosmos were unstoppable. Helen grabbed Aunt Bonnie's and Sweetheart's hands: Cosmos grabbed me and Miss Strange, who held on to Sappho. The two women got us in a line all holding hands. Helen was leading, with Miss Strange and the orang at the end. 'Come on,' called Helen, beginning to move us all, ducking under Artemesia and then dancing round Betsy for good luck. Judith stood at the side. As we passed her Miss Strange let go of Sappho and reached out her hand but Judith looked away.

It was late. Sweetheart went back to the house with Perry, Judith and Aunt Bonnie. Judith was beginning to say that she ought to go home but she clearly had no heart for it.

'Shouldn't you go home, Sugar?' Miss Strange asked.

I didn't say about Mother going. I just shrugged and said, 'I don't want to.'

She shrugged back. She didn't ask about my family and I didn't tell her. I didn't want to. We slept that night amongst the hay and the elephants. I dozed for a while. Cosmos was whittling at a piece of wood and I slept to the steady sound of her knife. When I awoke Miss Strange was sitting above the deep end looking down at our new charges. Cosmos lay on her back staring at the ceiling. Her whittling lay beside her. Helen slept on a hay bale, her arms and legs outstretched like she was making angels in the snow. She smiled in her sleep. Artemesia and Betsy slept side by side, standing up. The air was full of deep contented breathing.

'Both female,' said Miss Strange, looking at the elephants.

'Yeah, like not even a cute couple,' agreed Cosmos. 'Be no good in Siam. The men in Siam would no more ride a female elephant than you'd get a guy to ride a donkey in the Memorial Day Parade.'

'I think having two females is great,' I said, feeling very defensive.

'Sure. It's great,' agreed Cosmos. 'We're not like, in Siam.'

I lay down next to her and stared at the ceiling. A god on a snake stared down at me.

'That's Vishnu,' explained Cosmos. 'Reclining on the Ananta-Sesha serpent as he floats on the cosmic ocean. He is dreaming his cosmic dream. Every now and then the world is destroyed and Vishnu must recreate it in a dream. See, from his navel on a long-stemmed lotus is the god Brahma, the creator. It is his job to create what Vishnu dreams – everything in the universe.'

'Vishnu has the great vision then he gets the builders over,' chuckled Miss Strange.

Cosmos was not distracted. 'It is said that from the many petals and stamens of this miraculous lotus the gods Vishnu, Siva, Brahma and Agni eventually created the various castes or families of elephants, the celestial ancestors of Artemesia and Betsy.'

Miss Strange shook her head. 'Betsy! What kind of a name is that?'

On the walls a mosaic of mountains and trees spread up to the gods. 'Look there,' commanded Cosmos. 'There, sheltered in the Himalayan Mountains, is the mythical Himaphan forest, where many real and fabulous creatures including the elephants live.'

It was a dream world. We lay in a dream of elephants and mythical forests. This was where I wanted to stay always.

'Here, Sugar,' said Cosmos, 'I made you this.' She handed me the most perfect wood carving of Betsy playing. 'It's a Shinto-baku – a tiny elephant kept by believers near their bed to ward off nightmares.'

'Harry will close us down, Cosmos,' said Miss Strange, quietly changing the subject. I clutched my new power against evil.

'No,' Cosmos replied. 'We have something he does not. We have the power of concentrated calmness over unreason and brute force.'

'What does that mean?' I asked.

Cosmos looked at me and smiled. 'Buddha had enemies. They sent wild Nalagiri elephants to trample him to death, but Buddha subdued their ferocity by the power of his inner strength. The elephants came toward him and he simply raised his hand to calm them. We shall do the same.'

And I believed her.

Sweetheart sat smiling at the elephants. 'Just think what John Junior would have made of this. What a show he would be planning.'

Miss Strange laughed. 'He could make a show out of a dead elephant. Culpeper-Meriweather's Great Combined Circus.'

Sweetheart nodded. 'Boston. Fourth of July fair.'

'What happened?' I asked. Miss Strange smiled at me.

'Our Great Asiatic Caravan, Museum and Menagerie was due into Boston for the fair when an old elephant we had – this was before Toto and Ellen – died. So Culpeper heard about this and started advertising his event with the slogan *Come See the Only* Living *Elephant at the Fair*. John never worried for a second. He put up posters saying *Come and See the Only* Dead *Elephant at the Fair*. And they came. The public ate it up.'

Sweetheart shook her head. 'Not as much as the pig-tailed macaque monkey which inhaled when it smoked.' It was another world.

The next day was all hands on deck. None of the

women sat and watched. Aunt Bonnie and Judith came out from the big house with Sweetheart and Perry. Judith looked real pale but she had stopped crying. Her hair hung straight now and she had no make-up on at all. I thought it was much better. She looked younger. Troilus followed in her footsteps. Everyone gathered on the lawn. Women from all over the town. Even more than the night before. Women I had never seen before. No one had said anything. All Miss Strange did was bring Artemesia and Betsy out on the lawn. There was a long pause and a lot of murmuring and then everyone just kind of got on. Half the workforce immediately set to completing the enclosure. Everyone else was on food detail.

Helen gave out the shopping list. 'Okay, now, mainly vegetarian, please, ladies. We are looking for one hundred pounds of hay and twenty-five pounds of fresh fruit and vegetables per elephant per day. Bark, grass, hay, apples, cabbages, carrots, bananas, oranges, bread, and, before you rush out and think you're on to a winner – they don't like peanuts. Delicacies and treats include grapefruits and sweet-potato tops.' She grinned at the women. Helen had taken on a new life. I went with Sweetheart to the A&P. I just knew Alfonso would help us out. Then there was Frank's Franks – he always had lots of bread left over.

It was hot, unbearably hot in the enclosure. Gabriel arrived early. He never said a word to Helen and she didn't speak to him. It was as if nothing had happened the night before between them and yet everything had. Helen was a new person. She had her brown cords back on but she had tied a bright pink scarf from the cabin trunk round her neck and it stood out against her usual clothes. Gabriel got on with the job and on with sweating. About halfway through the morning the chain broke on his tow-truck. He tried to fix it but it was no use.

'No can do,' he said with his gift for language.

There were still a dozen or more pieces of track to come over from in back of the house. Helen didn't stop for a minute.

'Isn't the old harness still in the house?' she asked Miss Strange, and the two of them went off. When we got back Artemesia was wearing a large leather harness and doing the work of the truck. It seemed like nothing to her. She used her tusks like a forklift to get the track in place. Then Gabriel would fasten it to the harness so she could pull the load round to the enclosure. She and Gabriel seemed to have got into a rhythm so that Artemesia could even hold the pieces in place while Gabriel welded. Seemed kind of a strange trick, getting her to build her own stockade. She worked with great precision, apparently understanding the concept of balance and symmetry in loading and stacking the metal pieces.

Judith had moved herself sufficiently to take over providing the drinks, and Aunt Bonnie was working in the field. She didn't need to play with Perry any more. He had a new friend. Perry and Betsy played together every hour there was. Neither one seemed to know they were boy and elephant babe and maybe not ideal playmates. Certainly Betsy hadn't got the idea at all. Despite having the wizened look of a little old gnome she saw the whole world as a thrilling adventure. She would get so excited that her ears flapped, and then she would bounce up and down with her two forefeet together. Quite often it was while bouncing like an India-rubber ball that she would try sucking her trunk. She usually stood on it instead and fell over. Her feet and legs lacked coordination. They seemed too big and long for her tiny body.

When Perry took time off to play on the swing outside the barn, she stood and watched. Then she moved toward him and waved him away with her trunk. Perry got off and Betsy backed up to the swing and tried to sit down. The swing swung out of the way of her substantial bottom and she fell backward as Perry laughed. At least half an hour went by with Betsy trying to use her tail to hold the swing steady.

She tried using her trunk but to no avail. That brilliant elephant arm was no use to her yet. A piece of flesh sensitive enough to read Braille but at the moment incomprehensible to the young calf. One hundred fifty thousand muscles and Betsy didn't know how a single one of them worked. Eventually it would be flexible sideways, upward and downward, slightly telescopic, but not yet. One day it would be able to pick up a needle in a haystack. She twirled it like a long bobble cap placed on her head by Artemesia to keep her warm. It made everyone giggle, even Judith. Artemesia, however, knew exactly what she was doing. Her trunk was a six-foot-long, one-foot-thick third eye.

The women detailed to shopping had filled a huge shed near the field with different foodstuffs and bolted the door. Helen was busy organizing it all. She had fixed a pulley system to a tree and was busy hanging vegetables off it to make feeding as interesting as possible. 'Imagine you were in jail and all your meals just came on a tray.'

Sappho handed me an Oreo cookie. I wasn't sure it would be so bad. I don't know if the women were either. A lot of them had spent twenty years cooking family dinners. The thought of anything arriving on a tray was probably pretty attractive. Helen carried on organizing. She hung brackets for 'multi-level feeding' and a big trough for vegetables.

'Don't cut it up,' she ordered her brigade of women. 'The elephants need to pick and sort the food themselves. Just like in Africa.' There were other notions too about making the elephants at home. It was the coconut matting which finally got Judith involved. Until then she hadn't done anything. She hadn't left either, but she hadn't really helped. Cosmos had a thing about 'abrasion'.

'I'm right, aren't I, Helen?' she called out. 'You see, elephants need abrasion. Their skin is used to it in the wild so we need to make some. Help keep them in good trim.' Cosmos held up some coconut matting from a *Welcome* doormat. 'Maybe I could . . .' She tried fixing it to a log. For the first time Judith took an interest. She stood up. This was fabric. This was her area. She took the mat and she and Troilus went to get string and a strong needle. Soon she was sewing in abrasion all over the place. I'm not sure that Artemesia appreciated all the effort.

During a short break Sweetheart and Aunt Bonnie handed out drinks to everyone. It must have been a hundred degrees out and everyone was feeling it. Artemesia and Betsy stood side by side with Artemesia sheltering her calf from the sun. Cosmos sat on the ground looking at them.

'It's so weird,' she said. 'These huge creatures. I mean, like, they have all these feelings but they can't tell us about them.'

Aunt Bonnie giggled. 'Bit like men then.'

'Exactly like men,' chortled Sweetheart. Everyone laughed.

'Show us some of Artemesia's tricks,' called one of the women.

'What did she do?' called another.

Miss Strange patted Artemesia and looked her in the eye. 'Tightrope-walking,' she sighed.

'Did you see it?' I asked, trying to imagine such a thing. I mean, an elephant on a tightrope. It was incredible.

'Once,' replied Miss Strange. 'She had a special rope. Maybe twenty foot long, six inches in diameter and four foot off the ground. It was ridiculous. She would walk along the rope, get off, play the organ, blow a whistle and fire a cannon.'

'Anything else?' asked Doreen.

'I don't know. Isn't it enough? What do you want her to do? Write her name with a piece of chalk? Drive a car?' Miss Strange wiped the sweat from her forehead. It ran in strange patterns down the right-hand side of her face. A kind of glacial facial movement.

'I can drive,' I volunteered, but it was a grown-up conversation.

'They shouldn't be doing it at all,' said Cosmos. 'It's humiliating. I hate it. Animals shouldn't like be trained to behave like people. They're not amusing slaves. They are dignified creatures deserving our respect. They're too smart for it. You know there were like, some young elephants in Burma who kept raiding the banana groves near their owners' house at night. The owners put bells round their necks so they could hear when they were coming. The elephants stuffed mud in the bells and came anyway. Now that's smart.'

Artemesia wasn't listening. She had stood and watched for a while and then moved off. Using her trunk, she opened the latch to the food store, lifted the bolt and flipped it across with a quick movement of the tip of her trunk before pulling the door open. She helped herself to some oranges. After her snack she moved to the water tap. She turned on the tap using her front right foot and trunk. There was a hosepipe attached but all she did was raise it to her mouth and pour the water straight down her throat.

'Artemesia, what the hell . . .' started Miss Strange. Artemesia put down the hose and looked at Miss Strange. Very slowly and gently she lifted up one massive foreleg to rest on a crossbar and be petted. It was impressive. Miss Strange fed her one of Frank's hot-dog buns. Mrs Torchinsky looked on in wonder.

'Imagine never having to diet,' she said.

'Never having to wear a corset,' said another.

Sweetheart nodded. 'It's too damn hot for corsets. Too damn hot.' As she spoke she wriggled in her dress and slowly and deliberately removed her girdle. The women giggled in the hot sun. Then Doreen did the same, and then Ingrid. Each removal caused a great cheer of triumph. It was weird. Women I had got to know quite well suddenly changed shape in front of me. Up till then they had all looked pretty much the same. Now they bulged in all kinds of places. Helen began gathering up all the discarded garments and throwing them on the still-glowing bonfire. Women's lib had come to Sassaspaneck. Betsy managed to pick up an eighteen-hour version with her trunk and throw it up on her head. She was so proud of her new headdress that she began running pell-mell with it round the enclosure. This caused much shouting as Perry ran after her trying to grab it. Eventually Betsy lay down with the corset over one eye. She had a ridiculous, satisfied expression on her face which no doubt Harry had never managed to achieve with a customer before.

Then it started to rain. Gentle, cooling summer rain. Artemesia gave a trumpeting bellow and flapped her ears. Cosmos copied her and soon all the women were running wild round the enclosure. Spreading out their arms in the falling water. It was kind of crazy. It's not often you see a human being as ecstatic as a dog about to go for a walk but it was like that. Artemesia and Betsy ran through the middle of it all, twirling, flapping their ears and trunks and trumpeting with gusto.

Even Judith looked up from her sewing and grinned. For a second she caught Miss Strange's eye and they looked at each other. Miss Strange gave that half-smile she had, but then the moment was gone. Still, I think the rain was important. I think there was no going back after that.

That night was the last before the enclosure would be ready. We put Artemesia and Betsy back in the pool. Everyone was tired. The women drifted home in their new shapes. Those of us that were left – Helen, Miss

Strange, Judith, Aunt Bonnie, Sweetheart, Sappho, Troilus and me – sat on the edge of the deep end and watched our new friends. Judith was busy making some tapestry with elephants on it.

'We should go home,' said Aunt Bonnie, but she was too tired to move. We were all exhausted.

'Artemesia did a brilliant job today.' Sweetheart smiled at the huge creature. Down in the empty pool Artemesia stepped delicately on an apple. She split it open and rubbed the pieces into her hay before passing it to Betsy. It looked for all the world as if she was flavoring it. She was smart all right. Miss Strange nodded.

'Great creatures. They hauled planes in India in the war, they helped build the River Kwai Bridge. Hannibal took forty thousand men and thirty-eight elephants over the French Alps. When he crossed the Rhine some of the elephant rafts overturned. The attendants drowned but the elephants, weighed down by heavy foot chains, swam to the shore. The noble elephant. Symbol of the Republican Party.'

Helen sat with us now. 'Can you imagine the elephants marching with Julius Caesar? Arriving in Britain? The first elephants to set foot in Britain in ten thousand years. No wonder he conquered.'

Cosmos was struggling with a black and white TV. She banged the side of it and *I Love Lucy* spluttered into view. Artemesia looked up. She paused for a moment then pushed her trunk out and shook her head with a loud slap of her ears against her neck. Cosmos looked at Artemesia and changed channels to *Bewitched*. Artemesia paused for a moment and then rapped the end of her trunk smartly

271

on the ground. It made a hollow, metallic sound like some old theater effect. She did it again, causing a current of air to emit a sharp sound like a sheet of tin being rapidly doubled.

'What's that about?' asked Aunt Bonnie.

'Patently she doesn't like *Bewitched*,' said Miss Strange as Cosmos retuned the TV again.

'Really?' I asked.

'We'll never know, Sugar.'

Artemesia and Cosmos finally settled down to *The Johnny Carson Show* and there was quiet. Whether it was because they were exhausted or corsetless, the women sat more relaxed than I had ever seen them. Artemesia too seemed entirely content. She stood with her trunk curled and resting on her tusks. Her body stood easy but the folded tip of her trunk seemed to form two eyes, endlessly watching, perhaps smelling what went on. She seemed very old to me. Vast and gray like old Father Time. Betsy slept below her. She lay flat out, in the exhausted sleep of the puppy or the baby. She had covered her eyes with one ear folded over her head. From her trunk came small bubbly, snoring noises. I wondered what she dreamed of. Whether she dreamed at all. Could an elephant dream of possible happiness in the future? She was a baby but seemed to me to have been born old. She looked as if she had already been let in on some great secret. Perry lay near by, snuggled down in some hay.

Aunt Bonnie pulled on her cigarette. 'Aren't those tusks incredible?' She had never been much for animals, but sitting this close no one could help but admire.

Miss Strange looked at the lengths of ivory on which

Artemesia rested her trunk. I knew it was smooth and cool to the touch. It was a funny word, 'ivory'. Made it sound like it was nothing to do with the elephant.

'Pistol grips, baubles, bracelets, baroque beer mugs, hairbrushes, opulent fans, chess-pieces, dice boxes, knife handles, figurines, furniture, combs, perfume flasks, joints in bagpipes, well-balanced billiard balls, piano keys, mah-jong sets, carvings and trinkets, holy crosses, umbrella stands, rosary beads, bookends, porno scenes on ivory plaques ... that's what people see when they see ivory. More blood, human and elephant, has been spilled in the quest for this "white gold" than any other raw material.'

If I hadn't known it before, I knew then that I would fight for Artemesia and Betsy. That no one would make billiard balls out of them. I think that is when I thought of the telegram. I know I didn't tell anybody, but I think that's when it was.

Helen had found an extraordinary book in the library. It was the *All Purpose Swahili Phrase Book from the Society for the Propagation of the Gospel*. She was giggling as she read. 'I don't think this is going to help, Cosmos.'

Cosmos dragged herself from the TV. 'No, really,' she said. 'It might be comforting. Artemesia came from Africa. Swahili was probably like, the first language she heard.'

Helen read out a phrase.

'What does that mean?' I asked.

'The idle slaves are scratching themselves.'

Miss Strange nodded. 'Now that is useful.'

'How about this? "Six drunken Europeans have killed   *273* the cook. Do not pour treacle into the engine."' We all grinned although I wasn't quite sure why it was funny.

I was reading one of the huge leather-bound books about elephants. I wanted to know everything about them. Wanted to speak to them. I read out loud.

'Did you know that the area a bull elephant sniffs to ensure a female is ready for mounting is called Jacobson's organ?'

The women fell about.

'We'll have to tell Gabriel!' roared Miss Strange, weeping with laughter.

I didn't get it. There was such helpless jollity when Joey came in that I'm sure he thought it was about him. He shuffled in the door in his uniform looking hot and tired. He paused at the sight of Artemesia watching TV with Cosmos, but he didn't say anything about it.

'I caught the dog,' he declared. 'The one that killed the goose.' Judith stroked Troilus at the news. Joey smiled at her and she smiled back. It was the first normal thing she had done since she arrived.

'Uh ... Miss Strange ... I have kind of a strange announcement I have to make.' Joey cleared his throat, unaccustomed to quite so much attention. 'I want you to know that I don't think it's right. I have tried to phone the state office for advice but no one seemed to know and . . .'

Little Joey was sweating as he shifted from foot to foot. It was Judith who finally smiled at him and asked, 'What is it, Joey?'

Joey pulled his pants up and brushed back his hair for an official announcement. 'As dog catcher it is my duty to inform you that the Mayor of Sassaspaneck has today issued an order in relation to all domestic pets and their licenses. From today all animals in the town will be classified as domestic pets and will require a license.'

Miss Strange looked at him. 'What do you mean, all animals?'

'All,' muttered Joey.

'I see. And who provides these . . . licenses?'

'That would be the Mayor.'

Miss Strange carried on. 'So an elephant would now be a domestic pet?' Joey nodded. 'And if I don't have a license for, say . . . an elephant?'

Joey carried on nodding as if he was trying to get the idea into his own head. 'I would be required to bring the animal in . . . and have it destroyed.' Joey looked desperate. 'I'm sorry, Judith. I don't know what else to . . .'

It was brilliant. Not only could Harry close down the zoo by refusing all the licenses, he could humiliate Joey at the same time with the task of enforcing a ridiculous local law. It was a beautiful piece of work. But so was my telegram.

Chapter Thirteen

Maybe it was the heat toward the end of that summer, but everyone in the town seemed to go kind of deranged. Judith still refused to go home. She sat sewing and sewing. She and Troilus were quite a couple now. I didn't think it was one of Joey's rainbow bridges, but it was pretty close. It had been a couple of weeks since the enclosure was finished. Aunt Bonnie had been back to defrost stuff for Uncle Eddie and see he was okay. I went along to check on Father and Perry came for the ride. Straight across the harbor from the Dapolitos' house was Harbor Island. A small island on the harbor which had not been named by a literary genius. The island sported the only piece of almost-beach in the area and it was here that kids when not at camp were sent for swimming lessons. A series of floating docks, like Uncle Eddie's, had been anchored in place to box in the beach and make a safe area for the lessons.

Father and I had tried to have a conversation. He had

grown very thin over the summer and for the first time I thought he looked old. I guess I should have paid him more attention. Been a better daughter.

'I've been thinking about school,' he said. 'You need a proper school.' I wanted to talk about my place in the cosmos and not being an Et cetera, but it didn't seem like the moment.

'When's Mother coming back?'

'Yes. She isn't.'

'Why?'

'Yes. She needs some time.' We sat not speaking for a little.

'I have to go now,' I said.

'Yes.'

As I got up and walked past Father he took my hand. 'I'm sorry, Dorothy,' he said. I should have hugged him, something, but I couldn't.

I went across Sweetheart's yard to the Dapolitos' to get a ride back with Aunt Bonnie. She was sitting in the garden with Uncle Eddie. Perry was playing by the back stoop.

'Bonnie, Judith needs to come home. You know Harry is all talk. He needs her to come back. It's making him crazy.' It was a long speech for Uncle Eddie. Aunt Bonnie sat with her usual cigarette but she wasn't drinking. She didn't drink half so much now.

'Harry has to back off the zoo. You should come, Eddie, it's – well, it's wonderful.'

'He's mad, honey. Pearl . . . it's all made him a little crazy.'

Harry came round the corner. He was wearing one of

his election boaters, but not with any confidence. It drooped on the back of his head and he looked terrible. I thought he was just going to sit down but as soon as he saw Bonnie he started yelling.

'What the fuck have you done to my wife? She won't fucking come home. I thought you were my friend and look at you – out there with that crazy old broad. What's the matter with you? I thought you were on my side. Hey, Eddie, you know I've been fucking your wife? You know that?' Uncle Eddie stood up real quiet but it didn't feel good. Perry had looked up at the commotion from his screaming grandfather. Now he ran to Aunt Bonnie for protection. Harry grabbed him by the arm and held the boy out to Aunt Bonnie.

'What are you doing with that nigger kid? Huh? Are you trying to wreck my life?'

'He's your flesh and blood,' yelled Aunt Bonnie.

Harry screamed back. 'He is not. Look at him, for God's sake. He is nothing to do with me.'

Uncle Eddie had his own agenda. 'Have you been sleeping with Harry?' he asked, his voice beginning to rise.

The shouting went on. I hid behind a bush and waited for it all to be over. People, grown-up people, are supposed to keep an eye on kids. That's how it's supposed to work. They're supposed to love you and make sure you're okay otherwise something might happen. In Sassaspaneck all the kids went to camp. They got sent away to be looked after. All of them except me and Perry. No one was watching us. If you don't watch people then something will happen. I don't know whether Perry thought he wanted to swim or he just fell. Anyhow it seems he swam under the floating dock and never found his way up again.

It was a while before anyone noticed Perry was missing. They looked everywhere for him. Then, when it was getting dark, Uncle Eddie called out the volunteer fire brigade to help. The blasts measuring out the signal for our street hollered across the harbor and over at Main Street you could just see the lights going on at Torchinsky's. The Dapolitos' garden was all lit up with the Japanese lanterns Aunt Bonnie had got on special the summer before. I stood on the patio with the lanterns playing orange and red figures in the water. The night was still and it should have been real pretty. I guess after a while everyone knew Perry had to be in the water. It was Uncle Eddie who found him. Uncle Eddie, the son of a gondolier, who dragged him from the water. The tide had turned and they had been dragging a grappling hook behind the boat to stop Perry floating out to sea. We could see him pull the little guy up from the deep, his shiny skin glistening in the lantern light. Uncle Eddie held him in his huge arms. He came ashore crying. For some reason that was the worst thing of all.

Harry stood watching the whole time. He never moved. Uncle Eddie walked across the lawn with Perry in his arms, tears streaming silently down his face. He got to Harry and reached out to give him the child. Harry looked down and then he turned and walked away. I was sobbing and I didn't understand. I didn't even know where Perry had gone. He never even had a chance to find his place on the list. What was that all about? I had heard about death with Billie and Phoebe and Pearl, and had even seen the dead Cressida, but this was different. Aunt Bonnie and Uncle Eddie watched Harry go. Then Aunt Bonnie reached out her arms and pulled me in. We stood for a while under the Japanese lanterns. In the harbor the water was still. It had done its bit.

Aunt Bonnie took me with her when she drove out to the zoo with the news. There was silence as Judith sat sewing and sewing. Sweetheart and Cosmos started weeping. Miss Strange looked very odd. Pale and angry. No one said anything till she got to her feet and went to stand in front of Judith. Judith didn't look up until Miss Strange reached out and tore her needlework from her hand. She threw it on the floor.

'You have lost your daughter and your grandson. What does it take with you?'

Judith cowered as if Miss Strange was going to hit her.

'Don't. I lost my dog. I lost my dog.' Judith reached out to pull her loyal Troilus toward her. It set Miss Strange off.

'Who gives a fuck? Stop grieving over a fucking animal. There are people involved here. What's the matter with you? Didn't he look right? Is that it? Didn't Perry look right for you? What kind of person are you? Look at me. Do looks matter so much to you? Do they?'

Sweetheart moved to stem the tide. 'Grace,' she said quietly but there was no holding Miss Strange.

'Look at me,' she demanded to Judith. 'Look at me. I never looked right for you, did I? The scary mother. Look at me!'

She grabbed Judith's face and pulled it up, drawing a

thin line of blood with her fingernail as she did so. Judith looked her straight in the face and hit out. The blow came from nowhere. It hit the right side of Miss Strange's face and sent her reeling back. Judith stood shocked for a moment and then a complete change went over her face. It crumpled and she ran to Miss Strange. She knelt and put her arms around her.

'Mommy, Mommy,' she moaned as the two women clung to each other and wept and wept.

Everything was different after that. Aunt Bonnie blamed herself and she went real quiet. No one saw the funny side of anything any more. We went to the funeral together. We weren't family, Helen, Cosmos, Sweetheart, Miss Strange, Judith, Aunt Bonnie and me, but it felt like it. Uncle Eddie and Joey were the only men who turned up. Judith looked so pale and Aunt Bonnie wouldn't speak. Judith kept hugging her and telling Aunt Bonnie that it was an accident, that she was the one who had been wrong. The minister wasn't feeling too well so Cosmos said a few words.

'I would like to share with you the last words of Crowfoot, great Blackfoot warrior,' she said, clearing her throat as tears poured unbidden down her face. '"What is life? It is the flash of the firefly in the night. It is the breath of a buffalo in the wintertime. It is the little shadow which runs across the grass and loses itself in the sunset." We'll miss you, Perry. You were our family.'

Uncle Eddie and Joey carried the coffin. It wasn't easy – they were such different heights – but they gave it what dignity they could. Afterwards Uncle Eddie spoke quietly to Aunt Bonnie.

'Be careful. Harry's gone kind of crazy.'

Aunt Bonnie stroked Eddie's arm and said, 'Eddie, go up to the camp. Bring home the kids.'

Things changed after that. For example, I don't remember Judith wearing make-up again. She stopped doing all that stuff to her hair and even borrowed some pants from Helen to wear.

Maybe it was guilt – I hope so – but Harry was definitely loony after that. We got news that he was moving to enforce an order against the zoo. Miss Strange hadn't bothered with even trying for the licenses and now he was coming to close the place down. If he did then all the animals would be destroyed. We got together in the barn. Things didn't look good but Helen was driving everyone on.

'We need a plan,' she said, pacing in front of us.

'Forget it, Helen, it's hopeless,' sighed Miss Strange. Judith sat close to her mother, her head hung in despair.

'Maybe we should just give up,' agreed Judith. Sweetheart nodded and pulled her cardigan close around her.

Helen shook her head. 'We are not giving up on Artemesia and Betsy. Grace, this place is your life. You can't give up on it now. Perry wouldn't have wanted us to.'

It was not a good moment to invoke the dead. More tears followed. I thought it was a good time to tell them about my telegram.

'I made a plan,' I said. Everyone looked at me. I think sometimes they forgot I was there. 'It's a military thing.

My father told me. There was this General called Ha Ha Shepherd.'

'Ha Ha?' inquired Cosmos.

'Not now,' said Miss Strange.

'No, really. Anyway, he was supposed to take this bridge from the Germans who were advancing on it, do you see? So General Shepherd sent a telegram pretending he was the German colonel, saying don't worry about reinforcements, I've already taken the bridge. So they never came. You have to pretend that you have already won when you haven't. So anyway, I sent one to the news people.'

Sweetheart looked at me. 'Sugar, what are you talking about?'

'Well, Harry is a Republican, right? And Miss Strange said the elephant was the symbol of Harry's party. The Republican elephant? So I sent a telegram to the news people. I watch it all the time, and they like little funny stories. Sometimes they show them on Johnny Carson. I sent them a telegram from Harry saying there was no truth in the rumor he, the Mayor of Sassaspaneck, was trying to destroy Artemesia, symbol of his party. In fact, he was trying to save her from the town. As they will never have heard about it I thought it might make them interested. They might send someone to check it out. Harry would have to stop and explain himself. I don't think it would look too good.'

'A telegram.' Miss Strange patted me on the head. I knew she didn't think it would work. No one was really paying much attention to me by then. Death was a big, grown-up thing and I guess they were beginning to think I should go home.

The fire siren began to blast across the water. Two then four then one. It was the signal for the zoo.

'Harry's coming,' said Helen. 'We have to do something.'

We went together to the locked entrance gates and waited. Christabel Pankhurst's words hung above our heads as we waited. Judith, Helen, Cosmos, Sweetheart, Aunt Bonnie, Miss Strange, me, the goose and the orangutan. We could hear the wail of a police car and the big fire truck approaching. Helen was sitting curled up again. She was scared. We all were.

'They can't get in, right?' asked Aunt Bonnie. 'I mean, it is locked?'

'I can't do this, Mother, please,' implored Judith, looking straight at Miss Strange. 'Harry's my husband. I have . . .'

Miss Strange looked at all of us.

'Did you know,' she began, 'that it was a Judith who saved the Jewish people? The people were under siege so Judith used subterfuge, the subterfuge of a woman. She flirted with the attacking general, drank him under the table and she and her maid . . . what was her name?'

Helen shrugged.

'No,' Miss Strange nodded. 'History doesn't like women to have names. Anyway, she and her maid whacked off the general's head, stuck it in a picnic basket and escaped back to the Jewish camp. They staked his head high over the gate so when soldiers charged the camp they saw their general leering down at them and ran away. Judith set her maid free and all the women danced in her honor.'

'We can hardly put Harry's head on a pike, can we?'
said Aunt Bonnie, not entirely averse to the idea. The
sirens were right outside now and there was a rattling at
the gate.

Miss Strange stood up. 'Maybe not, but we will
dance.'

Harry's voice boomed out through a megaphone:

'This is the Mayor speaking. You are required by Town
Ordnance Four Hundred and Sixty-two to let me in
and examine the premises.' The megaphone fell silent
and you could just hear Harry yelling, 'Go on, Joey, go
on.' The megaphone burst back into life. 'These animals
are being held illegally without license and must be
destroyed.' He had completely flipped out.

Miss Strange looked at us. She took Judith's hand and
pulled her to her feet. One by one we moved together to
the gate and looked out. Harry was standing on the fire
engine with the lights blazing at us. Either side were two
patrol cars and next to one of them was Joey's van. Joey
looked nervous.

'Get your gun, Joey,' commanded Harry.

Joey yelled back. 'I don't need my gun.'

'You gonna do this job or what? Get the fucking gun.'

Joey looked at the gathered men. The whole of the
football team stood lined up behind Harry and
the brigade. Other men from the town had come in pick-
ups, cars and trucks. Mr Torchinsky stood over to one
side next to his hearse. About a hundred men facing the
zoo entrance. Joey opened the back of his van. He
reached in and took out a shotgun. He leaned against the
car cradling the gun in his arms.

Miss Strange spoke quietly to Cosmos.

'Open the gate.'

'Are you sure?'

'Yes.'

Cosmos stepped forward and took the chain and padlock from the gate. She pushed the heavy metal entrance to swing open as Miss Strange turned on the floodlights. Now Harry and his crew could see what they were up against. Seven females, a goose, a gray parrot and an orangutan.

'Give it up, Grace,' bellowed Harry. Miss Strange lifted her head and matched his voice with no megaphone to aid her.

'You cannot win,' she called to the men. 'This zoo has been here for forty years and it's not going.'

'This place is a danger to the community. There are animals missing. Dangerous foreign animals. You do not know how to control wild creatures. Even as we speak a government inspector is on the way,' yelled Harry. 'You are a threat to the community.'

'You will not touch a single creature,' replied Miss Strange, standing completely still.

The bright lights had woken up Girling the Gorilla in his cage behind Miss Strange. In the unnatural silence he began to beat the bars of his pen and make wild, threatening noises. Miss Strange calmly removed a plastic icecube tray divider from her pocket and held it aloft. Girling fell silent instantly. It was a pretty impressive use of an icecube tray divider. No one really knew what to do.

'You will not harm us,' said Miss Strange firmly.

'Yeah? Says you and whose army?' called a lone

male feeling safe behind the fire truck.

'Say I and great women down through the generations. We shall stand here like Lady Mary Banks, who held Corfe Castle against parliamentary forces with only her daughters and gentlewomen to defend her. In charge of our own destiny, like Queen Adelaide, Queen of Italy and Holy Roman Empress; Princess Aelgifu, ruler of three countries; Zoe, Empress of the Byzantine; Queen Asma, ruler of Yemen; Agnes of Courtney, Crusader Queen of Jerusalem; Blanche of Castille, Queen of all France; Caterina Corner, ruler of Cyprus; Anne of Beaujeau, Queen of the Bourbons; Grace O'Malley, Irish war leader; Rosa Parks, Harriet Tubman . . . Sojourner Truth . . .' Miss Strange was beginning to fade a little. 'And . . .'

'. . . Lily Tomlin,' added Sweetheart, slightly off the point.

It was probably the only name Harry recognized. Mr Honk screeched approval at the top of his raucous voice. He wasn't perhaps in tune with how serious everyone was, as he then paraded up and down between the warring factions showing off his plumage.

'Come on, men. Joey, bring the gun.' Harry moved forward with the football team slow on his heels.

'Bollocks,' called Mr Paton, changing his repertoire for the occasion.

Helen began to chant in Swahili. I knew she was actually saying, 'Six drunken Europeans have killed the cook. Do not pour treacle into the engine,' but it sounded very impressive. A deep primal tone which Harry could not fight.

'Order,' cried Harry over the noise.

'We don't give a fuck for your order,' I yelled.

This caused a moment's frisson. No one on either side was quite sure that this was okay. I mean, I was ten. There were those who were perhaps unaware that I was merely being historical. It was then that we saw the women. Dozens of them, some walking, some in cars, all moving up the drive to the zoo. Some carried candles and others had children with them. They moved silently but with great purpose. Judith looked at them and then at her husband. In a calm, dignified and loud voice she began to speak.

> 'Remember the dignity
> of your womanhood.
> Do not appeal,
> do not beg,
> do not grovel.
> Take courage,
> join hands,
> stand beside us.
> Fight with us.'

Harry turned and looked. The women of the town moved without speaking. They walked silently past the engine and the police cars, past the men and the young football squad. As they walked, the men parted and quietly let them in the gates of the zoo. Standing in front of Mr Girling, Mr Kruger and Mr Goss, who all paced in their cages, the women began to hold hands. The world was being destroyed and we were in a cosmic dream. The women stood united, facing the men. It was a powerful moment. Better even than press-ups in the wind.

'Come on, men,' yelled Harry with some desperation but no one moved. Harry jumped down from the fire truck and moved slowly toward us. As he came through the gates, Sappho, not aware of the tension of the moment, reached out and flipped his boater off his head. Harry was incandescent with rage. He leaped backward screaming, 'See, see. That animal is dangerous. It's out of control.'

It probably didn't help that a few people actually laughed.

'Joey! Joey!' Harry sounded like a desperate little boy. 'Joey, do your duty. For Christ's sake! Go on, you nancy idiot.'

Joey moved forward carrying a large net. He looked ridiculous. Sappho reached out and flipped that away too. Then the orangutan picked the net up and started after Joey. All the men laughed as Joey ran back to his van. He was humiliated. He began loading his gun and organizing ammunition. Harry started screaming.

'Can't you do anything, you ridiculous asshole?'

Joey was sweating now. 'Don't call me that. I am not ridiculous.'

'You've always been ridiculous, you dwarf. You can't do anything right. Look at you, you're nothing. You think people in this town aren't laughing at you? The dog catcher who thinks he can be mayor. You're not even a good dog catcher. You're a coward, Joey. You can't deal with more than a goddamn poodle. No wonder you never married, huh, Joey? Who the hell would have you? Judith didn't want you, did she? Did she?'

Joey had begun weeping. 'I stood by you, Harry. In school when they teased you, I was always there for you. You knew Judith was mine. You knew that and you took her from me. Helen didn't want you so you took Judith. You weren't good enough for Billie's daughter.' Joey pushed his way through the throng to his van, where he stood holding his gun and sobbing.

The women stood still. Silently facing out. Harry was shaking with rage. 'This is insane. You women, go home. You are ruining this town.' No one moved. 'Do as you're told!' he screamed, but no one moved. 'Right,' he called, 'fire up the engine. You asked for it.' Harry gestured for the engine to start and Mr Walchinsky from the hot-dog stand moved to get in the driving seat.

'Hey, Frank,' I called. He stopped and shielded his eyes from the lights.

'Dorothy?'

'Yeah. Only hot-dog stand in America designed by an architect.'

He looked at me and nodded. 'That's right.'

'You gonna knock down John Junior's zoo? And Mr Torchinsky.' I put my hand on the bronze statue of Billie which loomed above us. 'Most beautiful thing you ever saw. Remember? Come see the elephants, Mr Torchinsky? Frank?'

Harry was trying to get back into election mode. 'This town needs a stadium, a place for family . . .'

Hubert from the Pop Inn stepped out of the crowd.

'Where's your grandson, Harry?' he called.

Harry swallowed hard. 'I don't have a grandson.'

'He's dead, ain't he, Harry?'

'Oh . . . go back to Africa,' yelled Harry at the town's only black man. A general murmuring began. Hubert looked at him. Ingrid was standing with us. Slowly Hubert moved to his wife and stood beside her. Torchinsky and Frank followed. Then Alfonso, my fruit man, moved from the crowd of men and made his way through the gates to stand with Miss Strange.

'You goddamn . . . feminists,' yelled Harry. The murmuring continued. 'Will everyone be quiet . . . look.'

I could see Father on the edge of the crowd outside. He was shouting something to me but of course I couldn't hear. I have no idea whether it was support or disgust. Desperate to gain any kind of control, Harry resorted to his megaphone.

'People of Sassaspaneck, I appeal to you. Apart from this zoo being a health hazard, the fine young men of this town deserve better. Now I have——'

That's when the whistling started. Cosmos put one of her flutes to her mouth and began to play her strange tune. Next Helen pursed her lips and joined in. Gradually everyone did the same. Because this was America and tunes from the Sudan don't travel well, what they eventually whistled was the Battle Hymn of the Republic. You couldn't hear Harry at all. I don't know whether they were whistling for the elephants or for themselves. But I knew that these women had done the undoable. That they were a source of wonder. We had defeated the Mayor, the fire department, the police and my father. As the women whistled the Pleiades looked down on us. It was the closest to a religious experience I have ever had.

That was the moment two things turned up. The television crew and the missing salamander. I don't know why either appeared. Perhaps it was the whistling. Harry, still trying to be heard, had moved forward just as the news team got out of their truck. The bright lights from the camera were focused on the man with the megaphone when he stepped back and fell over the salamander. It was not an insubstantial creature. Maybe five foot long with the look of a dragon about it. Its appearance caused Joey to panic. He took aim and fired. Missed and started to reload. Harry, not sure where the gunshot had come from or who had felled him from behind, stayed down with his hands over his head. The salamander moved off but the TV people were hot on the story. The shot had stopped the whistling and everyone now stood watching.

'We're here in Sassaspaneck, New York, where as you can see the entire town has turned out for a most unusual election rally.' The reporter was wasting no time. 'It's not often that a Republican gets a chance to stand up and defend the very symbol of his party – an actual elephant – but that is what's happening here.'

While the man spoke, a minion from the news company was racing around. 'Where's the Mayor? We need the Mayor,' he kept demanding.

'He's on the floor,' said Hubert, disgusted with the entire proceeding. The minion pointed Harry out to the reporter, who moved forward.

'Mayor Schlick?'

Harry looked up. To say he was surprised doesn't quite cover it. 'Yes?'

'Is it true that you are actually willing to lay down your

life in order to save the elephants of this town?'

'Well, I . . .' Harry got to his feet, blinking in the light.

'That you are defending the very symbol of your political party with your life?'

Harry swallowed hard. Faced by this sudden burst of fame on one side and the entire town on the other, he had no idea what to do next. Joey grabbed the megaphone.

'No, it's not true. My name is Joey Amorato and I have been officially ordered by Mayor Schlick to destroy the elephants. Indeed all the animals. He has ordered me so I have to do it. The mayor wants the elephants dead.'

The reporter sensed a good story. 'A Republican shooting elephants. Mayor Schlick, do you want to comment?'

Harry scrambled to his feet.

'No, wait, there's been some misunderstanding. I don't want to kill anything.'

Joey clenched his gun and looked his old friend in the eye. 'You gave the orders, Harry. I'm just following orders. If they die it will all be down to you.'

The TV minion whispered in the reporter's ear.

'As you can see, the tension in this town is fantastic. Joey Amorota, Democratic candidate . . .' The words gave new inspiration to the humiliated Joey.

'I am going to get them fucking elephants, Harry, and it will be your fault.'

'Uh, yes . . . determined to eliminate the wild creatures. Mayor, your reaction.'

Caught in the lights, Harry blinked. 'There's been a mistake. Joey!' he called after the irate dog catcher, but there was no holding him. Joey was off into the zoo as fast as his small legs could manage. The reporter once more thrust the mike at Harry. 'I didn't mean it. Oh God,' he managed.

Miss Strange moved fast. 'Come on. We have to get to Artemesia.'

All hell seemed to break loose. The women split up from their whistling ring and the men moved in. Harry was still trying to deal with the cameras and Joey was already at the entrance. Helen, Judith, Miss Strange, Sweetheart, Cosmos and I began to run but Joey was ahead. We ran in past the gorilla cage and up to the penguin pool. That was when we heard another shot. In the enclosure Artemesia's ears were as wide as a sail as she trumpeted with alarm. A small trickle of blood ran down her right flank. Joey stood with a shotgun. Cosmos got there first and threw herself in front of Artemesia. Betsy was hiding behind some coconut matting, shaking and calling to her mother. As the rest of us ran up, Joey turned, aiming the gun at anyone coming near.

'Think I'm ridiculous, don't you? All of you. I can do this, you know.' Cosmos made a slight move toward Joey but he swung the gun back at her. Cosmos lifted up her hand and put it out toward him. I knew she was trying the Buddhist power of concentrated calmness over unreason and brute force but I didn't think it was a good time. Anyway, it was at that moment that a small mouse decided to run across the field. Cosmos saw it first, shrieked and stepped back. Then it caught Artemesia's eye and she wasn't keen either. She stood up on her hind legs in horror. Joey didn't see the mouse. He could hardly believe the power he was exerting. Women and elephants terrified by his massive testosterone-pumped power. He turned to grin at the rest of us just as Gabriel tackled him. Joey hit the ground and another shot went off.

'Get the elephants out of here,' yelled Harry, racing up as Gabriel scrabbled with Joey. Faced with TV fame he had completely changed his mind about the creatures. Miss Strange moved fast. She rounded up Betsy and opened the gates. Cosmos and Artemesia hightailed it out of there and headed for the house. We could still hear Joey and Gabriel fighting. We were all running as hard as we could.

'We have to hide them,' called Judith.

'Where the hell are we going to hide two elephants?' yelled Helen.

'The Himaphan forest,' said Cosmos.

'For Christ's sake, Cosmos,' yelled Miss Strange.

'It's okay,' I shouted. 'She means the woods, the woods over the river.'

We ran that way in the dark. Troilus couldn't keep up and we heard his whimpering honks behind us. At the riverbank we came to a halt. There was no bridge now, just the tracks which I had often used to come over. Sweetheart was last to arrive. She was wheezing.

'This is impossible.'

'No, it isn't,' I said. 'Tightrope-walking.'

Miss Strange nodded. 'Tightrope-walking. Come on, Artemesia.' Miss Strange stepped out on the track to lead the way. Everyone was panting and shaking but the great gray beast was calm. The nick in her right flank didn't seem to bother her. With very precise footsteps she   *295* stepped out on to the track. Her hind legs moving to rest precisely in the spoor of the front. It was an entirely silent walk. The sole of her foot spreading out to take the weight at each step. Perhaps Betsy knew the importance of what was going on. For once she got her trunk to work. She reached out and grabbed her mother's tail and began to follow. Strong lights picked them out on their steel tightrope as the TV van careered across the grass and up to the riverbank. The reporter leaped from the truck, still in full flow.

'The elephants are on the run. The question is whether . . .' Confused by the light, Artemesia paused for a moment. Suddenly we heard Harry scream in the dark.

'Joey! No!'

A shot came from behind and Betsy lurched forward. Artemesia turned to save her but the baby elephant fell forward with a hoarse, deep cry into the river. It never occurred to me that I couldn't save her. That's why I jumped in. I had been to Boat Safety. I thought I knew what to do. The river pulled at Betsy and she floated off to a sand ledge near the middle. She was bleeding from her left shoulder. Her head was being swamped by water as she lay on her side. I got to the middle of the river and tried to push her up on to the sand. I remembered about Resussa-Annie. I kept trying to remember what to do.

'You put your hand on her chest like so, then take a deep breath and blow, one, two, three.' I began to blow into her mouth. Her chest was supposed to rise up. I knew it was.

'Head to the side, blow out, one, two, three.'

I didn't even care about cooties. I thought her lungs would suddenly fill up but I didn't have enough air. No matter how much I blew I couldn't cover her baby mouth. I started crying, my tears mixing with the river water. I thought I knew how to do this and I didn't. The river was pulling on me and I couldn't hold on. The water snatched at me, pulling me away from the baby elephant. I didn't know that my father had been following. He knew his way without a map. I didn't hear him call to me but he saved me. My silent father leaped into the waters, reached out for me and pulled me safe. It was the closest moment we ever had.

From behind me I could hear Artemesia giving a great scream of pain as she turned back to land. The elephant knows about revenge. Artemesia ran at Joey. He didn't have a chance, and when she was done she knelt by the riverbank uttering choking cries with tears trickling down her cheeks.

Judith put her arms around her mother and rocked and rocked her.

'Mr Mayor, your comment,' called the reporter and Harry just stood there. He looked back at the big house and at Joey on the ground and at Miss Strange and then he began to cry.

'Billie! Billie!'

Betsy did not die. The fire brigade saved her. Once again Uncle Eddie came to do salvage.

The whole thing kind of shocked everybody and it took a while to settle down. The mayoral race was held over. No one had the appetite for it. The news people found out the truth about Harry and there was a great deal in the papers about Pearl. The elephants had made Sassaspaneck famous and for a while the town was full of strangers. Harry resigned from the fire brigade and didn't go out much. Aunt Bonnie's kids came back from camp and she went back to her regular life. It was about two weeks later that there was a town meeting. Judith addressed everyone. She looked so different now to the woman I had met when we first arrived. Strong and determined. Harry sat meekly beside her while she spoke.

'My mother, Grace Gerritsen, has been running the zoo for as long as any of us can remember. Perhaps it is time for a change, but it needs to be the right one. Does anyone have any suggestions?'

I looked around the gathered townspeople. Mr Torchinsky who had romance even though his wife had a mustache, Hubert who was a cool dude and had stood by us when it mattered, Frank Walchinsky, Alfonso and Gabriel who had been my friends. But mostly I looked at the women – Doreen Angelletta from the pizza parlor, Mrs Torchinsky the undertaker's wife, Ingrid who married a black man, Miss Strange, Sweetheart, Cosmos, Judith, Helen, Aunt Bonnie – and I knew I had found my place in the cosmos. Not necessarily in Sassaspaneck, but in myself. I could be anything. Run troupes of roller-skating bears or tame tigers or write or whatever. Being a girl was just fine if you got to end up like one of these women.

Helen stood up. 'I think Artemesia and Betsy need to go home. I think they need to go home to Africa.'

Abe from the ice-cream parlor stood up, shaking his
head.

'Are you crazy? Those elephants are the best thing ever happened to this town. People are coming from all over. This could put us on the map.'

Mr Torchinsky slowly got to his feet. 'You know, Abe,' he said, 'there is definitely money in it. We could all make money and God knows that would be nice but I'm a lousy businessman. Boots and bicycles, there's money in that, but the elephants have to go home.'

And that settled it. The whole town chipped in so they could go home, home to the bush, away from the people. There was a parade when they left. The two of them leading a great march through town. Everyone whistled and waved flags and Artemesia set off the cannon on the high-school lawn. Even Mr Paton flapped his wings to the high-school band. Judith, as stand-in Mayor, made a speech and then everyone marched off to the railway station. There were flags up everywhere. Even the funeral parlor was looking bright with flags. As we passed Mr Torchinsky's the most wonderful thing happened. A cloud of beautiful plumage rose up from the glasshouse at the back. Mr Torchinsky had released every one of his birds. It was a mass melody of thanksgiving as each of Shakespeare's birds took to the air and to freedom. The bizarre human grouping stood on the street and watched with wonder.

Grace went to Africa with our elephant friends. As she leaned out of the train to say goodbye she called:

'Sugar, I thought of something. Betsy – I didn't like the name, but there was Betsy Ross. She sewed the first American flag. It's okay.' And it was.

Nature gauges time not in tens but in thousands of years,

and in the great scheme of things what happened that summer in Sassaspaneck was not earth-shattering. But it changed some lives. Saying goodbye to Grace was hard. I loved her beyond all measure. She was not an Et cetera. She belonged to the Emperor. She was first on the list. Any list. I'm not sure what happened to everyone else. Father sent me back to England to boarding school. It was a British way of valuing me and it was its own kind of drowning. I never got back to Sassaspaneck. Helen had a baby. A boy who was both beautiful and big, which is what you get when a butterfly mates with a bull elephant. She called him Billy. She and Cosmos closed the zoo and opened an animal sanctuary and a home for unmarried mothers. At last love came back to the big house. Judith and Harry divorced and eventually she was elected Mayor. Troilus fell in love with an emu and went to live in the sanctuary. Grace slipped into her sleep under the stars in Africa. It was all a long time ago but I know that we were none of us Et ceteras.

I guess somewhere in the bush there is an elephant called Betsy who would remember. I still have my carving of her that Cosmos made all that time ago. Sometimes I wake in the night clutching it and whistling as if my life depended on it.